OBSIDIAN HUNGER

OTHER BOOKS BY ANNA DURAND

OBSIDIAN HUNGER

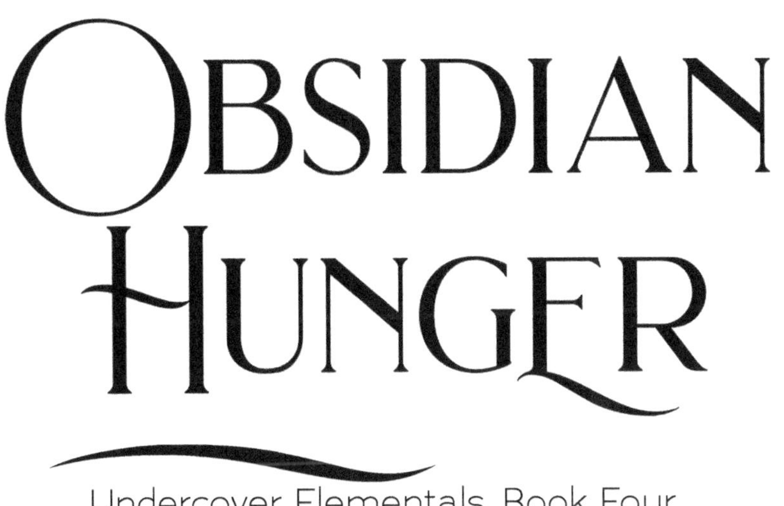

Undercover Elementals, Book Four

ANNA DURAND

JACOBSVILLE BOOKS — MARIETTA, OHIO

OBSIDIAN HUNGER

ISBN: 978-1-949406-27-6 (paperback)
ISBN: 978-1-949406-28-3 (ebook)
ISBN: 978-1-949406-29-0 (audiobook)

Manufactured in the United States.

Jacobsville Books
www.JacobsvilleBooks.com

Publisher's Cataloging-in-Publication Data
provided by Five Rainbows Cataloging Services

Names: Durand, Anna.
Title: Obsidian hunger / Anna Durand.
Description: Marietta, OH : Jacobsville Books, 2020. | Series: Undercover elementals, bk. 4.
Identifiers: ISBN 978-1-949406-27-6 (paperback) | ISBN: 978-1-949406-28-3 (ebook) | ISBN 978-1-949406-29-0 (audiobook)
Subjects: LCSH: Shapeshifting--Fiction. | Magic--Fiction. | Fairies--Fiction. | Women heroes--Fiction. | Fate and fatalism--Fiction. | Romance fiction. | BISAC: FICTION / Romance / Paranormal / Shifters. | FICTION / Romance / Fantasy. | FICTION / Romance / Suspense. | GSAFD: Love stories. | Occult fiction. | Fantasy fiction. | Suspense fiction.
Classification: LCC PS3604.U724 O37 2020 (print) | LCC PS3604.U724 (ebook) | DDC 813/.6--dc23.

CHAPTER ONE

Harper

MURDER, THAT'S WHY I'VE COME HERE—TO COMMIT MASS MUR-
der. I've been accused of insanity before, and I believed it—until that
day so long ago when I finally understood I have never been crazy. Everything I remember is true. Another world exists, one parallel to ours but
completely alien and separate from everything most humans believe can
exist. Craven beings inhabit that world, dangerous and powerful creatures
capable of the worst acts imaginable and some acts no human could ever
conceive of in the most horrific nightmares.

I don't need to imagine it. I experienced it all.

And today, I've come to their doorstep with one goal: Destroy the Unseen
realm.

I sneak around the perimeter of the gravel parking lot, staying low so
nobody will notice me. Tourists don't pay much attention to the woods,
anyway. They focus on the corrugated-metal building with the barn-red
paint job. A vibrant sign affixed to the side of the building declares it "Rock
the Keweenaw, Upper Michigan's Premier Geology Superstore."

Rocks and copper flakes? Leave them to the tourists. Knickknacks hold
zero interest for me.

The temperate weather has encouraged some of those sightseers to wander
into the rock garden behind the building so they can admire the concrete stat-
ues of fantastical creatures. I steer away from the garden, away from the well-
worn dirt path that winds its way through the woods. I'd scoped this place out
online. The website for the shop offered three-sixty views of its interior, but also
of the sights outside. Those photos showed me the path that leads to the modest-
size waterfall hidden among the trees as well as to the healing vortex.

Sweat dribbles down the back of my neck, though the day isn't hot. Wearing black leather pants and a black leather jacket makes me heat up faster, but it's the stealthiest shield against attacks. Leather hides my weapons too.

I slip into the woods, skirting the public trail but keeping a discreet distance from it. The last thing I need is lookie-loos tailing me. I'd hunkered behind a large boulder on the edge of the parking lot for two hours until I saw my opening. The proprietors of the rock shop were giving a presentation about the geology of this area, known as the Keweenaw Peninsula. It's part of Michigan's Upper Peninsula, and it does have an interesting history, but none of that matters to me. The fact that the presentation drew most of the tourists into the shop and away from the woods does matter.

I have my opening. My chance to reach the portal to the Unseen.

But first I need a supernatural taxi service—aka an elemental being who will take me through the portal. Piece of cake, right? I mean, so what if I have no idea how to find one of those creatures in these woods.

A woman's voice shouts, "The show's about to start! Get inside if you want to see it."

The last stragglers exit the rock garden and head for the shop's back door.

I rise a few inches from my half-crouch, spotting a brunette woman at the shop's back door. She holds the door open for the people rushing down the gentle slope from the rock garden. After everyone walks into the shop, the woman starts to go inside and shut the door but hesitates.

She scans the woods, her gaze sharp, her mouth tight. She rests a hand on her swollen belly as if protecting her unborn child.

I duck down again.

After a moment, the woman shakes her head like she's wondering what she thought she saw, then she disappears into the shop. The door clanks shut.

No one is outside, at least not in the vicinity of the shop. A visual survey of the woods reveals no obvious activity. I seem to be alone out here.

Perfect.

I skulk deeper into the woods, careful not to step on twigs or anything else that might result in a noise. Since nobody is around, I veer onto the groomed dirt path. It takes me further into the deepening gloom under the canopy of evergreens and hardwoods. The scent of caramel teases my senses. Certain bushes can smell that way, I know. The desert sometimes smells that way too. Here, the culprit is most likely wild blackberry bushes like the ones I'd noticed near the shop.

Up ahead, boulders vaguely shaped like benches form a semicircle around a patch of bare earth. That's the healing vortex.

A familiar burning sensation creeps across my skin on the back of my shoulder like pins and needles dipped in acid pricking my flesh.

I resist the urge to scratch it and stop beside the vortex, eying the naked ground with curiosity. Yes, I believe empty air can hold the magical power to heal injuries and maybe even resurrect the dead. Sometimes myths are true. I haven't experienced the healing power myself. If I'd known what a vortex could do thirteen years ago…

Nothing would've changed. Kelsey would still have died.

My throat constricts. My eyes burn, but I won't cry. I haven't cried since I was fifteen, and I refuse to start again today. I reach down to lay my hand over the dagger sheathed on my thigh, held in place by a scabbard strapped on with leather ties. My other hand drifts to the shoulder holster concealed under my leather jacket, my fingers seeking the cool metal of the handgun. Various pockets and holders conceal the knives I've brought with me.

Though I wanted to bring my sword, they kind of frown on bringing swords onto airliners, and it wouldn't fit in a reasonable size box either. So I'd mailed my smaller weapons and left the rest back home. Since I couldn't ship a handgun here, I'd bought it after I arrived. The expense was worth it for the extra layer of protection.

Whatever it takes, however many weapons I need to acquire, this time all the monsters will die.

I straighten and march down the path to the waterfall. Its flow cascades over a cliff twenty feet high to splash down in a small pool. It may be small in diameter, but the darkness of its waters hints at its hidden depths. A wooden bridge spans the nearest end of the pool. A natural stone ledge carves a line across the cliff, six feet above the churning, foaming waters.

The dull rumble of the falls drums in my ears.

And those hot needles prick at my back again. I'm close to the portal. The burning sensation proves it.

Rustling originates from behind me.

With my hands on my gun and the dagger, I whirl toward the sound. Knees bent, I survey the woods.

Nothing.

Rustling. Close by. To my right.

I turn slowly in that direction, peering into the shadows between the trees, tiptoeing closer to a large pine.

Behind you.

The instinct warns me too late. I spin around.

And a huge, naked, manlike beast seizes my shoulders.

He licks his lips, then they slide into a lustful smile. "Well, isn't this interesting? A succulent morsel served up right when I need it most."

The stranger speaks with a British accent, but he's not from England. Nope, no way in hell.

Heat radiates off his body. His tanned skin sports a coppery sheen that almost shimmers in the sunlight filtering down through the trees. Tiny flecks of gold, reminiscent of glitter, glisten on his skin. He towers a foot taller than I am, and my five-six isn't exactly short—in the mortal world. His hair, so dark brown it seems almost black, tumbles down to his shoulders in shiny, lush waves. Maroon streaks shoot through the locks.

But it's not his hair or his Roman nose that commands my attention.

He is buck naked, and his long, thick penis dangles between his thighs.

Yep, that's the part of him I can't stop staring at even while his hot fingers massage my shoulders, and the strangely alluring scent of him envelops me. Maybe I would be more shocked if I were an average human, but I'm nothing close to normal.

"That's right," he purrs. "Look your fill, love. You'll have this inside you soon enough."

He cups his dick with one hand.

Is he seriously hitting me up for sex? Here in the woods?

Jerking out of his grasp, I stumble backward into the pine tree. I trip over a large root but catch myself and move sideways to get away from the tree. The last thing I need is an impenetrable object barring my path.

The creature follows me, stopping a few feet away.

My gaze roves over him of its own volition. Damn, his body is impressive. Acres and acres of large, defined muscles ripple beneath his coppery skin. I can't stop my body from getting warm and tingly in places I don't want to feel this way, even though the sensation is much more pleasurable than the burning prickle I'd felt in my shoulder a moment ago. He might resemble a man in many ways, but he is not human.

I let my focus slide lower, past his outrageously taut abs, and lower still to his groin.

Oh great. He's getting an erection.

I jerk my gaze up to his face.

He smirks. "Like what you see? Of course you do. Every woman wants what I've got."

This beast is arrogant, aroused, and oversize in every way. Maybe I made a slight error in judgment when I marched out here alone. It's not like anybody would've come with me. I don't have friends, and my family wrote me off a long time ago.

The creature's smirk deepens. He tips his head to the side. "You've been looking for me."

I start to deny it but stop. He must be an elemental, one of the beings that live in the Unseen. He looks nothing like the ones I've seen before, but nobody of this world looks like he does either. I have been looking for him, kind of. Not him specifically, but his kind.

"Here I am," he says, spreading his arms wide. "Devour me."

My brows squish together, tightening the skin above my nose. Devour him? Is this guy serious? *He's not a guy, Harper, remember that.* This kind of talk can't seriously work for him.

I curl my fingers around the grip of my gun. My jacket hides it from this creature's view.

"Thanks for the offer," I say, "but I had a big lunch. Too full to devour anything."

Certainly not his big, stiffening—

I yank my gaze away from his manly parts. *Get a grip, woman.*

My attention wanders to the waterfall, visible behind him. It must be a portal. The burning sensation has come back, stronger than before, which confirms I am within a stone's throw of a doorway to the Unseen.

"You can do something for me," I tell him.

He perks up, his smirk widening into a sensual smile. "What's your pleasure, *dulcissime?*"

Though I have no idea what *dulcissime* means, it doesn't matter. "Take me to your world."

"I can take you to another world without leaving this spot."

"No thanks. Take me to the world you live in."

He cants his head, studying me. "What other world do you think I come from?"

"The Unseen."

His full lips flatten into a line. "What do you think you know of my world? Mortals aren't supposed to notice it exists."

"I noticed," I snap. "Take me there right now."

The creature raises his brows. "Demanding, aren't you? And what will you do, pretty little mortal, if I decline your request?"

"Bring the pain, that's what." I yank my gun out and train it on his chest, where I assume his heart lies. If he has a heart. "I'll shoot you point blank with jacketed hollow point ammo. You'll be a big red smear on the grass."

He glances down at the weapon nudging his chest. One side of his mouth curls up. Keeping his head down, he peeks up at me through his thick, dark lashes. "Do all mortal women like to fire tiny explosive projectiles? I thought it was only Lin—only some of you."

I whip my dagger out of its sheath and raise it between us. "I've got more weapons than you know about. Take me to—"

"No, *dulcissime.*" He closes his fist around the gun's barrel. "I don't appreciate threats of violence, even empty ones."

"It's fully loaded, not empty."

The gun vanishes.

Poof, it's gone. One second, I'm gripping it. The next, I hold air in my hand. Stunned, I stare at the space where the handgun had been. Sure, I knew beings from the other world could teleport, but I hadn't realized they could vanish objects too.

They are far more dangerous than I'd ever known.

I thrust the knife at the creature.

He waves his hand. The knife disappears.

"What did you do with my weapons?" I demand. "Those cost money, you know."

"Your concern, not mine."

"Give me back my gun and knife."

He fists his hands, then loosens them, gritting his teeth. "Enough of this. I'm taking you nowhere, unless you want to come to my lair for a night of erotic pleasure."

"I am not having sex with you. And it's daytime, anyway."

His lips slide into a dangerously seductive smile. "You'll be in my bed for the rest of today and all night, well into tomorrow and possibly the next day. No woman ever gets enough of me."

I snort. "Full of yourself, aren't you?"

"You'll be full of me soon enough."

To hell with this. I'll go back to the rock shop and wait an hour or so, then come back out here to find someone else who can take me into the Unseen. This creature is insanely obsessed with sex.

I back away from him inch by inch, glancing sideways to make sure I get lined up with the path to the shop. On the count of three, I'll run for it. One, two—

The beast flies at me. No joke, he *flies* at me. His hands close around my upper arms, and without slowing his speed one iota, he flies us both into the pine tree.

A belated gasp bursts out of me.

I'm pinned to the tree by his huge, hard body. His head is above mine, and the bulk of him surrounds every inch of me. The strange scent of him overpowers my senses, awakening me in very inappropriate ways. I detect whiffs of mysterious spices and a hint of ash, but it's the indefinable essence of him that sends a deliciously hot shiver through me and makes my breaths quicken. I can't place the scent, but it makes me yearn for…him.

Oh no. Oh no, no, no. I cannot be ensorcelled.

He grasps my waist and lifts until my face is level with his. My feet hang suspended several inches above the ground. He sniffs my hair, my cheek, my hair again. Then he dives his face down to my throat and sucks in a deep breath through his nostrils.

"By the gods," he hisses, "you smell like…everything."

My lady parts tingle. I want him to—No, I will *not* finish that thought.

Oh shit, this is bad. So very, very bad. *Bespelled by a lunatic? Really girl, is that what you've come down to?*

After all these years of searching for a way into the Unseen, of encountering various creatures from that world, I've succumbed at last. I've been ensorcelled, made a slave to this wicked beast who stumbled onto me in these desolate woods.

No, he'd been searching for me.

Which is totally insane. Nobody knew I was coming here.

He growls low in his throat and drags his tongue up my neck, inch by inch, with a leisure that implies he enjoys it way too much. He groans deep in his throat, the sound resonating in his massive chest, an expression of unadulterated hunger.

The heat of his tongue, the dampness of it, makes my breath hitch. But the sensation of his scorching-hot skin plastered to my body sends my pulse into overdrive.

He raises his head.

If I had any breath left, I would gasp. His eyes burn bright red, the rims of his irises shimmering with pure silver. Little red sparks burst inside his pupils like fireworks.

His nostrils flare. His chest heaves.

And his erection is jammed into my belly.

"Calm down," I say breathlessly. Me, breathless? Never, not for any man. But this creature is not a man, and he's done something to me. "Set me down, okay? I won't run."

"Yes, you will." His voice has gone rough, and his body is strung as taut as a cable on a suspension bridge.

"No," I tell him, striving for a calmness my body refuses to grant me. "I will not run. Please put me down."

He stares at me for several seconds, not blinking, while his eyes begin to churn with shades of red and yellow like a malevolent maelstrom in the ocean. Beyond the brilliant colors lies a dark, fathomless abyss.

"*Futuo*," he hisses, and he sets me on my feet, his eyes flaring wide.

I don't know what that word means, but his tone suggests it's a nasty curse word.

He stumbles backward a few paces, shakes his head, and jams his hands into his hair. "What the—No, I won't do it."

"Do what?"

He straightens and spears me with his swirling gaze. "Stay out of these woods if you know what's good for you. There are worse things than me lurking out here."

"But—"

He's gone before I can finish my sentence. Gone as in poof.

CHAPTER TWO

Max

I SNARL A LITANY OF CURSES IN EVERY LANGUAGE I KNOW—LATIN, GREEK, Spanish, Italian, French, every variety of English from Old to Middle to the modern version, plus a few tongues known only to denizens of the Unseen realm. I'd said "*futuo*" in front of that vexing female, though I doubt she knows the Latin word means "fuck." I had been about to do whatever it took, even force myself on that pretty little mortal, to gorge on her sexual energy. A rapist? Is that what I've become? Have I really sunk to the lowest level of filth known to the multiverse?

The delectable little mortal has no idea how close I came to defiling her, with or without her permission.

Bloody hell, I've turned into a demon. A monster. The thing humans check under their beds for at night.

I slam my fist into the nearest tree, punching a hole straight through it.

The aspen teeters for a moment and then crashes to the ground. Its weight takes down three smaller, surrounding trees.

"Not one for being surreptitious, are you?"

I groan as I turn toward the being who spoke. "Bugger off, Janus. I'm not in the mood for your high-and-mighty banter."

The god Janus aims his gold eyes at me—genuine gold, not a golden color. His eyes are bizarre even to a long-time resident of the Unseen like me. They glimmer like solid, polished gold even while they spin like molten metal. On top of that, he wears a white toga with a shiny gold belt around his waist and gold torques around his biceps.

He is a freak.

Not a half-bad bloke, but a freak. And bloody annoying at times.

Janus glances at the tree I demolished. "Are you practicing for a fight with a gnome? Or do you simply revile trees?"

"Even I'm not daft enough to fight a gnome for the fun of it."

Despite their fanciful depictions in mortal popular culture, gnomes are neither small nor harmless. They're enormous beasts who can cause earthquakes by stamping their feet. I battled them once, but not for pleasure. I did it for the only mortal who has ever made me feel like I'm not a monster.

I flap my hand at Janus. "Didn't I say bugger off? Haunt another portal and leave this one to me."

The god folds his arms over his chest. "You may have free rein to come and go from the mortal realm as you please, but that does not give you leave to destroy this world."

"Not destroying it." Not on purpose. I punch a hand into my hair instead of into another tree. "I've had a strange experience, that's all. Nothing I can't handle on my own."

"Your urges are growing stronger, aren't they? You knew this would happen if you continued refusing to feed."

"I'm not discussing this with you."

Or anyone. I'm an incubus, but that doesn't mean I have to like talking about what that entails. Feeding on sexual energy? Not the sort of thing a gent wants to discuss with anyone except his lovers. Since I have no lovers, not lately, that means I am not talking about my sexual needs.

Certainly not with Janus.

"Piss off," I tell him. "And stop acting like you know everything about everything. You might be a god, but until a few months ago, you were powerless and stuck in limbo. Your godly friends hated you so much they destroyed you, remember? So I don't think I'll be taking advice from you."

Janus has regained his powers, and maybe I should fear what he might do if I annoy him too much, but I don't. Let him destroy me or smite me or whatever gods do to lesser beings. I deserve it.

"As you wish," Janus says with a sigh. "We will not discuss your problem, even though you nearly ravaged a mortal today."

I grind my teeth. "What are you talking about?"

"What else? I refer to what transpired moments ago between you and that lovely human female."

"Are you spying on me?"

"No, but you were near a portal when it happened and thus within my domain. I sensed a disturbance and employed my vast powers to check on it."

So that's why he tracked me down. To make sure I'm not losing my mind.

Maybe I am. A little bit. Nothing I can't handle.

Bloody liar.

Naturally, the god-arse has made sure to remind me of his "vast powers."

"The mortal has left the vicinity," he says. "But you have another problem."

I groan. "What now?"

"She is looking for you again."

His words strike me like a physical blow. I don't need to ask of whom he's speaking. Only one "she" would bother to hunt me down.

"She's a goddess," Janus says. "You cannot avoid her forever. And this time, she seems to be far more determined to find you." He shakes his head. "You are her favorite toy. What did you do to engender such infatuation?"

"Nothing. The bird is insane."

Janus surveys the woods. "I do not understand why so many elementals choose to inhabit the forests of the mortal world."

"Because we can."

I've had enough of this conversation. Amid a burst of flames, I shift into my alternate form. The god becomes a giant from my viewpoint nearer to the ground.

Janus bends over to peer at me. "Yes, tiny salamander, scamper off to your former mistress. It is where you always go when you are avoiding the goddess."

Lindsey is my friend, you tosser. I can't speak the words since I have no vocal cords in this form. Salamanders in either world can't talk.

"I will be watching you," Janus says.

He vanishes.

And I… Well, I do scamper away. With tiny salamander legs, it's all I *can* do. Teleporting in this form is much more difficult, and it gave me a pounding headache every time I've tried. Being tiny and adorable has its perks, though. Women love it. They pick me up and pet me, murmuring sweet words to me, not realizing I'm as randy as a demonic goat and looking for a chance to seduce them.

Once I get well away from the irritating god, I revert to humanoid form and whisk myself straight to the shop, though I hang back just inside the rear door in the shadows.

Lindsey stands behind the sales counter chatting with a customer.

I still haven't gotten used to thinking of her as Lindsey O'Roarke instead of Lindsey Porter. Her husband is a former elemental, the onetime king of the sylphs, who adopted a full name and fabricated personal history when he became a mundane human. Lindsey was the Janusite and sort of babysat Janus's powers for a while until the Four Winds decided he'd earned a second chance. These days, Lindsey is a mere mortal again and very pregnant.

The summer heat swelters, making the mortals sweat, but I notice it as nothing more than an annoyance.

A mosquito whines near my ear.

I swat it away, throwing out a minuscule burst of flame to roast that little beggar. Insects are one of the most irritating things about this world. The most bothersome aspect of popping into the mortal realm is, without doubt, the need to wear clothing. I glance down at the ensemble I've selected, charcoal slacks and a green T-shirt. But gods, the shoes. They're torture devices for certain. I chose gray socks and a pair of loafers. Why in the hell do humans call things that constrain their feet "loafers" as if they're relaxing and enjoyable to wear?

Lindsey's customer departs. She turns her attention to a stack of mail, tossing most of it in the rubbish bin. When she comes across a catalog, she starts flipping through it but pauses to scrutinize one page.

Resisting the urge to rip the blasted loafers off my feet, I amble up to the counter. "Good morning, mistress."

Her head pops up, and a brilliant smile lights up her face. "Maxie, where have you been? We haven't seen you in over a week." She wags a finger at me. "You missed family dinner night."

I resist the urge to grimace. If any other elemental finds out I attend a thing called "family dinner night" here in the mortal realm, if they realize I consort with puny mortals at all, I'll never hear the end of it. Everyone knows Janus visits Lindsey and her family, but no one dares to criticize a god, especially one who was destroyed and resurrected at the whim of the Four Winds.

I lean against the tall counter, one arm braced on it. "You're not the Janusite anymore, and I'm not your familiar, but you still order me about like your salamander slave."

"And you still call me 'mistress' even though I never liked being called that." She blows out a breath that flutters her chestnut bangs, then flaps her hand in her face. "Damn bugs."

"Don't curse in front of the baby." I glance at her swollen belly and wonder what childbirth is like these days. When I'd been a mortal in the Roman empire, childbirth was not safe or pleasant for the woman.

Lindsey rolls her pale-blue eyes at me. "Honestly, Max, the baby doesn't know I'm swearing. But it's cute that you care about his well-being."

"His? How do you know it's a boy?"

"A new-fangled invention known as ultrasound. I'll show you the picture later." She points her finger at me again. "You are coming to dinner tonight."

"Yes, oh wise mistress, I shall attend." I study her for a moment, and something occurs to me. "Didn't you sense me approaching? You have that—what did Janus call it?—an innate instinct that alerts you to the presence of elementals."

"I think pregnancy hormones are messing with my mojo."

Mentioning Janus makes me remember what he said earlier. He warned me the goddess herself is after me. Hathor always gets what she wants in the end. I evaded her for a long time, thanks to the fact a sorcerer had enslaved me and hidden me from everyone else's detection. The Janusite-familiar bond protected me after that, but not anymore. I no longer have any sort of protection against Hathor. If she wants me, she will get me.

But I don't have to make it easy for her.

Lindsey picks up the catalog, biting her upper lip while she examines the pictures on the page that had captured her attention earlier.

Slanting over the counter, I peer at the page. "What's so fascinating about rocks? They're pieces of compacted dirt."

"Not all of them. Some are created in other ways, like volcanic glass." She squints at the catalog page. "This is some kind of black rock with pretty, iridescent colors in it. It's expensive, but I might buy one anyway to use as a display item only, for the tourists." She skims her thumb over the picture. "Feel like I should buy it. What do you think?"

"Yes, whatever." Who cares about a pretty rock? Lindsey does, naturally. It's her job to care about chunks of hardened dirt and volcanic glass.

She puts down the catalog and settles her hand on my arm. "What's wrong, Maxie?"

I groan. "Don't call me that. It's embarrassing."

"Don't be grumpy, and that's an order." She squeezes my arm. "Are you still worried you don't deserve love? You do, sweetie, trust me. Your fated mate is out there somewhere."

"Lindsey, for pity's sake." I groan again. How am I meant to refrain from groaning when she insists on calling me emasculating pet names? And she brought up the subject I dearly wish I had never mentioned to her. I push away from the counter, shoving my hands into the pockets of these awful trousers. "That bollocks about fated mates is…well, bollocks. It must be. Why in the name of Jupiter would the Oversoul want to force a female to love me?"

She clasps her hands on the counter and gives me a motherly smile. "Oh Maxie, any woman would be lucky to be your mate. You're the sweetest, kindest, bravest, most loyal companion anyone could have. I'm grateful to have you as my friend."

"Kind? Sweet?" I growl, which makes her snicker. "Why don't you slice off my genitals and have done with it?"

She laughs a bit more, her blue eyes sparkling. "Your girl is out there somewhere. I know you're going to find her, and maybe she's the one who can convince you that you're not a depraved monster."

"Of course I am." I lean in, giving her my wickedest incubus grin. "I'm a sex demon, remember?"

Her brows raise gradually. Her eyes widen a hair.

Then she bursts out laughing. "Max, you are so silly."

Why do I spend time with this woman? She makes me feel like an errant child. But it's no mystery why I love her—as a friend. She saved me from the sorcerer's enslavement and gave me a purpose in life. Best of all, or maybe worst of all, she showed me what the term humanity truly means. Lindsey risked everything to save both worlds, not once, but three times. Her husband Nevan died during the last battle, and despite having the power to rewind time and change it, she let his death stand because altering the past posed too dire a risk to the greater good. The Four Winds sent Nevan back to her, but she hadn't known they would. She made the most gut-wrenching sacrifice out of a pure, unselfish desire to save two worlds.

Can I ever hope to be as good a person as Lindsey?

No, I can't. I've done terrible things for which I had no excuse and certainly no altruistic motives.

I say goodbye to Lindsey—she hugs me, naturally, and kisses me on the cheek—then I return to the falls. Normally, I leap over the wooden railing and onto the rock ledge to exit this world via the portal behind the rumbling cascade. But now, I stand motionless at the railing. My gaze becomes fixated on the tumbling, swirling waters below me. Through the foam that drifts across the pool's surface, I imagine I see a familiar face. Golden-red hair. Eyes as blue as lapis lazuli. Silky-soft skin as pale as porcelain but with a faint, natural blush on her cheeks.

Aurelia.

I squeeze my eyes shut. My fingers clench the railing. She isn't in the water. She isn't anywhere. Aurelia no longer exists. Because of me.

Thwack.

A sharp object slams into my back. Pain ricochets through me, hot and sharp and fierce. The force of the impact propels me forward. I stumble into the railing, shattering it, and tumble headfirst into the churning waters.

Stunned, I stare up at the face of the person who has sprinted to the broken section of railing. Golden-red hair. Lapis-blue eyes. Pale skin. The face glaring down at me, I recognize it.

No, it's not Aurelia. It's the well-armed mortal who wielded a gun and a dagger at me, and who made my lust flare up like never before. When I recover from the pain, she will suffer for this.

A ribbon of blood-red unfurls from my body as I sink down, down, down.

Fortunately, I'm not that easy to kill.

CHAPTER THREE

Harper

INCH CLOSER TO THE BROKEN RAILING, GAZING DOWN INTO THE depths of the pool. The swirling waters and foam make it hard to see anything below the surface. Have I killed him? I draw back a little, gulping against a sudden tightness in my throat. Why should I care if I killed him? He's one of the evil creatures from the other world, and he tried to assault me. This demon, and every last creature like him, deserves to die.

"You backstabbing harpy."

The deep voice behind me makes me jump and spin around.

He's there, fifteen feet away. Dripping wet. Naked. His coppery skin glistening. He reaches behind his back and pulls the knife out of his shoulder, wincing. Through clenched teeth, he says, "That stung."

I open my mouth but have no clue what to say.

The beast throws the knife at me. It sinks into the earth between my feet.

"What are you playing at?" he asks.

"I was trying to kill you."

His mouth twists into a nasty smile, and his laughter is dark and feral. "You're a bloody stupid wench, aren't you? Whatever you think you know about my world is woefully inadequate." He bends forward, his gaze narrowing on me. "I'm immortal, you silly chit. You can't bump me off the way you would a human."

I kneel to pull the knife out of the ground, then plunge it back into the dirt and out again three times. The action cleans the blade. I rise and sheath the knife. "I'll do better next time."

He shakes his head. "You still don't understand the forces you're dealing with, do you? None of your weapons will destroy me."

Why did I try to kill him? If I'm ensorcelled, I shouldn't want to murder him. He must have ensorcelled me. Why else would I want him? It's a spell, not genuine lust.

Yet when I spotted him, wham, the need to do away with this beast gripped me. He's an alien creature from a parallel world. The Unseen gives birth to only monsters, which means he is a monster too. My world will never be safe until every last one of *them* is dead.

Maybe that ensorcellment has a chink in it.

The fact he didn't die proves I have no clue how to destroy one elemental, much less an entire world full of them. How had I thought I could raze the Unseen? I hadn't thought. The impulse took over like it had countless times over the years, and I'd chosen a location at random. Somehow, I knew would wind up here, close to a portal. The burning, prickling sensation confirms it.

I need to believe my choice of location had been random because the alternative is too terrifying to consider.

The beast tilts his head to the side. "How did you know it was me? I was still in glamour, looking reasonably human. I was also facing away from you and wearing clothes."

Good question. I'd been headed for the waterfall, determined to find the entryway to the other world, when he appeared. He poofed in facing away from me. With nothing but his backside to base my assumption on, I knew it was him. I just *knew*.

"Lucky guess," I tell him. "How many outrageously large men are walking around in these woods?"

I may not know the precise number, but I do know one thing for certain. My attention flits to his groin. He's the only male that well-hung who haunts these woods.

He crosses his arms over his broad chest. "Why do you want to visit my world?"

"None of your damn business."

"If you want my help, try a little sweetness." He grits his teeth, making a vein in his temple throb. "What am I saying? You haven't got a clue about being sweet."

My phone chimes.

I glare at him while I pull out my phone and tear my focus away from his crotch long enough to check the new text message. *Can you fill in for Mia tomorrow?* my boss asks. *She's down with the flu.* I type my response: *Sure, I'll be there.*

Stuffing the phone in my pocket again, I resume glaring at the creature before me. At his face, not his crotch. I've wanted into the Unseen realm for so long, and I'm standing so close to someone from that world who can take me there, but I have to give up. For today. For this one time. My normal life needs me. I need the job, so I can't say no. But I'll probably have to pay a fee to reschedule my flight home, not that I can whine to my boss about that. Sally won't give a hoot about my problems, and I don't care to explain where I went or why.

Saving my crappy job comes with a price.

At least I discovered where to find a portal. I can come back another time.

I'll get them, Kelsey, I promise you that. Someday I'll get them all.

"Well, this has been a blast," I say, pretending not to give a crap about anything. "But I have to go. I'd say I'm sorry for stabbing you, but I don't like to lie. If you want to crawl into a hole and die voluntarily while I'm gone, feel free."

He smiles like a feral beast. "If you think it's that easy to get away from me, you are sorely mistaken."

My spine snaps straight. "If you try to rape me, I will find a way to dismember your body piece by piece starting with your favorite organ."

I glance at his groin to make sure he understands.

He chuckles darkly. "Sounds like fun, *dulcissime.*"

Growling under my breath, I whirl around and stalk off down the trail toward the shop. At least that's what I intend to do.

He seizes me around the waist and hauls me into his massive body. My forehead just reaches his chin. He bends his head, his gaze riveted to mine while a ring of red fire spins around the edges of his irises, and within their depths lies a fathomless blackness.

A chill skitters up my spine. I've seen a blackness like that before—in the eyes of the creatures that murdered my best friend thirteen years ago.

The creature holding on to me today scrapes his tongue over his lips. "What do you want with my world?"

Murder, that's what. I won't rest until I've razed the entire Unseen realm.

But I still have no clue how to do that. *Shit.*

"None of your business," I say. With his body pasted to mine, I feel…strange. My lips tingle with the need to feel his mouth on mine, and my skin tightens in anticipation. "I'll pay you to take me through the portal."

"Pay? Money?" He chuckles again, his breaths heating my skin. "I don't need money, darling. There are no shopping malls in the Unseen."

"What kind of payment do you want?"

He slants in even closer, his nose brushing mine. "A kiss."

I swallow, my throat suddenly blocked by a hard mass. A kiss? That sounds innocuous enough, but then, I'm dealing with a supernatural creature from a parallel world. I can't trust anything he says. Still, he is offering to take me into the other world, for the price of one kiss.

My tummy flutters. It's anxiety, not excitement at the prospect of feeling his lips on mine. This beast is crude, obnoxious, and vile.

And sexy as hell. Which might be literally true.

His muscles flex against my body as he adjusts his hold on me.

And my stupid, traitorous tummy flutters again.

"Here's the deal," I say carefully. "One kiss. On the lips. No tongue. It will last two seconds, tops. Understand?"

"Yes." His voice gets deeper and rougher, like a distant rumble of thunder. "I agree to your terms. But in case you're thinking this is a magically sealed bargain, remember, you're on the mortal side of the veil. We can't seal a bargain here."

"I know about bargains and debts, but I suppose I'm taking your word for it that you won't exceed the terms we've agreed to."

"My, I do love a woman who tells me not to exceed her terms." He tightens his arm around me a smidgen. "It sounds almost erotic."

"Nothing I say is erotic." I squirm but can't get any leverage. "You disgust me. I'm agreeing to this kiss for the sole purpose of crossing the veil. You promised to do that. Now get the kiss over with and take me into your world."

The fiery rings in his eyes flare bigger and hotter.

He molds his lips to mine, slowly, gently. His mouth feels silky and hot, and the faintest flavor of spices trickles between my lips to tantalize my tongue. He moves his lips over mine, never breaking contact, never sneaking his tongue out to taste me. Is he actually following my rules? Why would he do that? I expected him to steal a deeper kiss. His tongue would slip between my lips, agile and velvety and—

Then I would have kneed him in the balls. Yes, that's what I would've done.

A groan resonates through his chest as he presses his mouth more firmly to mine.

I melt against him, everything south of my waist growing damp and hot.

He lets go of me and steps back.

Tiny orange flames erupt all over his body, and his eyes flare crimson.

"Bloody hell," he mutters, and the flames on his body burst into a conflagration as tall as he is, obscuring him.

The flames snuff out.

In the spot where he stood, now a small, red lizard sits.

Blinking swiftly, I stare at the little creature.

The lizard grins at me, its tiny white teeth exposed.

Somehow, I know this is the large, muscular, manlike creature who kissed me seconds earlier. He transformed into a lizard. Not just any lizard, mind you, but a red salamander.

The creature disappears in a puff of smoke.

And I shuffle down the trail to the rock shop.

CHAPTER FOUR

Max

I EMERGE INSIDE THE CAVE INHABITED BY THE FAE WITCH ENNEA, AP-pearing in humanoid form rather than as a salamander. Why did I shift into my alternate form in front of the mortal girl? I don't know her name, much less how she might react to such a blatant display of shape-shifting. She knows the Unseen exists but seems ignorant of much about this world.

Shifting into salamander form was…what? A stunt to shock her? Or was I showing off for her? I don't do that, not for obnoxious little mortals like her.

But that kiss. My blood sizzles at the memory of it. I've kissed many wom-en in my long existence, but never have I felt anything like the sensations evoked by her lips on mine. Soft, sensuous lips. The scent of her filled my nostrils even as the barest taste of her sneaked into my mouth. I fought hard, fought with every shred of self-control within me, to stop myself from ravag-ing her. The thought of thrusting my tongue deep, of devouring her flavor and exploring every millimeter of her mouth, made my balls ache.

I had to pull away. To get away. Before my control snapped, and I did something I swore never to do—give in to the lust. For an incubus, lust isn't simply sexual desire. It's a seething hunger that eats away at my soul, as real and powerful as any living thing.

To fend off the hunger, I need help. That's why I've come here, to this cave.

Ennea is bent over a cauldron with her eyes closed, fanning the steam toward her face and inhaling it. A faint smile curves her lips. The steam has dampened the hair around her face.

She cracks one green eye open to glance at me. "Hey, hon, what can I do for you?"

My friend Lindsey describes Ennea's accent as "like Chicago and the Bronx had a love child." I know Chicago is a city in the mortal realm and the Bronx is a region within New York City, or something like that, but I don't have a bloody clue where those places are. I limit my trips into the mortal realm to visiting Lindsey and Nevan.

Ennea straightens, letting out a gusty breath. "Potions smell so damn good, sometimes I want to drink them up."

"I assume that would be a bad idea."

She nods toward the cauldron. "This one is a stun potion. You wouldn't believe how many elementals want the power to stun their enemies, even for a couple of seconds. This potion is my bestseller."

"Fascinating," I say as I walk toward her, though her potions do not fascinate me in the least. I'm obsessed with the memory of kissing the strange mortal female. The ruthless hellion threw a knife into my back, yet I want to see her again. Need to see her again. And that need has disturbing implications. As I come up alongside Ennea, I tell her, "I need your assistance."

"If you want a stun potion, I'll give it to ya for free."

"No, I need…something else." I scratch the back of my neck, evading her gaze. "I need a spell or a potion or whatever. Something to curb the, ah…hunger."

"Hunger? Are you talking about the incubus kind?"

I blow a breath out my nostrils. "No, I'm asking for your help in procuring a pepperoni pizza. What do you think I mean?"

She raises her hands, palms out. "Take it easy, hon. I'm just making sure I understand what you want before I start chanting."

Groaning, I cover my face with my hands. "I'm sorry."

"Forget about it. You haven't been yourself lately." She peels my hands away from my face. "It's gotten really bad, hasn't it?"

I nod.

"Okay then." She steps back, surveying the tables around us, each one filled with an array of magical implements. "Let's whip you up a little something-something to take the edge off."

"The edge has become long and cold and razor-sharp."

"Don't underestimate my magics, Max."

I will never do that. Along with our odd group of friends, both elemental and human, we had saved the world twice. Lindsey was the driving force behind those successes, but the rest of us provided essential support.

Maybe I hadn't been as essential as the others. The first time around, I'd been enslaved by a regrettable bargain with a nasty sorcerer. The second time, I was disabled by the hunger. It's worse now than it had been all those months ago. In the meantime, I've been sating my need in ways I prefer not to think about.

Ennea cants her head at me. "Mind if I ask why you don't go back to that goddess? She gets you fueled up good, doesn't she?"

"I can't go back to Hathor. She is insane and obsessed with me. She has her minions hunting for me as we speak."

"A magical stalker, eh? That sucks." Ennea moves toward one of the tables and begins rummaging through its contents. "You want me to add a little stalker protection to the spell?"

"Yes." I hadn't known that was possible, but then, I know very little about fae magic. Ennea is the prettiest witch I've ever met, blessed with the cuteness of the leprechauns, her tribe of fae. Yet I've never felt the slightest inclination to seduce her. I want that annoying mortal. "Hurry up, would you? I have somewhere to be."

The words pour out of me before I consider their meaning. Where do I need to be? A shudder ripples through me as I realize the answer.

I need to find the mortal whose lips have transfixed me.

Ennea smirks. "What's the rush, lover? You got a hot date?"

"No, I—it's—gah!" I throw my hands up. "Can you do the bloody spell or not? I'm in no mood for a chat."

"Man, you are strung out, aren't you? No worries. I can get this done lickety-split."

Sometimes Ennea reminds me of Lindsey, the way she talks and the way she's completely unfazed by my condition.

"Have a seat," Ennea says, gesturing toward a large chair in the corner. "It'll be just a minute."

I can't sit, can't hold still, and certainly can't wait much longer. An itch deep under my skin torments me, and I must keep moving to keep from going barmy. So I pace the length of the room, my bare feet slapping on the stone floor.

Ennea thrusts a hand out to halt my pacing. "What happened? You're way more bent out of shape than the last time I saw you. How long have you gone without sex?"

"A few months."

"Shouldn't you be okay for a while longer?" She moves in front of me and rises onto the tips of her toes to look me in the eye. "What's going on, hon? I need all the info to get this spell right. You wouldn't want me to accidentally turn you into a toad or wind up with your manly parts shriveled up like raisins."

I roll my eyes.

"Not joking," she says, stabbing a finger into my chest. "Talk, Max, or I'm not doing a thing for you."

I wander to the big chair and sink onto it. Scrubbing my face with both hands, I exhale a long breath that deflates my shoulders. When I meet Ennea's gaze again, I feel deflated in more than my posture. "I encountered a woman."

Her expression brightens. "That's wonderful! Is she your fated mate?"

A string of snarled curses explodes out of me. I take a deep breath and try to regain my composure. Honestly, it's been many months since I've had much composure at all. I try anyway.

"The woman," I tell Ennea, "is a bloody irritating little mortal who wears enough weaponry on her person to take down a gang of motorcycle enthusiasts."

Yes, I'd sensed all those weapons though she kept most of them hidden.

A laugh snorts out of Ennea. "It's called a biker gang. You've been hanging out with humans a lot over the past year. How come you still can't get their slang?"

"I don't obsessively watch mortal television shows like you and your snarky brother do. Once a month is enough for me." I glance around. "Where is Tris, anyway? He didn't accost me the second I crossed the veil, the way he loves to do."

"Triskaideka is…unavailable. My sister Pendi took over manning the vortex for the time being."

"Why are all your siblings named after Greek numbers?"

"Ma and Pa couldn't keep track of all us kids, so they named us in birth order."

"I see." I slump down in the chair. "Why is Tris unavailable? I've gotten used to him annoying me with his moronic insults."

"He's got something to deal with, and it's none of your beeswax."

"You're all barmy."

"Whatever. Tell me more about the well-armed girl."

Grumbling, I drum my fingers on the chair's arms. "She tried to kill me."

"Obviously, she failed."

"Her weapons are not endued." I massage the spot on the back of my shoulder where the knife had slammed into my flesh. "It bloody hurt."

"Aw, poor Max." She sashays up to me and leans over my shoulder to inspect the wound. "I'm guessing this is where she hit you since you were rubbing it. All I see is a faded white line. Boy, you salamanders sure heal fast." She steps back. "What else happened with the sexy mortal chick?"

"What makes you think she was sexy?"

"Come on, I'm not dumb. You wouldn't be looking for a lust-reducing spell if you weren't hot for the girl you met today."

I grumble again. "She wanted me to bring her into the Unseen. Wouldn't tell me why. I said I'd do it for a kiss."

Laughter splutters out of Ennea. She laughs so vigorously her eyes start to water. When she, at last, stops her guffaws, she wipes at her eyes with her fingers. "Oh Max, you really are the cutest. Lindsey's right about that."

"I am not cute or cuddly or sweet." I shift in the chair, unable to get comfortable. "That little mortal threatened to dismember me starting with—" I gesture toward my groin. "My favorite part, as she called it."

Ennea laughs again. "I think I like this girl. But did you kiss her?"

"Yes."

"And?"

I prop an elbow on the chair's arm and drop my forehead into my raised palm. "She tasted better than any female I've ever encountered. Kissing her inflamed the hunger, but there was something else underneath it. Something bizarre and confusing. For reasons I cannot fathom, I felt the need to show off for her by shifting into salamander form."

"Maybe she's your fated mate."

"Stop using that term. Fate is bollocks, and the idea any incubus might have a fated mate is pure myth."

"Unless it isn't."

I lift my head to frown at her. "Sarcasm is not helpful."

"Not being sarcastic."

"Forget about fate and the infuriating mortal woman." I push myself up in the chair, straightening my spine. "Make the ruddy potion or spell or whatever it is."

"All right, all right. No need to get upset."

Ennea returns to the table full of magical stuff and gets to work.

I slump onto the chair again, my thoughts spiraling back to the woman and the kiss and the spark both ignited inside me. I try to think about other things, like Hathor and whatever bounty hunter she might've sent after me, but I can't stop my mind from traveling back to the falls and the girl.

Fated mate? Sheer nonsense.

But if I were to have a fated mate, I have no doubt the powers that be would choose the most irritating, frustrating, impossible female in the universe for me. After the things I've done, in my previous life as a mortal and after the forging as an elemental, I deserve nothing less than to be punished for the rest of eternity. The good I'd done with Lindsey and her allies can't begin to make up for the past.

Ennea marches up to me carrying a small, mud-brown ceramic bowl. She holds the bowl in both palms, offering it to me. "Suck it down, sweetie."

I peer down at the putrid-green liquid inside the bowl. "Can't you do a spell instead?"

"This is part of the spell. You drink it, then I chant."

When I lean in, a cloud of steam envelops me, its stench acrid and sour. I recoil, resisting the urge to pinch my nostrils shut with my fingers. "There must be another way."

"How can you be so squeamish? You ingested nasty dark magics voluntarily to help Lindsey."

"That didn't have a taste or a smell." It had set me on fire from head to toe, but since fire is the element every incubus is bound to, it hadn't hurt me. Much.

She thrusts the bowl closer, and in a stern voice says, "Drink it, Max."

I accept the bowl. Sucking in a breath, I lift the rim to my lips and tip the bowl up. The vile concoction pours into my mouth and burns down my throat. I fight my gag response until I've downed the entire bowlful of sickening muck.

Then I break into a fit of hacking.

Ennea ignores me and begins to chant. Her words are unfamiliar, but then, I've never bothered to learn the fae tongue or any of the primordial languages used by witches, sorcerers, oracles, and similar beings.

Realizing I still clutch the bowl, I set it on the floor.

The witch's eyes glow like sparkling emerald fire. Her hair lifts and feathers out as if a wind disturbs it, but I feel no air movement at all. Her chanting grows louder, faster, her voice infused with a strange echoing quality.

Abruptly, she falls silent. Her hair flops down, and her eyes return to normal.

Ennea pats my shoulder. "All set."

"It's done? That quickly?"

"Yeah, Max, it's done. Now scoot so I can get back to my paying work."

"Are you sure it worked? I don't feel any different."

"I'm sure."

Since I can't thank her without incurring a magical debt, I kiss her cheek instead. "Take care of yourself."

"You too, hon." She wags her eyebrows. "Good luck with the sexy mortal."

I growl and vanish.

When I reappear at the portal, I gaze down into the small pool below the burbling boulder, the only sign that a portal resides here on this side of the veil. Ripples in the water warp my reflection. Am I a monster? None of the friends I've made in the past year think so. Lindsey insists I'm good, and she wouldn't lie. What I want to do now would test Ennea's spell to its limits. I should give up the idea, but I can't.

That kiss. Her soft, delicious mouth.

Even my vivid recollection of the moment when I kissed Harper fails to inflame my hunger. It's there, yes, but it simmers at a low level the way it should when I'm not starved. I understand the spell masks the need but doesn't erase it. I'm still starved for sexual energy, but I can get by for a time without feeding.

And the only thing I want to feed on is *her.*

Golden-red hair. Lapis-blue eyes.

If she wants to get inside the Unseen realm, she'll have to give me what I want—what I need—first. She lusts for me too, I felt it. Since I refuse to take a woman by force, I'll have to win her over the mortal way.

Lindsey calls it "dating."

Yes, I will "date" the annoying mortal who stabbed me until she gives in to her lust and I get what I need. I'll haunt her until she can't stand it anymore. She will succumb to my charms, eventually. I have eternity to seduce her, while she has only a mortal lifetime to keep resisting me.

I rush through the portal into the mortal realm.

The second I emerge from the cave behind the waterfall, drenched and resolved in my mission, a strange sensation shimmers through me. I sense…her. I can find her wherever she goes, the signal is that strong. Fated mate? I still don't believe in that, but something binds me to her and drives me to track her down.

For sex. Nothing else.

You'll be mine, little mortal, sooner than you think.

CHAPTER FIVE

Harper

WOULD YOU LIKE FRIES OR ONION RINGS WITH THAT?" I ASK THE PUR-
ple-haired teenage girl who stands across the counter from me, staring
blankly like I've spoken nonsense. Am I the only person under thirty who
doesn't go catatonic when someone speaks to me? It seems to be an epidemic
these days. Maybe younger people have spent too many hours per day with
their gazes glued to the tiny screens on their phones, tablets, and other devices, and their brains have liquefied.

I stare at my phone as little as possible. It makes me go cross-eyed after
five minutes.

"Ummmm," the girl says, her dark eyes flitting everywhere but to
me. "Fries. With the jalapeno chili cheese dip."

Jeez, I miss the days when fries were just fries. No sriracha or jalapeno
cheese, no nothing except salt and maybe ketchup. Why does the modern
world have to complicate the hell out of everything?

"Sure," I say and punch the rest of her order into the digital cash register. "Would you like a receipt?"

The girl goes blank again, though her nose crinkles, shifting the silver
ring that pierces it. "Receipt?"

*Yeah, you brain-dead slave to trends, you know what a receipt is, don't you? It's
a little slip of paper with numbers and letters printed on it.* Okay, I might have gotten a bit cynical. But honestly, I have trouble taking anyone seriously when they
have a kitten tattoo on their arm. Some tattoos are beautiful and artistic, but
this girl's design is downright goofy. The only mark on my body that hasn't been

there since birth isn't something I volunteered for. It's a permanent reminder of the most horrific time in my life. The day my best friend was murdered.

The girl shakes her head. "No receipt."

"Okay, then, you're all set." I hand her one of the V-shaped plastic thingies that have numbers printed on them. "We'll bring your order to your table."

The girl shambles off.

Since it's past the lunch rush, I don't have any other customers. The drive-through is still busy, but I get a brief break from the burger-hungry hordes.

Feminine laughter echoes to me from the back of the employee area, past the food-prep stations and the bathroom. It originates from the direction of my boss's office. Sally, the manager, must have left her door open again. She's interviewing a potential new employee in her office, but I've never heard her laugh during an interview before.

The laughter erupts again, this time mutating into girlie giggles.

Sally? The tough-as-nails manager? Giggling?

No way. Somebody else must be in her office. Maybe the interviewee is a woman, and she's the one giggling. I haven't seen the person since they'd already been in Sally's office when I arrived for my shift half an hour ago.

Caden, my coworker, wanders past me carrying a package of drinking cups. He wears his usual serious expression. Aren't college kids supposed to be living it up? He always seems to be worried about something.

I snag his arm. "Have you seen the person Sally's interviewing?"

He pauses just long enough to shake his head and say, "Nope."

Before I can speak again, Caden hustles away from me.

A customer walks through the front door, and I return to my duties as a diligent member of the service industry. Diligent and underpaid. Underemployed too. I have a frigging bachelor's degree. Do what you have to do to get by, that's my motto.

That and "destroy the Unseen realm."

Uh...how will do that again?

Sally's laughter gets louder—and closer.

"There she is," Sally says. "Come over here and meet my best employee. Nobody works harder than this girl. She's a laser-focused labor machine."

I'm not sure I like being compared to a laser and a machine, but I dutifully turn to face Sally.

All the blood seems to drain from my body like a vampire has sucked me dry. I gape at the man standing beside Sally because I know him. Sure, he's altered his appearance somewhat, but there's no mistaking who he is.

The crazed creature from the woods. In Michigan. Over two thousand miles away from where we currently stand in the middle of the Nevada desert.

How the hell did he find me? And how did he get here? There are boundaries or something, that's what I'd been told. Invisible lines no elemental being can cross. The boundaries surround every natural water feature on earth, forming a one-mile radius beyond which only humans can live. I moved to Nevada for the sole reason that there are no natural water features in the middle of the desert.

"Max Nero," Sally says, glancing at him and then at me, "meet Harper Goode. Harper, this is Max, the newest member of our team."

Fabulous. Now the supernatural psycho knows my name and where I work.

The creature holds out his hand to me like he wants to shake mine. "It's a pleasure to meet you, Harper."

He still speaks with a British accent, and he infuses those simple words with enough sensuality to make my mouth go dry.

With my boss watching me, I have no choice but to be polite and pretend he's just an average Joe—if average means enormous and mind-blowingly hot.

He's not hot. He's dangerous and evil.

I gingerly slip my hand into his.

He surrounds it with both of his palms. "I look forward to working with you, Harper."

Christ, I wish he'd stop saying my name. It sounds ridiculously erotic spoken in his deep voice with that accent. He towers over me, over Sally, over everything and everyone in the vicinity. Good thing this restaurant has tall ceilings.

Max keeps holding my hand.

Warmth tingles through me from my scalp down to the tips of toes, but it settles the heaviest between my legs. I stare into his eyes, not because I want to but because they seem to draw my focus like a magnet.

His irises start to glow faintly with swirling shades of copper and crimson.

Does anyone else see that? Apparently not.

His black hair has lost its maroon streaks and is brushed back, while his skin has lost its coppery sheen. Instead, it looks tanned, like he's spent a day at the beach. His muscles have shrunk just enough to make him look impressively ripped, but not unnaturally muscular. He put on some clothes too—skintight indigo jeans and a golden-brown T-shirt. A pair of white sneakers cover his large feet.

And his eyes... They stop swirling, reverting to the honey-brown color they had been before our gazes intersected. His irises appear human now. Gorgeous, but human.

Stop thinking of him as hot and gorgeous, you moron. He's evil.

Yes, he *is* evil, and he wants to use sex to get to me. For what purpose, I have no idea.

Sally lays a hand on Max's bicep, fondling it more than is appropriate for a boss-employee relationship. She almost coos when she says, "Harper will show you the ropes and get you a uniform. I'll see you later, Max."

My boss, a forty-something woman with a husband and three kids, bats her eyelashes at the creature posing as a human. My God, she's flirting with him.

He pats her hand. "Thank you, Sally. You are a love."

She smiles and giggles again, then waves to Caden. "Come here and take over for Harper. She's getting our new employee settled in."

My boss finally leaves.

After I introduce Caden to Max—and Caden calls him "a real bro," whatever that means—I seize Max's arm and drag him back to the employee break room. No one else is here. I shut the door and round on Max.

The beast, I mean. I shouldn't use his name because it makes him seem more human. He's a vile creature.

"What the hell are you doing here?" I demand. "How did you find me?"

He braces a hand on the wall beside the door and leans toward me. "We're connected, darling. You can't get away from me, not even if you try to kill me again."

"You and I are not connected." Darting my gaze around the room, I search for something I can use as a weapon, something I can ram straight through his skull. But I see only plastic utensils. A spork doesn't seem likely to do the trick.

"We are connected," he repeats. "That's the only way I could find you. I sniffed out your metaphysical signal."

"Bullshit."

He squishes his lips together, his nostrils flaring. "You know about the Unseen. You know magic exists. Yet you refuse to believe I can track you? You're a fool, Harper."

Okay, he might have a tiny bit of a valid point. Mostly, I don't want to believe he can do that because it means I will never get away from him. He's dangerous by the mere fact of coming from the other world. His presence bumps me off-kilter in ways I prefer not to think about right now. Or ever.

So instead, I turn away from him and head for the cabinet in the far corner of the break room. Yanking the cabinet door open, I rummage through the stacks of plastic-wrapped shirts and pants, the components of our uniforms. Jeez, will any of these fit him? He's enormous. All those muscles would strain the fabric of even the largest sizes we have.

"What are you doing?" he asks, his tone casual.

"Getting you a uniform. If you insist on working here—"

"I do."

"Then you need a uniform." I pick up a package containing the largest size of shirt and study it. Will this fit him? Probably not.

"Don't bother," he says. "I am ready."

"Everyone wears a uni—" I glance over my shoulder and freeze. Though my mouth opens, no sound comes out.

He's wearing a uniform. White polo shirt emblazoned with the store logo. Navy-blue pants. White-and-navy hat. He even has a name tag.

I scuffle up to him, halting a few feet away. "How did you..."

He leans against the wall, arms crossed over his broad chest. "I glamoured it, love. Do try to catch up with reality. Magic is real, I am real, but the clothes I've glamoured are not real."

"Neither is the way you look. Your body, I mean."

A slow, sly grin stretches his lips. "Noticing my body, eh? I knew you'd be up for it soon, but I did expect it would take longer than ten minutes."

"Up for what?" I shake my head and throw my hands up. "Never mind. I don't want to know. I do want to know how you got past the boundaries."

"Which boundaries? There are so many kinds in the mortal world."

"You know damn well what I mean. The boundaries around the portals."

He eyes me with what seems like appreciation. "Ahhh, so you aren't clueless after all. Clue-deficient, yes, but not devoid of any clue."

"Answer my damn question."

"Do all mortal females curse at the men they desire? It seems to be a common affliction in the ones I've met."

"I do not desire you, asshat." Hands planted on my hips, I glare at him. "Answer the question. No more sneaky, snarky evasion."

A long and melodramatic sigh gusts out of him. "How did I cross the boundaries? The answer is, it's none of your bloody business."

"More evasion." I inch closer, jabbing a finger in the air near his chest. "What did you do with my weapons?"

"Which weapons? You have so many of them, though not on your person at the moment. I'd sense it if you were armed."

That's disturbing, but I put aside my unease and push for answers. "You took my gun and my knife. Poofed them away. I want them back."

"Firearms and blades won't do you any good in the Unseen." He absently rubs his jaw. "Afraid I can't return them, anyway. I sent them into an erupting volcano."

"You—How?" When he starts to reply, I throw a hand up to silence him. "Never mind. What did you do to Sally to make her gaga for you?"

"Gaga? I've not heard that one before. I gather it means she's lusting for me."

"Yes."

"Can't help that, love. No matter how I glamour my appearance, I cannot mask the intoxicating pheromones I give off."

I clench my fists and growl. "You are the most obnoxious, infuriating creature I've ever met. What are you going to do with the pay you get from working here? You said you don't want money because there's nowhere to spend it in your world."

"That's right. I do not need mortal money." He surges forward and grasps my upper arms, slanting in so close his hot breaths reflect off my face and flutter my hair. "Stop calling me a creature. Unless you'd like me to call you dinner."

"Go ahead and maul me. Prove you're the monster I think you are."

His lips twist into a feral smile. "That's not how I feed, *dulcissime*. You don't even understand what I am, do you?"

"You are not the first fairy I've met."

"Fairy?" He lets go of me and steps back, gesturing at himself. "Do I look like a ruddy fairy? They're called the fae, at any rate. But I am not one of them."

He really, really does not look like the fairies from storybooks or even the ones I ran into so long ago. The ones who destroyed my life. I know they're called fae, but I need to torment this beast so maybe he'll get fed up and go away.

"Okay," I tell him, "I give. What are you?"

"A salamander." He gives me an imperious look. "Since you are dangerously clue-deficient, let me explain it to you. A salamander is a type of elemental being. We are bound to fire, one of the basal elements, because we are older than the younger races, like the fae, who are bound to chemical elements. You would know us by the Latin name that mortals invented."

"Which would be?"

"I'm an incubus, *dulcissime*."

He lunges for me, wraps his arms around me to pin my arms to my sides, and hauls me into his hard, hot, muscular body. I swallow a yelp. My heart hammers, my skin tingles, and every breath he exhales shimmers across my face.

My feet dangle a foot off the floor.

"Let me enlighten you," he purrs, his voice husky and dark. "I feed on sexual energy, and the pheromones you're giving off are testing my willpower. You will feed me soon, mark my words. You'll beg me to fuck you because you want me more than you've ever wanted anyone else."

I ought to deny it, to spit in his face and tell him to go to hell. My voice refuses to work. My muscles refuse to budge. Even my body betrays me with a heady desire that makes me lightheaded and settles low in my belly, right above where I've suddenly grown slick.

"Are you ensorcelling me?" I ask, my voice dismayingly breathless.

"I don't need to." He drags his tongue up my throat, slowly, sensually. "It's pheromones, love. Simple biology."

Nothing about this is simple.

And I'm in deep shit—up to my neck.

CHAPTER SIX

Max

HARPER IS BEAUTIFUL AND SEXY, BUT SHE SEEMS TO BE SLIGHTLY DE-ranged and in deep denial of her sexual hunger for me. I hunger for her too, and though Ennea's magic has curbed my lust for this woman, something about Harper tests my willpower and the bounds of the spell. At least I'm not on the verge of assaulting her anymore. Christ, if I'd hurt her back in the woods…

I hadn't. That's all that matters.

But if the spell founders…

Nothing will go wrong. Ennea is the most talented witch of any race I've ever met. Her spell will keep working.

Harper squirms in my arms. "Let me go, you disgusting ape."

"Incubus," I correct, enunciating each syllable with exaggerated care. "I'm an incubus, not an ape or a fairy. Call me a salamander if you prefer."

"Whatever you are," she hisses while glaring hot, molten daggers at me, "let go immediately."

"Or what?"

"I'll—I'll get you somehow."

I chuckle. Really, she is the most charmingly insane female. "Go on, then. Give it a go."

She jerks her leg, apparently trying to knee me in the groin, but she can't get enough leverage. Next, she tries to wrestle her arms free. Her effort yields nothing more than a frustrated noise.

I bend my head to sniff her throat. "You're not a virgin. I'd smell it if you were. So why are you this pent up?"

"Excuse me? I am not pent up." She squints at me, her mouth puckered. "What do you mean you can smell I'm not a virgin?"

"You are the densest mortal I've ever encountered." I release her and move backward a single step. "Incubus, remember? Sex is my forte. I can sniff out a lot about you." I slant forward to take a whiff of the air near her face. "For example, I can tell it's been a long time since you had a good shag. No wonder you're so uptight."

She glowers at me, her little hands fisted at her sides. "Forget about my sex life. It's none of your goddamn business. How did you get past the portal boundaries?"

Her curiosity is annoying, but it also presents an opportunity I can't pass up.

I amble toward the sofa that's shoved up against the wall and drop onto it. Linking my hands behind my head, I stretch out my legs and cross my ankles. "Here's my offer, darling. For every question I answer, you will answer one too. And I mean real answers, not a simple yes or no. I want informative, honest answers. Do we have a deal?"

"Bargains don't work in this world."

She does have some knowledge of my world, but I stand by my assessment that she is dangerously clue-deficient.

"I'm not asking for a magically enforced bargain," I say. "A simple agreement will do."

She chews on her bottom lip for a moment, then exhales a blustery breath and relaxes her hands. "Fine."

"I get the first question since I've already answered several of yours."

"Go ahead."

"Why do you want to go into the Unseen?"

"Ask me something easier the first time."

I narrow my gaze on her. "You promised to answer my questions. Are you a liar, Harper?"

"No, but since you won't tell me how you got around the boundaries, I don't feel like telling you my reasons for wanting to visit the Unseen."

Bugger me. She makes a good point. I backed myself into this corner and won't get out of it unless I tell her the truth about me and the boundaries.

I'll save that for later.

"All right," I tell her. "A different question. Do you have a boyfriend or husband? I assume you don't since you haven't been shagged in such a bloody long time."

"Why ask if you think you know the answer?" She moves to the cabinet she'd been rummaging through earlier and shuts its doors, then turns around to lean back against it. "No, I do not have a boyfriend or husband."

The confirmation of what I'd suspected sends an odd sensation rippling through me. I can't be...relieved. I have no reason to give a toss about her personal life. I've never seduced a woman who has a lover waiting for her at home, but for Harper, I would make an exception. I'd feel terrible about it, but I'd do it anyway.

She arches her back as if she's stretching to ease tight muscles. The movement pushes her breasts up. Those lovely, round, full breasts.

Maybe I wouldn't feel *that* terrible about it.

Luckily, I don't need to find out if I would seduce her even if she has a lover. She already confessed she has no man in her life. Well, no man except me. And I plan to stay in her life until I've had her and banished this all-consuming craving for her body.

"My turn," she says. "How big of a man-whore are you?"

I suspect she's hoping to confuse me, but I'm not quite as clue-deficient about the mortal world as she is about mine. "Man-whore? Ah, I do believe I've heard that one before. Once again, I am an incubus. Fill in the blanks on your own."

"That's not a complete, honest answer."

Damn her and her delectable body. I'm only putting up with her questions so I can get answers from her in return and get enough information to seduce her. Maybe this woman with her infernal questions, not to mention her hatred of all things elemental, is my punishment for the sins I committed in the past.

I lower my hands and shift uncomfortably on the sofa. "I have been an incubus for around two thousand years. Do you think I've kept track of every bird I shagged? Let's simply say it's far more than any mortal could comprehend."

Or accept. Not that it matters to me if she accepts my past.

She pushes away from the cabinet, and her gaze sharpens on me. "You've been an incubus for two thousand years? That statement implies at some point you weren't an incubus."

"You had your question. It's my turn." I fold my arms over my chest. "How big of a woman-whore have you been?"

She sets her hands on her hips, her mouth tight. "That's none—"

I shake a finger at her. "Uh-uh-uh. Question for question. That's the deal."

She moves her lips as if she's cursing silently. "I've slept with five guys."

"That's all? Is there something wrong with you?"

Harper flinches as if I've struck her. She lashes her arms around herself, biting down on her lip, and averts her gaze down to the floor.

I haven't struck her, but I have struck a nerve. Why? I itch to know the answer, though it shouldn't matter to me.

She straightens, rolls her shoulders back, and resumes glaring at me. "My turn again. How long do you plan on working here and stalking me?"

"As long as it takes, *dulcissime*. If you want me gone, the solution is simple." I reach down to cup my semi-hard shaft. "Once I feed, I'm gone."

"Ugh. Why me? Considering how you've enchanted Sally, I'm sure you could get any woman you want to spread her legs for you."

"I want you. Only you."

"Why?" She looks genuinely baffled.

I'm baffled too, but I realized after our second encounter in the woods that I need to fuck her or I'll starve. No other woman, not even the goddess Hathor, appeals to me anymore.

"No bloody idea," I say in response to her query. "All I know is I need to have you. Once that's done, I can go back to my life, and you can go back to yours."

"You'd better find another way to feed yourself because I won't be your dinner."

"Tell my cock that. It wants you."

"Can't you jerk off or something instead?"

I can't stop the bitter laugh that rumbles out of me. "My own sexual energy can't nourish me. If I don't feed, I will starve. Trust me, darling, you don't want to meet a sex-starved incubus. The way I behaved when we met was only the first sign of the hunger."

"Will you die if you don't feed?"

I toss my head back and groan. "I'm immortal. I can't die by normal means, not even by starvation."

"So, what happens if you never feed again?"

"Enough. I've answered several of your questions." I sit forward. "You know sex is all I want. Why won't you simply give me what I need so we can go our separate ways?"

"Sorry, you don't do it for me."

You're a liar, Harper. I know it, and I'm sure she knows, but she refuses to admit the truth.

"I will do it for you, Harper—very, very well—if you stop clenching every part of your body." I rise from the sofa and stride toward her, halting inches away. "I'm excellent at helping women relax. Once I'm inside you, nothing else will matter except the pleasure I give you."

"Never going to happen."

Someone knocks on the door.

Harper stalks over to it and flings it open.

The young man I met earlier, Caden, glances from Harper to me and back again. "Sally wants you to show Max the food prep first, then get him up to speed with the registers."

"Sure, fine," Harper says breezily, giving the boy a breezy smile to match her tone of voice. "I'll do that right away."

"Awesome."

Caden gives us both the thumbs-up sign and leaves us.

Harper slashes her hand through the air in a gesture clearly meant to encourage me to walk out the door. "I hope you like grease because you'll have it in your hair after a day of food prep."

"Nothing you say will discourage me." I saunter out the door and wait for her to follow. "Lead the way."

She frowns, then hurries past me.

The bossy little mortal has to be in charge. At work, she can get away with it. Once I have her alone, away from this infernal restaurant, I will take the lead.

How much time will I need to seduce her?

A day at most. I'm just that good.

CHAPTER SEVEN

Harper

"WHAT IS THIS?" MAX SAYS, HIS LIP CURLING AS I DROP A RAW HAM-burger patty onto the grill. "It's pink and squishy and looks like the arse-end of a dead gnome. Do mortals actually eat this rubbish?"

"Yes, we do." I glance around to make sure no one else heard him talking about gnomes and mortals. "This is raw meat. Once it's cooked, it looks a lot more appetizing and tastes a heck of a lot better."

Not that I particularly like the food here. The stuff I make myself at home is way better.

Max pokes the patty with the edge of the spatula he holds. "What am I meant to do with it?"

"Let it cook and then turn it into a burger with a bun and whatever else the customer wants."

The kitchen smells like food, everything from burgers to fries to chicken nuggets and even fried fruit pies. Somehow, though, I can still smell him through all the sensory garbage. The scent of him makes me antsy, almost excited.

Shit. He's right about those pheromones, and I hate it.

No way in hell will I ever sleep with him. The creep can starve for the rest of eternity. Makes no difference to me.

Once the burger is cooked, I hand him a bun. "Put it in here. Have you ever seen a hamburger before?"

"Yes, I've seen and eaten them. The ones I ate looked far more appetizing than this one." He scoops up the thin patty with the spatula. "This is a pathetic excuse for nourishment."

"We sell them. You don't have to eat them." I wave for him to hurry up. "Put it in the bun but leave the top off for now. I'll check the order."

He slides the patty onto the bottom half of the bun and holds it in his latex-gloved hand.

I find the order slip where it's clipped to the shelf above. "Looks like we need lettuce, tomato, and ketchup. I'll get the fries while you—"

When I turn toward Max, I freeze.

He holds a complete burger in his palm. Lettuce. Tomato. I even see the ketchup between the meat and the veggies.

I blink several times, but nope, I'm not hallucinating. Probably. "How did you…"

Max thrusts his chin out. "I conjured the red and green vegetables as well as the revolting red paste."

"Do I want to know where you got that stuff? Isn't conjuring when you get things by magic from who-knows-where?"

"Yes, but in this case, I know from whence it came." He points at the bins of vegetables and condiments above our heads. "I got it from there."

"Normal people grab stuff. They don't teleport it."

"I am neither normal nor a person."

Jeez, I keep forgetting he isn't a man. The longer I'm around him, while he looks pretty much normal, the easier it is to forget. Max is a monster. A demon that feeds on sex.

For the rest of the day, I let Max conjure whatever he wants as long as nobody sees him doing it. He blithely informs me that he can make them forget anyway, so what difference does it make. I need to get a touch bitchy to make him agree to hiding his peculiar talents and not wiping the minds of my coworkers.

He's done enough already, enchanting my boss.

At the end of my shift, I leave without saying goodbye to Max. He's chatting up Sally again while she bats her eyelashes and coos over him. The sight of it makes me nauseous. Does he actually enjoy casting spells on women to make them gaga over him? Sheesh, and he can't understand why I refuse to have sex with him.

Back in my apartment, I collapse onto the sofa and shut my eyes. Maybe I'll sleep here tonight. The bed is fifteen away, but my muscles don't want to budge another inch. The apartment is tiny, all one room except for the itty-bitty bathroom that has an actual door. It houses the toilet and the itty-bitty shower stall. The sink is outside the bathroom, part of the open area that contains the itty-bitty kitchen and the area that houses my bed, the little love seat I call a sofa, and a lamp. The closet is next to the bathroom sink.

Efficiency living at its most basic.

Laughter erupts outside the front door.

Right outside my apartment.

I heave my body off the sofa and shuffle to the door, peeking out through the peephole. Its fisheye lens distorts things a bit, but I still have no trouble recognizing the figure outside.

Max stands right in front of the door, smiling at the girls who loiter near the periphery of what I can see through the peephole.

They're the ones laughing. Giggling, actually.

I yank the door open.

Max's head swings in my direction, his smile softening and heating up when he spots me. "Hello, *dulcissime.*"

Though I have no idea what he keeps calling me—Is that Latin? Italian?—I refuse to ask him what it means. Probably don't want to know. He might be calling me something dirty. The thought of what filthy things he might say in another language makes my nipples tighten.

It's the damn pheromones, that's all.

The girls, a blonde and a redhead, giggle some more and sidle closer to Max to pet his biceps. The redhead coos, "Oh wow, you are ripped, aren't you? Come over to our place. We have way more fun than her."

The girl, whom I don't recognize, flicks her haughty gaze toward me.

Like she has any clue how much fun I have. We're strangers.

When was the last time I had fun? I can't remember, and that's pathetic.

"Thank you for the offer," Max says, "but I already have plans."

The blonde pouts. "Too bad. We could've had so much fun, the three of us."

Is she seriously suggesting a threesome with me standing right here?

The better question is why do I care. I don't. No way. Max can do whatever he wants with whomever he wants.

The girls sashay down the open walkway to the stairs that lead down to the parking lot.

Max leans against the doorjamb inches away from me. "Ahhh, alone at last."

"You may not come inside."

"Unclench, Harper, and let me in. If your willpower is as strong as you think, there's no danger of us accidentally shagging." He fingers a lock of my hair. "Unless you want me so badly that you're afraid you can't keep your hands off me."

"Not likely." I swat his hand away. "Go home to whatever cave you came from. I will not be your fast food."

"Oh no, love, you would never be fast food." He angles in, his breaths reflecting off my cheek. "When we fuck, I'll spend days giving you pleasure, making you climax over and over until you can barely move and then you'll beg for more. I'll spill myself inside you again and again until you can't imagine living without my cock buried deep inside your body."

"Dirty talk does not turn me on."

The proclamation is only half a lie. I've never liked it when guys talk dirty, but the way Max does it has my body growing slick and hot and achy. This is insane. I met him yesterday, when he'd been on the verge of assaulting me. He is a monster, a creature from another realm of reality.

Once, I'd been at the mercy of dark beings. Never again.

"Why are you so cheerful today?" I ask, barring my arms over my breasts. "Yesterday, you were crazed and ready to attack me. Today, you seem relaxed and way too pleased with yourself."

"I did not attack you, did I? Maybe my self-control faltered for a moment, but I reasserted it."

"Uh-huh. That makes me feel sooooo much safer around you."

He pushes away from the jamb, scratching his jaw, his head bowed. "I'm sorry I frightened you. I have never assaulted a woman, and I never want to. Starvation made me a bit...overzealous. I have it under control now."

Sure, I'll believe that—because I'm the dumb chick in a B horror movie.

I snort. "Awesome for you, but I don't plan on being the test subject for your self-control. Go home. Goodbye, good riddance, adios, adieu."

He perks up, his lips ticking upward at the corners. "Do you speak Spanish and French?"

"No. I watched *Looney Tunes* when I was a kid."

He tips his head to the side, his eyebrows pinching together. "You watched lunatics performing a concert?"

I can't help it. I laugh.

"No," I tell him. "*Looney Tunes* was a cartoon TV show. One of the characters spoke French, and another spoke Spanish. Only occasionally, though. If I remember right, it was a skunk and a rat." It might actually have been a mouse, but who cares. I paste on a big, totally fake smile. "Gee, you'd fit right in."

He frowns. "I am neither a skunk nor a rat."

"Doesn't matter. You are a creature from another world, and I will never have sex with you. Goodbye."

I slam the door in his face.

After a couple of seconds, I peek through the peephole.

Max's eye fills my view.

I yelp and jump backward.

His voice resonates through the door. "We will see each other again, Harper. You can't chase me off that easily."

Silence. It stretches for several seconds at least.

I risk peeking out again.

Max is gone.

But not for good. That creature—salamander, incubus, whatever—has become obsessed with seducing me. Good thing I have solid willpower. Iron-clad, actually. Never in my life have I slept with a guy unless I decided to do it. No amount of dirty talk, flirting, or sexy smirks will make me change my mind about Max.

I strip off my clothes and crawl into bed.

And I dream about Max.

CHAPTER EIGHT

Max

I WHISK MYSELF BACK TO THE WATERFALL IN MICHIGAN, THE ONE BEHIND the rock shop. I could've gone to one closer to Harper's home, but I feel more comfortable here. Why did I emerge at the wooden railing around the pool instead of on the rock ledge right next to the cascade? Why am I hesitating? I need to go home and rest up before undertaking another day of cooking meat that looks like the arse-end of a gnome.

Giving up on Harper is not an option.

For some reason, some insane and bloody annoying reason, my body wants her and only her. If I can't seduce her soon, if Ennea's spell wears off before I can do it, I'll be in trouble. The large, hulking kind Lindsey used to get into before she gave up her Janusite powers. Like her, I've done this to myself. She refused to believe in the supernatural until it smacked her in the face. I've refused to acknowledge my hunger until it became starvation.

I can't get a leg over with anyone else. It must be Harper.

And naturally, she despises me.

My charms are lost on her—so far. I need to work much harder to win her. To get her in bed, I mean. Not to win her. I don't care about doing that.

I sense a presence behind me, something dark and feral. *Bloody hell.* I thought I would have more time.

"How high is the bounty now?" I ask as I spin around to face the hunter who's come for me. A groan reverberates in my chest when I see him. Pasty skin. Red eyes. Long, pointed canines. "This is perfect. She sent a ruddy vampire? Hathor's standards have sunk to a new low if she's dredging up slime from the bottom of a cesspool."

"Do not insult the goddess," the vampire says in a voice that sounds like gravel scraping across sandpaper. "She is above us all, far better than you for certain."

Like all his kind, he speaks with a German accent. Mortals have so many things wrong about the supernatural world, probably because so few of them have ever seen it or met anyone who lives in it. Why do vampires sound German? No one knows for certain, but rumors suggest it has something to do with the origins of the first vampire. More rumors swirl around that story.

Yes, even the Unseen has a grapevine.

"Hathor is a hateful shrew and completely psychotic," I say. "Walk away now. I dislike getting my hands bloody, and the need to commit murder leaves me irritated for the rest of the day."

The vampire hisses, baring his fangs. "I have killed stronger elementals than you."

"Yes, I'm sure you are the baddest of the badass vampires." I roll my eyes—at the vampire, but also at myself for using a phrase Lindsey would've said. I've spent too much time with her and the band of allies she once called Team Lindsey. No wonder I can't seduce Harper. To the vampire, I say, "If you're going to behead me, may I at least know your name first? It's the polite thing to do."

He raises one finger, his long black nail glistening in the twilight. "I am Gundisalvus."

"I'll call you Gunny." I spread my arms, and small red flames burst out all over my skin. "Would you like to be grilled or flambéed?"

Gunny charges at me.

The flames on my skin explode into a conflagration around my body. I swat at the vampire's hair, lighting it on fire.

He shrieks and stumbles backward, desperately patting his head until the flames are doused. His scalp, once pale, has turned crispy black.

"Unless you enjoy being toasted Cajun style," I say, "leave immediately. I can do this all day, but you'll have trouble biting anyone when your teeth are charred little stumps."

I want to murder him, but elementals are difficult to kill. Destruction is the only method, and that requires a magical assist. Endued weapons, magically enhanced poisons, those sorts of things will get the job done.

But I have none of that.

Gunny throws his arms up, bends his head back, and howls at the sky.

Not only is he revolting to look at and the most irritating creature in either world, but he thinks he's a wolf too. Didn't anyone tell him vampires aren't meant to howl?

"You have quite the voice," I say, "but I'm growing tired of playing this game."

I rush at him, aflame from head to toe.

He disappears before I reach him.

Skidding to a halt, I curse under my breath. The damn vampire has teleported away. To tell Hathor, no doubt. Well, at least she has the power to destroy him. His abject failure to capture me will displease her greatly.

Others will come.

I can't go home. Staying outside the boundaries is the only way to stay out of Hathor's clutches. I return to the parking lot of Harper's apartment building, find a secluded spot in the bushes behind the structure, and sleep there. The impulse to pop into her apartment and have a peek keeps me awake for several hours. Somehow, I must convince her to like me, at least enough that she will stop fighting her obvious attraction to me and provide the sexual energy I need to refuel myself. After that, I can leave. The annoying, if succulent, little mortal can go on with her life.

After a few hours of rest, I'm awakened by the slamming of a vehicle's door. I've heard that sound many times before when I was in residence at the rock shop in Michigan. Tourists, especially the young ones, love to slam their doors.

I yawn, stretch, and zip myself to the door to Harper's apartment. To avoid being harassed by the mortal authorities, I'm forced to suffocate my body with clothing. I raise my hand to knock on the door.

Harper rips it open before my knuckles contact the metal. Her hair is rumpled, and she wears only a pair of extremely short shorts and a top with extremely thin straps. The entire ensemble is fashioned from a thin, almost translucent fabric. When I move a few inches to the side, the sun shines on her body, making the flimsy fabric even more translucent and revealing glimpses of her nipples as well as the hairs at the juncture of her thighs.

Why does she have to dress that way? I'm trying to behave like a gentleman. Well, sort of a gentleman. An incubus can never truly behave himself. It isn't in our nature.

"You look scrumptious," I say, unable to keep my lust from coloring my voice. "I'd planned to make you breakfast, but I'd much rather feast on you."

Her eyes widen for half a second, then she squints at me. "What do you want?"

"I told you. To make you breakfast."

"No thanks. I eat bran cereal every morning. No freaky fairy food."

Fairy food? I resist the urge to snap at her that I am not a fairy, but I've already informed her of that fact. She's trying to annoy me in hopes of chasing me away. *Not bloody likely, Miss Goode.*

Why is my potential fated mate named Goode? It sounds like a joke, or the title of a raunchy film—*The Incubus and Miss Goode.*

Miss Goody Two-Shoes is more appropriate.

Still, I have the feeling she'll be downright naughty when I finally take her body and feast on all that pent-up energy.

Her gaze flicks to my groin. "Sorry, I don't let horny goats into my apartment."

"At least 'goat' is a step up from fairy." I set my hands on either side of the doorjamb and lean in. "But I'm not planning to ravish you—yet. I want to cook for you."

"Told you no. I'm sticking to healthy bran cereal."

"I would feed you something far more sensual and satisfying."

"No."

She slams the door in my face. It barely misses my nose.

That woman is impossible. How am I meant to win her over? Nevan cooked for Lindsey shortly after they met, and she loved it. Harper acts like I suggested I want to feed her excrement and force her to drink piss from a cup. I might not be a master chef, but I can do better than that.

Excrement would be more appealing than the hamburgers I'll spend all day flipping on a greasy griddle and cramming into atrocious buns.

I give up and go to the restaurant, forced to wait outside with the other employees until Sally lets us inside. Harper isn't here yet. Yesterday, I noticed her name on the schedule for today but failed to note the time her shift starts.

As I walk into the restaurant, with Sally holding the door open, I ask, "When does Harper come in today?"

"Ten o'clock." She flutters her lashes at me. "Don't worry, Max, I'll be here all day."

She squeezes my biceps and winks.

Wonderful. I need a way to dampen my pheromones, need it badly. Somehow, I must survive from seven a.m. until ten a.m. while the lecherous Sally pinches my arse and makes suggestive comments. It isn't her fault. I know that, but it won't help me get through the hours until Harper arrives.

This is going to be hell.

Chapter Nine

Harper

BY THE TIME I GET TO WORK, MAX IS ALREADY BUSY PRETENDING to be a normal human doing a boring human job. All day, I watch him doing just that. When a toddler drops her ice cream cone, he cleans up the mess and tells a joke that makes the little girl laugh. He charms her parents too. Every time he delivers an order to someone's table, he chats with them a little bit, not so much that he's derelict in his duties but enough to make all the customers love him.

It's not pheromones, I'm pretty sure of that. It's him. People like the beast from another world. He knows how to schmooze, a talent I've never acquired no matter how hard I try. Maybe I've become too closed off, and that's why I suck at socializing. The things I'd gone through made it difficult to stay as open and friendly as Max.

He makes it look so damn easy.

Okay, I might be a touch jealous of that skill.

At one point, I come upon him sweeping the floor in the break room. Seeing him, an elemental incubus, performing janitorial duties leaves me speechless for a minute. I stand there watching him, confused by his determination to keep working here. I also get an eensy bit distracted by the sight of his ass flexing every time he bends to pick something up off the floor.

"Enjoying the view?" he asks without looking up.

Yes, I am. He doesn't need to know that.

"Why are you doing this?" I ask. "Sweeping, mopping, slinging burgers and fries all day. You have supernatural powers. You could just stalk me or ensorcell me or something."

On the day we'd met, I thought he had ensorcelled me. Now...I have no frigging idea.

45

He huffs, darting his eyes to peek at me. "Where's the sport in that?"

I shut the break room door and slump against it. "Why are you going to all this trouble?"

"Do you have early onset senility? I told you yesterday." He props the broom against a table and saunters up to me. "My cock wants you, no one else. It's bloody annoying, and if I could talk it out of this, I would. Unfortunately, my body is ignoring my wishes."

"But you don't need to work here." I cross my arms over my chest, hoping to create a barrier between us. Like that will ever work. He smells delicious even when he's coated with the grease that seems to infuse the air inside this restaurant. "Being dirty and greasy isn't a turn-on."

"No, and it isn't enjoyable either."

"I repeat, why are you doing this?"

He slants toward me, bracing his palms on the door at either side of my head. "I've told you twice already. If you make me say it a third time, I will kiss you. It won't be sweet and tender. I'll ravage you with a kiss of pure, unadulterated lust. Then perhaps you'll finally grasp what I've been telling you. Until we have sex, you're stuck with me."

Fortunately, someone knocks on the door. One of my coworkers wants to eat lunch. Since I'm blocking the door, both Max and I have to move.

Lena, a pert young college student, eyes us with a strange expression as she hurries over to the fridge.

I return to the cash register, and Max goes back to whatever he'd been doing.

That evening, I stumble into my apartment and flump onto the sofa. Groaning, I let my head fall back. My lids drift shut.

A knock at the door rouses me from my half-asleep state.

Yawning, I call out, "Who is it?"

"Who do you think? 'Tis I, dearest. Your knight in shining armor."

Aw, shit. What is that damn incubus up to now? My knight. Like hell. His sarcastic tone makes it clear he doesn't intend to pledge his chivalrous, chaste love for me.

I lever my body off the sofa and scuffle to the door. Engaging the safety chain, I open the door a few inches. "What do you want?"

"To come inside, of course." He smirks. "And I do mean that in every possible way."

"Must you always be so crude? Mr. Darcy would never say he wanted to fuck Miss Elizabeth."

Max braces his body against the jamb, bringing his face way too close to mine. "You think I don't understand your literary reference, but I've read *Pride and Prejudice*. Mr. Darcy was a bloody moron. If he'd gotten under Lizzie's skirts on page two, none of that other nonsense would've happened."

I blink at him. Several times. Rapidly. An incubus reads the classics? An incubus *reads*? Maybe I had some false impressions of the Unseen realm, considering my sole experience on that side of the veil was less than welcoming.

"Mr. Darcy was sarcastic," I say. "I'd think you could identify with that."

Max observes me for a moment, his expression unreadable. "I want to talk. That's all."

"If you want to talk about how you need to screw me, forget it. Not interested."

He takes a step back and raises one hand, palm out. "I swear I will not discuss sex unless you bring it up first."

No smirk. No snarky tone. He is the most confusing man I've ever met.

Creature, not man. He is a creature.

The more time I spend with him, the harder it gets to remember that.

Oh, what the hell. I'll see him at work tomorrow, anyway.

I swing the door open and gesture for him to enter. "Welcome to my tiny apartment. If you were expecting a spacious and luxurious condo, I'm afraid you'll be disappointed."

He walks inside, and I suddenly realize he's wearing his work uniform.

I also realize I'm still wearing mine. *Yech.*

"Have a seat," I tell him. "If you can fit on the sofa. I need to change clothes before the stench of grease chokes me."

Max looks down at his own clothes and grimaces. He flicks his wrist. The clothing shimmers and changes, becoming a pair of leather pants and a black, long-sleeve shirt. The pants, a shade of dark brown, cling to every muscle in his thighs and sculpt to his ass. The shirt fits just tight enough to accentuate his torso muscles while being loose enough to leave something to the imagination. The bulge at his groin clearly isn't a sign of excitement. It's just how big he is.

I swallow. Hard. No sock in those pants.

"What would you prefer to wear?" he asks.

"Huh?"

"Your clothes. What would you like to change into?"

"I don't know." I take one step, intending to head for the closet, but halt as a bizarre sensation shimmers over my whole body.

"There," Max says. "Much better."

A sense of dread trickles through me as I look down at my body.

My uniform is gone. In its place, I wear jeans and a billowy white blouse.

I skim my hands over my arms and belly, afflicted with a sudden sense of unreality. He conjured me clothes. Or maybe it's a glamour. All I know is these clothes I seem to be wearing didn't come from my closet. "Where did you get this stuff? Please tell me it's not a glamour that'll wear off and leave me naked."

"That would've been a marvelous idea, but no. I conjured it."

"Yeah, but where did it come from?"

"I've no idea. I don't get a receipt for the things I conjure."

That "ew" feeling is coming back, and I sidle past him to put the sofa between us. "How do I know you didn't steal these clothes from a corpse?"

He rolls his eyes again. "Are you always this suspicious?"

"Yes. Always."

Max flops his big body onto the little sofa. It jumps. He spreads his arms over its back and sighs. "I don't know where conjured items come from unless I consciously summon things that belong to individuals I know. However, a corpse is no longer a living being, so I can't steal from one. It would be abandoned property as far as I'm concerned, but I did not acquire your clothing from a cemetery."

"But where—"

"That's all I can tell you." He pats the sofa. "Sit, Harper. Let's have a conversation."

I really, really wish I had a bigger apartment with more furniture—or at least a bigger sofa. Sitting down will mean sitting inches away from him.

My gaze swerves to his groin and the not-sock inside his leather pants. Jeez, I've never seen a man with a stick that big.

He strokes himself through his pants. "Come, *dulcissime*. Let us talk, and then I'll let you fondle the part of me you can't seem to stop staring at."

I clear my throat, lift my chin, tear my gaze away from his groin, and march around the sofa to take a seat beside him. Despite the mere inches separating us, I stop myself from gawking at his body. Instead, I lean back and set my feet on the footrest.

"Well done," he says. "You managed to make giving in seem like a brave act of defiance."

"Gee, thanks."

He relaxes against the sofa, sinking into the cushions, but his arm stays draped over the back and his fingers graze my shoulder. "I'm going to answer your question. I'll trust that you will show me the same courtesy once I'm done."

"Okay," I say cautiously, not sure what he's up to this time. Elementals are, at best, sneaky bastards. At worst, they're evil.

Max is different from the creatures I've encountered before. Maybe he isn't evil after all.

A little shiver tickles my spine. If I don't think of him as evil anymore…

"The boundaries," Max says. "You want to know how I get around them."

"Yes."

He hooks his ankle over the opposite knee. "I have special dispensation. The portals and boundaries are governed by one being, the god Janus, and he grants me free access to the mortal realm. He does this because Lindsey O'Rourke asked him to do it."

"Who's Lindsey O'Rourke? I didn't think elementals had last names."

"Most don't, but Lindsey is not an elemental. She's mortal. Until recently, she was the Janusite, a human gifted with the powers of the Roman god Janus. He had been…shall we say, inconvenienced and unable to make use of his powers. Lindsey received them."

"Oh." I struggle to sort out his revelations. "Why was she chosen? Do other mortals have the powers of gods?"

"No. Lindsey was the only one." He gives me a grave look. "You can't tell anyone what I've just told you. If any elementals found out what Lindsey used to be, they might come after her in hopes she still has those powers. If anyone learned I can circumvent the boundaries, they'd come after me too."

"I won't tell anybody." I make a derisive noise. "Nobody would believe me, anyway."

"Elementals would, but most mortals are exceedingly ignorant of the supernatural." He eyes me with a narrowed gaze. "Why aren't you?"

He did share his secret with me. I suppose I owe him an honest answer in return. "I've been to the Unseen realm once. It was not a pleasant experience."

"What happened?"

Memories, once buried, spring to the surface. I crook my fingers on my thighs, the nails digging into my jeans. "I had gone for a walk with my best friend, Kelsey, and we accidentally wandered farther away from home than we intended. When we came to a small waterfall, we knew we were way off course. Before we could turn back, these…creatures leaped out of the water and grabbed us."

Beside me, Max has gone still and quiet, seeming not to even blink.

"They abducted us," I explain. "Fairies abducted me and Kelsey and murdered my best friend."

"Are you sure they were fae?"

"Yes. They told us we were their slaves and that we belonged to the obsidian fae."

"Obsidian fae?" Max purses his lips like he's thinking hard. "Everyone in the Unseen thinks they're a myth. For a thousand years, there have been rumors about a band of rogue fae who renounced their connection to the chemical elements and instead bound themselves to obsidian as a means of absorbing dark magics."

"Chemical elements? You mentioned that before, but I still don't get it. How are they connected to the elements?"

He gives me that look, the one that suggests I'm a foolish mortal moron. "Since you are clue-deficient, I'll explain. Every elemental being is bound to a particular element, hence the term elemental. The element becomes a part of their essential being. Their powers are connected to it, and they cannot live without that bond."

"You're bound to fire, right?" I remember the way he erupted in flames the other day, and a shiver rips through me. He really is wickedly hot. "How old are you? Yesterday, you mentioned you've been an incubus for two thousand years, but the term salamander didn't exist before the sixteenth century. Paracelsus came up with the names for the elemental beings who are associated with the basal elements, including salamanders."

"Ah, I see someone has been googling."

"You know what Google is?"

He sniffs. "I am not as ignorant of your world as you are of mine."

"You must've been born before Paracelsus. So why are you called a salamander?"

"Still so clue-deficient," Max says, shaking his head. "Paracelsus may be the best-known mortal to use those terms, but we existed long before he was born. How do you think a mortal knew those names? A salamander whispered in his ear."

"Was it you who told Paracelsus about elementals?"

"No, darling, it wasn't me. Legend says it was a succubus who loved Paracelsus and stayed with him until he died." Max winks. "Or perhaps he was forged and lives still."

"Forged?" I probably look as clueless as he claims I am.

"Let's talk about that later." He slides a touch closer. "Tell me why you want to visit the Unseen. It has something to do with your abduction and your friend's death, I imagine."

He won't stop asking until I give him an answer, but I can't tell him the whole truth. I want to destroy his world and every creature in it. So I tell him a sliver of the truth. "I'm going to hunt down the obsidian fae and kill them."

"Revenge." Max nods appreciatively. "A solid motivator. But you have no clue how to dispatch an elemental, as evidenced by your pitiful attempt to murder me with a knife."

"I don't suppose you'll help me."

He pats my knee. "Oh yes, darling, I'll find you an endued weapon so you can destroy the obsidian fae and me. I'm a very, very stupid salamander after all."

"Endued?" I angle toward him. "What's that mean?"

His eyes widen for a second, then he sighs and rubs his forehead. "Indeed I am a very, very stupid salamander. The stupidest of all, in fact."

The miserable tone in his voice matches the look on his face. He blabbed to me about something I shouldn't know. I have no idea what "endued" means, but it's obviously an important clue. Maybe the word is in the dictionary.

"Bugger," he mutters. "I might as well tell you. Not as if you can get an endued weapon on your own. The term endued refers to something that has been imbued with magical power. In the case of weapons, this means they possess enough power to destroy an elemental. There are also magically enhanced poisons and dark spells that can achieve the same result."

Interesting. Like he said, though, I can't get something like that on my own.

Might I convince him to help me?

Ugh. I know what I'd need to do to talk him into lending a hand. Any bargain between us will involve sex. He needs it to stay sane and healthy. The idea of sleeping with him should disgust me. Instead, thinking about it makes secret parts of me go warm and tingly.

Oh, I'm in deep, deep trouble.

But he is my only way into the Unseen.

If I destroy the other world, I'll be destroying Max too.

My throat constricts as I gaze into his spinning irises. Destroy Max? I ought to have no qualms about doing that, but suddenly, I'm not at all sure I want to do it.

I can think about that after I get into the Unseen. Only one thing seems likely to gain me his cooperation. Since I won't have sex with him, that leaves me with one possibility.

"What if we kissed?" I ask. "Would that get you fueled up?"

He jerks like I've surprised him with a jack-in-the-box.

Well, I did kind of throw that at him out of nowhere.

Max stares at me, his brows crinkling. "You want to kiss me?"

"Answer my question, please. Will a kiss help your situation?"

"Perhaps. I've never tried to quench my hunger with a kiss, but I suppose a right good one might do the trick." His gaze settles on my mouth, and his tongue slips out to wet his lips. "Let's try it."

His voice has gone deeper and rougher, sexy as hell and rife with hunger.

I swallow, but my throat has gotten tighter. Kissing him sounded like an easy way to get what I want. Red rings of flame encircle his swirling irises, though, and I know I've made a terrible mistake by suggesting this.

"One kiss," I say. "That's all. For the price of one kiss, you will take me to the Unseen. If you renege again, I will find you and make you suffer. Maybe I can't kill you, but I can stab and shoot you enough times to make you very uncomfortable."

He chuckles, the sound deeply, darkly sensual. "One kiss won't be enough for you, but I accept your terms."

"Who starts this? You or me?"

"The bargain is yours."

So I have to kiss him. A new, sharper tingle sweeps over my skin. My breath catches, and everything below my hips grows damp and achy at the mere thought of pressing my lips to his.

His lips part, and his tongue glides over his bottom lip.

I scoot closer. My knee bumps his thigh. My shoulder nestles in the hollow of his shoulder, but he doesn't move his arm off the sofa's back to put it around me. He waits for me to make the first move. It is my bargain, after all, so I have to get things rolling.

A vision flares in my mind. Both of us naked, rolling in the sheets on my bed, getting tangled up while we—

Oh hell no. I will not finish that unwanted fantasy.

My body wants it for sure.

"Hurry up," he says, his voice still an erotic rumble. "Or I might lose control."

I touch my lips to his. They're warm and soft, lush and delicious, the taste of them faintly cinnamon. He smells of caramelized sugar and toasted marshmallows, an odd combination, but I can't think about why he smells that way. Can't think at all. I lay my palms on his cheeks and sample his lips with my tongue, exploring, testing, teasing. He doesn't move, seems to have stopped breathing. His skin heats up, the slightest touch igniting a smoldering fire inside me. Oh God, he tastes like...pure sin.

Do I have the willpower to handle this?

No choice.

I slip my tongue inside his mouth. An explosion of flavors and sensations rips through me. Chocolate, honey, sweet wood smoke, burnt sugar. Desire hotter than anything I've known before sweeps through me, weakening my body and making me moan. I thrust my hands into his hair, clenching the silky locks in my fists. His tongue is silky too, slick and hot, and he answers my every swipe with one of his own but never pushes for more. His patience and the taste of him, along with the feel of his naked body against mine, drives me to the edge of madness.

His body. He's ditched the clothes.

With a throaty moan, I fling my arms around his neck and dive in deep.

A rush of air flutters my hair. I register that fact before I realize what it means. Max has repositioned us on the sofa in the blink of an eye. I now lay spread out beneath his naked body.

He shoves a hand under me to grasp my ass.

Tongues tangling. Hands groping. We kiss and kiss and kiss until my whole body burns and tingles and I feel sure I'll die if he doesn't take me right now. I latch my leg around his and clutch at his shoulders. My nipples have gone hard, and even I detect the aroma of my need.

Max groans deeply, the sound resonating in his chest and vibrating into my mouth.

Please. I would beg out loud, but I can't stand to give up this kiss.

He breaks away, gazing down at me with flaming eyes and parted lips. His breathing is labored, and his dick has stiffened against my belly.

Max disappears in a blink.

Chapter Ten

Max

I SLEEP IN THE WOODS THAT NIGHT. HARPER'S KISS HAS FED ME, BUT NOT enough to thwart the hunger she engenders in me. Her lips. Her tongue. Her supple body. I felt all of that when we kissed, and despite Ennea's spell, I'd been on the verge of taking Harper. I have no idea what might happen if I do. Yes, I need to fuck her. I should've given her what she wanted and taken what I needed, shagging her mindless all night long. Instead, I ran away.

What if I lost control during sex and hurt her?

The risk is too great.

You bloody coward. I can live with being a coward for the moment if it keeps Harper safe—from me. Hathor's minions can't penetrate the mortal world beyond one mile from any portal. Since this region known as Nevada seems to have no water, at least not in the vicinity of Harper's home or her workplace, I don't need to protect her from Gunny or his mates. I hoped Hathor might've iced Gunny, but even if she has, the deranged goddess will send other bounty hunters.

So I sleep among the cactuses and tumbleweeds. A snake considers taking a bite out of me, but one flash of my fire skin and the creature changes its mind.

In the morning, I head back to the restaurant. Harper has the day off, I'm told, and so do I. Yesterday, I forgot to check the schedule, and Harper neglected to remind me. I suppose I should forgive her for the oversight. My presence unsettles her. She wants me, yes, but she also seems to have a deep-seated fear of everything elemental. I can't blame her for that. Being abducted by the obsidian fae has clearly left her scarred.

After discovering I'm not needed at the restaurant, and after shaking off the advances of Sally, I exit the building through the back door. It leads into an alley where an enormous receptacle with an enormous lid holds the restaurant's rubbish.

The alley stinks of rotting food.

I'm staring at the revolting "dumpster," as I heard someone call it yesterday, when a figure appears nearby. I groan when I see who it is.

The incubus formerly known as Travis Blackwell, sheriff of Mandan County, Michigan, wears his favorite blue denim trousers—jeans, Lindsey calls them—and a shirt that hangs open. He wears no shoes.

"Finally giving up on footwear?" I ask. "About bloody time. You're an incubus now, not a mortal forced to endure clothing and the torture devices known as shoes."

Travis hikes up his brows. "You're wearing clothes. Guess you've given up the incubus lifestyle, huh?"

"Only for a time, and only for a specific purpose." I frown at Travis and wonder for the thousandth time why he insists on keeping his bizarre accent. Lindsey calls it the Texas twang. "What are you doing here?"

I don't need to ask how he got here. In her last act as the Janusite, Lindsey granted a few elementals, her closest allies and friends, the freedom to move about in the mortal world. Aside from myself, that freedom was granted to Travis and the leprechauns Ennea and Tris.

Travis hunches his shoulders. "You're my mentor. I kinda got used to you being around to give me advice."

"You don't need me. You've got a handle on your urges." Unlike me, which I do not say, though Travis damn well knows about my problem. "Go shag a nymph or something."

"Feeding ain't the problem." He scratches his neck, wincing. "I, uh, kinda flamed out accidentally and set a tree on fire. I conjured a bucket of water and got the flames doused, but I don't want that to happen again."

I stare at him for a brief moment, then burst out laughing. "That's your terrible problem? The one that required you to hunt me down in the mortal realm? We are salamanders, Travis. Fire is an essential part of our makeup, the element we are bound to. Mastering it should be simple."

"You forged me. Isn't it your job to teach me about this stuff?"

A chill races down my spine. Yes, I forged Travis. When he lay dying, murdered by an evil bitch, I made the decision to transform him into a salamander. Though I had sworn two millennia ago I would never forge another being, I did it again anyway. Travis was Lindsey's oldest friend, and her grief over his death coupled with our Janusite-familiar bond drove me to do the unthinkable.

Now, I'm stuck babysitting a nascent salamander.

Besides keeping his Texas accent, Travis has also refused to choose a new name to use in his new life. He clings to the past, to his old life, far too much.

"Go home," I say. "Spend your time thinking of a new name for yourself and forget about the fire issue. Once I've done what I need to do here, I will help you."

"Sure. Thanks, Max."

Travis disappears.

I exhale a long sigh, my shoulders sagging. My karma has come back to haunt me at last. The only woman my body wants is a mortal who hates elementals. The bloke I forged follows me around like an abused puppy. And a barmy goddess wants me back in her bed. I almost miss the days when I'd done my mistress Lindsey's bidding and risked my immortal existence to save two worlds. At least then I knew my place.

Where do I belong now?

I trudge down the alley toward the street, not because it's my only way out but because I need to keep moving. Physical exertion always clears my head. Running would be better than walking, but when I run, I tend to "flame out," as Travis puts it.

When I get within a dozen feet of the alley's exit, a figure appears in front of me.

The vampire Gundisalvus sneers at me. "Caught now, are you not?"

"No, Gunny, I'm not."

How the bloody hell did he get here? No elemental can travel more than one mile from any natural water feature, none except for me and the few others Lindsey gifted with free access to the mortal world. Gunny has no such immunity, not from Lindsey, for certain, and not from Janus either. The god would never permit it.

Gunny licks his lips. "Go on and run. I love a good chase. The prey tastes that much sweeter for the struggle."

"Hathor won't be happy if you eat me for lunch."

"She permits me a taste, an hors d'oeuvre if you will."

I've had enough of hearing about his dietary habits. I'll burn myself to cinders before I let a ruddy vampire have me as an appetizer. Besides, I have more important matters to discuss with this loathsome creature. "How did you bypass the boundaries?"

Gunny sniggers. "Proprietary information. I cannot share."

The only method I can think of that might allow an elemental to bypass the boundaries is dark magic. The darkest sort would be required to get past Janus. Since he's a god, his powers supersede those of ordinary elementals. They surpass even those of other gods.

I suppress a groan. That can mean only one thing.

"Hathor used dark magics," I say, "to get you past the boundaries. You must be chock-full of the rot." I inch closer to him, sniffing the way only an elemental being can. My lip curls at the putrid stench of the darkest magics. "You're soaked in them, aren't you? Black spells. They will poison you, mate, do you realize that?"

"Our mistress commands, and I obey." Gunny sneers again. "She commands you to return. You should fall at her feet and beg her forgiveness, not hide in the mortal realm like a quivering mouse."

A mouse? If that's the best insult this tosser can dream up, he needs to expand his imagination.

"Go home, Gunny. The mortal world is not for you."

What if he attacks humans and drains them dry? What if the putrid magics roiling inside him infect mortals? I need to get rid of him for good.

Right, no problem. I'll conjure an endued sword and run him through. Because it's so bloody easy to acquire one of those.

Maybe I can't destroy the vampire, but I can wound him enough that he'll need time to recover.

I spread my arms and activate my flames, my entire body ablaze.

And I hurl the flames at Gunny.

They bounce off him, spraying backward onto me.

What the…

Gunny grins the evilest grin I've ever seen, his fangs sharp and glistening. "Dark magics, remember, salamander? I have more power than you."

Why do the villains always have dark magics on their side? Maybe I should ingest some of those to even the playing field.

Harper wouldn't like me that way.

Why do I give a toss?

Gunny lunges at me, hissing and baring his fangs.

I kick him in the gut.

He staggers backward and snarls at me. "You will suffer—"

Enough of this. I swing a flaming fist up into the soft underside of his chin. My fist strikes with a crack of splintering bones.

Gunny howls.

I clench my fist for another blow.

He tears a pipe off the wall of the restaurant building and wallops me in the face with it.

Pain rips through my jaw and webs out into my head, stabbing white-hot knives of agony into my brain. I stumble sideways. The alley spins around me for a few precious seconds, and by the time I regain my equilibrium, Gunny is raising the pipe for another strike.

He jerks and freezes, eyes bulging. Blood pours from his mouth, streaming past his lips and dripping onto his chest.

This can't be. I haven't touched him.

Gunny's head lolls forward, hangs there for a moment, and tumbles to the ground.

I gawp at the headless body still standing upright. How the—what the—

Gunny's body crumples, landing on top of his head.

Where he had been, Harper stands.

I can't summon any words, stunned by her appearance. She wears the same leather outfit as the first time I saw her, complete with all the knives and other weapons. In her hand, she grasps a small sword, now stained with blood. It's not the dagger she tried to kill me with on the day we met. This blade is longer and inscribed with intricate, swirling patterns.

"How did you do that?" I ask. "Only endued weapons can behead an elemental."

"Endued? I don't have anything like that." She pulls a black rag out of her pocket and wipes the blade clean, then tosses the rag into the nearby dumpster. "As for how I lopped his head off, it's pretty obvious. I whacked him with this."

She holds up the sword, its cleaned surface glistening silver.

"But a mortal weapon can't do that," I insist as I step over Gunny's corpse to reach her and bend my head to sniff the blade. "There is no magic invested in this blade. I'd smell it if there were."

"Fascinating." She slides the sword back into its scabbard, which dangles from her belt. "Why are you obsessed with how I killed that guy? He was about to off you." She eyes Gunny's remains and winces. "What was he, anyway?"

"A vampire."

She draws her head back, her chin tucked, and examines the body again. "Are you serious? A vampire? Guess it shouldn't surprise me they're real since all you other freaks are legit."

I try not to bristle at her blanket use of the term freak, but honestly, how many insults can a man take without getting irritated? I must look irritated because Harper raises her brows.

"What's your problem now?" she asks.

"Let's see if we can solve that mystery together." I tap my chin, pretending to consider the answer. "You've called me a creature, a monster, and a freak. Why might I feel vexed about that?"

"You're awfully sensitive for a cr—an incubus that feeds on sexual energy. I mean, you like to walk around buck naked." She raises her hands. "I'm just saying."

"Saying what?"

Harper lowers her hands and sighs. "Never mind."

Whatever she thinks of me does not matter one whit. All I need from her is one bloody great shag. I don't care if she likes me.

I don't. Not one bit.

"Go on," I say, "scurry back to that dark little hole in the wall you call home. I'll clean up your mess and meet you there."

Harper rubs her shoulder, wincing a little.

"Are you injured?" I ask.

"No, I'm fine." She folds her arms over her chest. "You could thank me. It's the polite thing to do."

"Thank you for what?"

"Saving your life."

I scoff. "Gunny was no real threat. I would've had him shitting his pants and running back home in five seconds at the most."

"Uh-huh." She pats my cheek. "Believe that if it makes you feel better."

She saunters back down the alley and rounds the corner onto the street, out of my sight.

I survey Gunny's remains, both segments of them, and consider how best to dispose of the blighter. Will he stay dead? If her sword isn't endued, she shouldn't have been able to decapitate him. She did, though. How, I can ponder later. I need to treat these remains as if he might come back to life later. Dumping him in the nearest volcano ought to do the trick. Even if he revives after that, he'll need considerable time and energy to regenerate.

Ah, how I love my life. I've been reduced to disposing of corpses.

Recent events almost make me long for my life in the Roman empire. Even the vilest emperor couldn't ensorcell me.

I kneel to pick up Gunny's body.

The corpse vanishes, along with its severed head.

Hathor. That crazy, conniving goddess has a lot to answer for.

CHAPTER ELEVEN

Harper

I SHUFFLE INTO MY APARTMENT AND SHUT THE DOOR, SAGGING AGAINST it. The adrenaline rush of offing a vampire drained away on the drive home. By the time I trudged up the stairs to my apartment, I was ready to flop onto my bed and go to sleep with my clothes on. With the door supporting me, I'm tempted to just slump to the floor and sleep right here.

My shoulder still burns faintly, but the scorching, stabbing pains have gone away.

Why did decapitating a vampire trigger the pain? The scar acts up whenever I get within range of a portal. It seems to have an affinity to magic.

I shiver. Magic. I hate that shit and every creature suffused with it.

Do I hate Max? He's been oddly nice since he showed up at the restaurant. Last night, I was ready to get naked with him. Maybe he ensorcelled me after all.

No, I can't believe that.

And my refusal to believe it scares me more than the idea I might've been ensorcelled.

I sink to the floor, my legs splayed in front of me and my back glued to the door.

A figure winks in beside me, but all I can see is bare feet and gray slacks. I crane my neck back to gaze up Max's body to his face.

He kneels beside me. "Are you unwell?"

"Wiped out, not unwell." I rub my eyes with the heels of my hands. "Wiped out and freaked out."

"The encounter with Gunny upset you."

"Was the creep's name really Gunny? Doesn't sound very vampire-y, and he sounded German too. I thought all vamps were from Transylvania or something."

He lets out a long-suffering sigh. "A mortal with an overly vivid imagination dreamed up that nonsense. In fact, no one knows why vampires speak with German accents. I don't know the full story, no one does, so don't ask any more questions about it."

"Is the vamp dead?"

Max sits down beside me and massages his neck. "I would assume he's dead, but then, things often aren't as they appear where elementals are concerned. His body vanished at any rate."

"Vanished?" I twist my torso to look at him. "You mean like it disintegrated?"

"No, I mean that it vanished." He waves his hands in a vague gesture. "It went poof."

"What the hell happened to it? Where did it poof to?"

"Afraid I'm not privy to that information." He contorts his mouth into an irritated expression. "Though I have my suspicions it was Hathor. I had an anti-stalking spell installed, but she could still send her minions after me. I assume she found a loophole in the magics, perhaps because she wasn't stalking me herself. She had someone else do the dirty work."

"Hathor?" I rotate my whole body to face him, tucking my legs under me. "Do you mean the actual goddess? The one from ancient Egyptian mythology?"

Max goes stone-still, his face going blank for a moment. Then he slumps against the wall, groaning miserably, and shuts his eyes. "Yes, the goddess Hathor. She is insane and obsessed with me. I must be as knackered as you are to blurt that out."

"You do look a little green around the gills."

"I have no gills. My body functions much as yours does."

"That's a saying mortals use to mean you don't look so hot."

He manages a half-smirk. "But I am hot, always. Touch me and see."

"Already know your skin is hot. I meant—"

"I know what you meant. I've heard that saying before." He lets his head fall back against the door. "The green gills statement had me flummoxed."

"Why did Hathor send a vampire after you?"

"Because I took away her favorite toy." He hooks a thumb at his own chest. "Me."

"I don't get it. What does she want from you?"

He rolls his eyes. "What do you think? Hathor wants her sex toy back."

"Oh." My cheeks grow warm, partly from embarrassment, partly from thoughts of what Max and the goddess might've done together. I want to be the one playing with Max. God, do I ever want that. I bite my lip and focus on the carpeting, picking at loose threads. "So, why don't you go back to her? You need sex. Sounds like she's more than happy to give it."

"She is insane. If I go back to Hathor, she'll ensorcell me, and this time I might not get away from her. I can't be her slave again. I won't do it." He covers his face with his hands, then lets them fall away. "And in point of fact, I cannot do it. My cock wants only you."

The heated tone of his voice, the husky rumble of it, makes my breath hitch. I want him. How can I know it isn't his pheromones triggering my desire against my will? I glance up at him, and the molten, swirling colors in his eyes send a shiver of excitement rushing through me. Does it matter why I crave him? I can enjoy having sex with him and then walk away.

Unless he really did put a spell on me.

"How do I know you haven't ensorcelled me?" I ask. "Maybe I'm attracted to you only because you've made me feel that way with your supernatural tricks."

"I wouldn't know how to ensorcell you. Besides, if you were ensorcelled, you wouldn't be so snarky. You'd be a mindless slave to my will." His tight-lipped expression melts into a devious smile. "I might enjoy that, though. You at my mercy."

"No, you wouldn't. If you wanted me that way, you would've figured out how to put a spell on me days ago."

He jerks his head back. "That's what you think? What happened to 'Max, you're a freak and a monster and a creature'? You called me that less than an hour ago."

Damn, he's right. Why did I emphatically state he wouldn't ensorcell me? Because I meant it, I suddenly realize. Despite the fact I called him a freak earlier, I don't think of him that way anymore. "I guess I've…seen other sides of you lately."

"Ah, that sounds promising." He leans closer. "I can smell your desire, Harper. It's driving me mad."

Shit. I am getting damp down there, but I didn't think he could smell it. The idea that he does instigates a wave of warmth that spreads through my entire body while my skin grows so sensitive that I swear I can feel his breaths on my lips and almost taste it too.

He gazes deep into my eyes, and his voice drops to a sultry purr. "You will enjoy it, I'll make certain of that. Your pleasure feeds me, so I have excellent motivation to push you to the limits of your mortal body and beyond. You'll beg for more even while you lay limp and satiated in my arms."

My lids flutter shut of their own accord. I draw in a deep breath, sucking in the spicy, drugging scent of him. A low growl rumbles in his throat, the sound rife with a hunger that has me choking back a moan. Oh God, I want—need to have sex with him. Right now.

"Yes," I whisper, my breaths growing heavier. "Yes, Max, please. You smell so good, I don't want to wait anymore."

He says nothing. Does nothing.

I force my lids to open.

Max wears a tight-lipped expression, the hot colors in his eyes dimming.

"What's wrong?" I ask.

He screws up his mouth, his lips working like he's struggling for words. "Max—"

"Dammit," he hisses. "I can't do this. Not now, not this way. I—" He unleashes the longest, most pitiful groan I've ever heard. "It's my pheromones you want, not me."

"So what? You're an incubus. Pheromones are what you do."

He runs a hand over his mouth. "Yes, but this time is different. I don't want—Never mind."

And with that, he winks out.

"You've got to be shitting me," I say to the air where he'd been. "I throw myself at you, and you take off? Don't expect me to do that again." I scramble to my feet and snarl at the empty space in front of me. "You screwed up, Max, and I won't say yes again."

Except I can't actually swear to that. My body wants to shout "yes-yes-yes." If he pops back into my apartment right now, I'll give in.

Damn pheromones.

I shamble into my bedroom and flop onto the bed on my stomach, taking time only to throw the covers back before I collapse. I kick my boots off too and shed my weapons, but I leave the rest of my clothes on. Too tired to undress. Too tired to stay awake. Max's seductive ways woke me up for a brief time, but now the weariness crashes down on me. I drift into the blessed oblivion of slumber.

Even in sleep, my mind torments me with visions of Max.

We're in a small open area within the woods, where green moss forms a pillowy cushion beneath our feet. The air smells of caramel and fresh-cut grass and…spicy Max-ness. He's naked before me, his erection waving in the air between us. I glance down at my own body and realize I'm naked too, my nipples erect and the evidence of my lust dribbling down my inner thighs.

Max growls, the sound soft and ravenous.

I can't catch my breath. He's beautiful, otherworldly, sexy as hell, and ready for action. So am I. Why do I want him this much? I barely know him and yet… Answers don't matter. I created this dream for myself, didn't I? This fantasy grants me the chance to explore my desire for him without giving in to it, not in reality.

Enjoy Max with no risk? Hell yeah.

He moves closer, pulling me tight against his body. "Say it again."

"What?"

"You know what." He rakes his hot tongue up the column of my throat and curls it around my earlobe. "Say it again."

His voice has gone rough, his need coloring his tone and hardening his muscles.

With his lips on my ear, I only need to turn my head to whisper, "Yes, Max, please."

A groan, deep and carnal and almost feral, resonates in his chest.

In an instant, we go from standing upright to lying on the ground with me beneath him. The full length and breadth of his incredible body covers mine. His heat penetrates my skin, the scent of him drugs me, and the wildly swirling colors in his eyes transfix me. Threads of maroon, the same shade as the streaks in his hair, unfurl in his eyes.

"Mine," he growls as he slithers down my body, kissing and licking and sucking every part of me he can take hold of with his mouth.

By the time he reaches my hips, I'm writhing and knotting my fingers in his hair. Desperate noises bubble out of me, spurred by a mounting need.

He nuzzles the hairs on my mound, inhaling deeply. "I'm going to eat you up."

"Yes, Max, please."

"Feed me your pleasure."

He shoves his head between my thighs and—

A bolt of black energy slams into his back. His body convulses, his head snaps back, and the fiery colors in his eyes are doused. He drops onto the ground beside me, his eyes wide and his chest heaving. His breaths come in wheezing gasps.

"Max!" I shout as I scramble to my knees, glancing around to find the source of the black energy bolt. It had sizzled with white sparks, its branching body shimmering with dark copper. Its primary color had been black.

No, not just black. Obsidian. Shimmering, roiling obsidian.

The scar on my shoulder burns like a branding iron has been rammed onto it. Cold sweat beads on my forehead and trickles down my temples. I struggle to move, but I can't. The scar, the brand, seems to pin me in place.

A figure appears on the other side of Max.

I swallow, but my throat has gone dry and tight.

The figure, the manlike creature, gazes down at Max without expression. The being's obsidian flesh seems to consume the light around the creature even while his skin shimmers. He aims his eyes at me, their depths a fathomless black, their rims composed of spinning rings of deepest sapphire.

For the first time in thirteen years, I've come face to face with an obsidian fae.

A bodysuit of silver-tinged black forms a kind of second skin that shields everything save for his hands, feet, head, and neck. His hair is gray as ash. When he crouches to peer at me straight-on, the obsidian centers of his eyes begin to whirl.

"You belong to the obsidian fae," he says, his raspy voice as bizarre as his appearance. "No other may have you. Harper Goode belongs to the darkness."

I grasp Max's hand, seeking solace in the contact, but there will be no solace. Not as long as the obsidian fae exist.

"Forget this one," the fae says, pointing one dark finger at Max. "Dispatch him with the weapon we gave you so long ago if you wish to spare him the pain of what is to come. His pain matters naught to us, but your survival is the key to our plans. We will not allow you to give all your goodness to him. It belongs to us."

"If you try to kidnap me again, I'll get away somehow."

The being laughs, the sound dark and without humor. "You think to escape us? No, child, you will be free only if we allow it. You need to…simmer for a while. Once you have reached the point of optimum potential, we will harvest your soul."

His statement and the hungry undercurrent in his voice shoot ice through my veins. Every hair on my body stiffens from the awareness of what those words mean. Harvest my soul. They intend to kill me.

"Do not fret," the fae says. "It will all be over soon."

"No. I'll fight you."

"You will fail." He slants toward me and aims his long finger at my shoulder. "Our brand marks you to this day. It compelled you to search for the Unseen, to seek a way into it and find us again. You never had any free will, child. We have pulled your strings since the day we took you into our world. When the time is right, you will come to us willingly."

"Never."

"You will see. The brand will show you."

The fae vanishes.

I wake with a jolt, the breath exploding out of me. My heart thuds. The room whirls for a second or two, then the hallucinatory motion diminishes until it fizzles out altogether. I lie on my back on the bed, still clothed, sweat dampening my hair and oozing over my skin.

The obsidian fae want me. One of them invaded my dreams to assert their claim on me.

My whole body trembling, I push up into a sitting position.

I will die before I ever let them have me.

Chapter Twelve

Max

I SLEEP OUTDOORS, AGAIN, IN THE MORTAL REALM, AGAIN. AFTER GUN-ny's foray into the human world, I'm no longer certain of my safety here—or of Harper's. I don't think the loathsome vampire has seen her, but if he can cross the boundaries, who knows what else the bastard can pull off. Maybe he possesses the ability to see through the back of his skull. I do not want to know what dark and vile magics Hathor imbued into the vampire to give him free access to this world.

So, to protect myself from bounty hunters, I sleep with a pile of sand and rocks covering my body. Even as a soldier in the Roman legions, I hadn't needed to camouflage myself this way. The legions rampaged. We didn't hide from our enemies. As a salamander, I helped save the world twice. Now I'm reduced to hiding from a ruddy vampire and a mad goddess, conceal-ing myself under layers of dirt. Soon, I'll be living in a sewer with rats and cockroaches, coated with filth and slime.

No wonder Harper doesn't want me.

Well, she wants me. But she doesn't want to. I am a beast, a creature, a monster, a thing.

I wake at dawn and walk the streets of this town until the restaurant opens. This morning I arrive there a few minutes before Sally, hanging about in the alley near the staff entrance and within sniffing distance of the odoriferous dumpster. Sally shows up a few minutes later. When she aims her dreamily lustful gaze at me, I cringe and scratch my arms. I wish to hell I could turn off these bloody pheromones. Sally doesn't want me. She craves the high she gets from my pheromones. My life would be so much easier if I could just shag Sally and go home to hide in my warded lair. Hathor can't get me there.

Christ. What a bleeding coward I've become.

Well, I can't shag Sally, anyway. My damn body won't let me.

Fated mate? What a pile of rubbish that is. If Harper is fated to be mine, why does she despise me?

Sally unlocks the door and holds it open for me. "Sexy beasts first."

I stare at her. Beast? I doubt she means it as an insult, and she certainly doesn't know Harper keeps calling me that name, but the word stings like a slap to the face.

My employer winks. "We're all alone for another fifteen minutes."

Bloody hell.

As I cross the threshold into the building, I ask, "Where is Harper? She's usually the first one to arrive."

"Harper quit last night."

I halt just inside the doorway. "What? Why?"

Sally shrugs. "She wanted more time off, claimed it was a family emergency, but she's already used up her vacation time. Besides, I've heard all her excuses before. I told her if she didn't come to work today, she was fired. She quit instead."

I round on Sally, towering over her on purpose. "You did what? Harper needs this job. She works harder than anyone else in this ruddy grease-filled hellhole, coming in at whatever hours you assign her, working double shifts, doing whatever you ask of her without complaint. But you couldn't give her a few days off?"

My voice sounds harsh even to my ears, but I can't help it. I watched Harper doing her job, smiling at customers even when I know she must've been exhausted. Studying the posted work schedule showed me how often she works double shifts. Sometimes she takes an early morning shift after working until midnight the night before, then stays late to cover for someone else.

Sally's eyes bulge. Her mouth falls open, and her face pales.

Reflected in her eyes, I see my own flaming a deep crimson.

I shut my eyes and back away from Sally. The beast has shown his true face.

"P-please," she whimpers. "Don't hurt me. I'll give Harper her job back."

"Don't bother. She's better off away from this place." I open my eyes to fix them on her. "Still want to fuck me, Sally? I'm fireproof, but I doubt you are. It will be, quite literally, scorching sex."

Panic contorts her features as she flaps her head violently.

Why the hell did I feel the need to terrify her? I've never flambéed a woman during sex. But Sally hurt Harper, and I cannot stand for that.

"Relax," I tell her. "You'll never see me again. I quit too."

With that, I zip away to the one place where I know I'll be welcome, teleporting directly there the second I cross through the portal.

Lindsey yelps.

Nevan flings a blanket over his wife to cover her nakedness. She remains seated on his lap. They both gawp at me, Lindsey with shock and Nevan with annoyance.

"Sorry," I say. "Didn't think you'd be, ah, doing whatever it is you're doing."

"Having sex," Lindsey snaps. "How can an incubus not figure that out?"

"It's seven a.m. I assumed you'd be asleep."

Lindsey dismounts her husband, hugging the blanket tightly around herself. Nevan lies there stark naked, glaring at me.

"He doesn't seem to be up for it," I inform Lindsey. "Literally."

Nevan springs into a sitting position, his nostrils flaring. "What do you want?"

Though he speaks with an Irish accent, he's no more Irish than I am British. I can't explain why either of us has a modern mortal accent. No elemental can. It's one of the great mysteries of the Unseen.

I glance at Lindsey and her very swollen belly, then frown at Nevan. "She's very pregnant, you know. Should you be mauling her? It might harm the baby."

Nevan's mouth opens, but Lindsey speaks before he can. "Honestly, Max, did you come here to yell at Nevan for having sex with me? Or is there some legitimate reason you blipped into our bedroom?"

I rub my jaw. "I was aiming for the living room. My targeting is a bit off today."

Nevan eyes me up and down. His lips kink into a smirk. "The apparel suits you. I particularly like the name tag. Is that blood on your shirt?"

Oh bollocks. I'm still wearing my work uniform. I glance down and notice the red stain Nevan had spotted. "It's ketchup. The yellow bits are mustard, and I think that brown splotch is grease."

Lindsey raises her brows. "What have you been doing lately that involves ketchup and grease?"

"Working at a fast-food restaurant in Nevada."

They both stare at me blankly for several seconds.

Until Nevan bursts out laughing.

Lindsey slaps a hand over her mouth, but her attempt to stifle her laughter results in her entire body shaking and her eyes watering.

"Yes, have a good laugh," I say. "I've been humiliating myself, pretending to be a mortal and swimming in greasy foods every day, in a desperate attempt to get the only woman my body wants to shag to want to shag me. I've even mopped up vomit. Hilarious, isn't it?"

I stomp over to the wooden chair in the corner of the room and slump onto it.

Lindsey grabs a satin robe off the headboard and shimmies beneath her blanket as she dons the garment. Then she dumps the blanket on Nevan's lap and pads over to me, kneeling in front of me with her hands on my knees.

"Poor Maxie," she says. "You're having a hard time lately, aren't you?"

"I'm in hell."

Nevan grunts. "I've been to Hell. Trust me, you are not there yet."

Lindsey flashes him an irritated look. "You're not helping. Can't you see Maxie is bummed out?"

I let out a long, miserable groan. "Would you please stop calling me Maxie? And what in heaven's name does 'bummed out' mean?"

"She thinks you're depressed," Nevan explains. He scrutinizes me for a moment, his brows cinching together. "You are a mess, aren't you?"

"Yes."

"And you came to us for assistance."

"Not you. I need Lindsey's help." I slouch deeper into the chair. "No offense, mate."

He lifts one shoulder. "As long as you don't try to have sex with my wife, I take no offense."

"Nevan honey, you suck at consoling Max." Lindsey pats my knees. "Now, what can I do to get you out of the dumps?"

"The whats?"

"Being in the dumps is another term for being bummed out." She rubs her lower back and arches backward. "Ooh, I really can't squat on the floor these days."

Nevan leaps off the bed, scoops up his wife, and deposits her on the mattress where a stack of pillows props her upright.

"I'll make breakfast," he says, "while you and Max talk."

He exits the room.

"Okay," Lindsey says, "tell me what the problem is. You mentioned wanting a woman who doesn't want you."

"What I said was my body wants her, but she doesn't want me." I let my head fall forward as I sigh. "Ever since I first saw her, she's the only female I want to f—to have sex with."

Lindsey's mouth curves into a closed-mouth smile, her cheeks dimpling. "You can say the F-word in front of me. I'm not that delicate. Or are you still worried about the baby overhearing curse words?"

"A bit of both."

"It's so cute that you worry about us." She adjusts her pillows while making little grunting noises. "There, that's better. I'm so glad you found your fated mate. Tell me all about her."

"What makes you think she's my fated mate? That's nonsense, anyway."

"She's the only woman you want. Sounds like fate to me."

"Then fate has a bloody awful sense of humor." I shove both hands into my hair and grumble. "Her name is Harper Goode. She hates elementals and thinks I'm a monster, a creature, and a thing. It's not entirely accurate to say she doesn't want me. It's more that she doesn't want to want me. My pheromones force her to feel desire for me."

"Are you sure about that?"

"Yes. That's why I have pheromones, to attract women so I can feed on their sexual energy." I heave myself out of the chair and begin to pace the width of the room. "Never before in my two thousand years as an incubus have I wished I didn't have magical pheromones."

"But now you do."

"Last night, Harper was ready to get a leg over. What did I do? I ran away and slept in the desert with the snakes and scorpions."

"Why do you think you did that?"

I pace faster, flicking my fingers, eliciting tiny blue flames from their tips and snuffing them out before flicking my fingers again. "I want her to want *me*, not my supernaturally enhanced pheromones."

"Maybe she does."

"Even if that's true, I can never know for certain."

Lindsey pats the mattress beside her. "Sit, Max. Your pacing is making me dizzy, and I really don't need you setting the bed on fire with your finger flicking."

I obey her, even though she isn't my mistress anymore. I came here for her help, and she seems ready to give me advice.

"Can your pheromones travel long distance?" she asks.

"No, I have to be in relatively close proximity."

"Perfect." She slaps her hands on her thighs. "I have the solution. Call her."

"Even if she came when I called, which she can't, I'd still have the phero-mone problem."

"No, Max, I don't mean a supernatural shout-out." She grabs her cell phone off the bedside table and offers it to me. "Call her on the phone."

Hmm, that might work...except for one problem. "I don't have her number."

"No problem." She sucks in a deep breath and hollers, "Nevan! I need my laptop. Pronto."

Nevan brings her laptop computer, which I've seen her use before. I've never touched a computer in all my existence, but she flips up the lid and swirls her finger on the little rectangular pad beneath the keyboard.

Lips scrunched, she peers at the screen. "Let me find the app Ennea gave me. Ah, there we go. Now I just type in Harper Goode in Nevada and..." She flings up her hands, grinning. "Voila! We have her cell number."

"Ennea gave you an app?" Whatever an app is.

"An enchanted app that makes sure I find whatever I'm looking for with the first search." Lindsey types on her phone, then offers it to me again. "Just hit the green button, and it'll dial Harper's number."

"I—" My gaze flies to Nevan, who hovers nearby, and back to Lind-sey. "I'll need privacy for this. May I borrow your phone for a while? I'll bring it back later."

"Sure, take it."

"You're a real mate, Lindsey."

I whisk myself to the other side of the world, to a spot that's precisely opposite where Harper is. Punching the green button on Lindsey's phone, I hold it to my ear. It rings three times before she answers.

"Hello?" she says sleepily.

"It's me, *dulcissime*."

A long pause follows. "Max?"

"Yes, it's me." I lower my voice to a rumbling whisper, the voice that women always love. "How badly do you want me right now, Harper?"

Chapter Thirteen

Harper

MY HAND TIGHTENS AROUND MY PHONE, MY BREATH CATCHES IN MY throat, and my entire body awakens with a rush of heat. I'm standing beside the sofa, dressed in my sleep clothes—satin shorts, satin top with spaghetti straps, and a knee-length satin robe, all of it black and edged with lace. I wonder if Max will like this outfit and then wonder why I care. If I'd been sleepy a few seconds ago, that haze evaporated the instant Max's voice rumbled straight into my ear, into my brain, the effect of his sensual voice reverberating through me. How badly do I want him? I could lie, but he damn well knows how he affects me.

"I want you," I admit, "more than I've ever wanted anyone."

"Even now, when I'm on the other side of the world?"

What is he doing on the other side of the world? Maybe he means it as hyperbole, and he's just back in Michigan. Doesn't matter.

I struggle to pull in a ragged breath. "Yes, Max, I want you right now. As much as ever. More, actually, because I was ready to get naked with you last night, but you ran away."

"Sorry about that. It won't happen again."

"Twice you promised to take me to the Unseen if I kissed you, but you reneged."

"I apologize for that too."

Holding the phone away from my ear, I stare at it. He apologizes? I press the phone to my ear again. "I thought gratitude was a big no-no in your world."

"Yes, but we're in the mortal realm at the moment." His voice drops back into that husky, erotic register. "Shall I pop over there and ravish you?"

My sex throbs, definitely liking that idea. "You'd better not run away again."

"I won't. You have my word."

"Then yes, get your ass over here."

He appears behind me, making me squeak with surprise, and wraps his arms around my waist to tug me against his hot, muscular body. I let my head fall back against his chest as I toss my phone onto the sofa and clasp my hands over his on my belly. The silk of his white shirt feels delicious on my skin, and his leather pants barely contain the bulge inside them.

"Tonight," he says, his lips brushing my ear, "I'll take you anywhere you want to go."

"Just take me, Max. Now."

A ravenous sound vibrates through his chest as he skims a hand up under my top, his red-hot skin evoking delicious sensations in its wake. "Going to feast on you for hours and hours."

The only sound I can make is a strangled moan. He turns me into human jelly, everything inside me taut and ready even while I dissolve into him, weak with the need he engenders in me.

Still, my brain manages the occasional coherent thought.

"Why did you call me first?" I ask, not minding at all that the words come out breathy.

"To make sure you want me." He seals his hand over my breast. "And not just the pheromones."

"Does it matter? You need sex, I want to get naked with you, and your pheromones make that happen."

"I'm aware of that."

He sounds a little irritated, but I have to ask, "Why do you care?"

"Because I—" He blows out a breath. "Stop talking, Harper. I'm trying to seduce you."

"Get on with it, then."

"You are the most contrary female in any realm, and the most demanding."

"Are you planning to do me sometime this century?"

He growls again and rakes his thumbnail across my nipple.

I gasp.

"Starting now," he murmurs into my ear, flicking his thumb back and forth, "the only words I want to hear from you are 'yes, Max, please' or 'make me come, Max' or other things of that nature. Moan as much as you like. And when you come, you will scream my name."

I open my mouth to speak but lose the capacity for language and for coherent thought when he releases my breast and thrusts his hand into my shorts, cupping me intimately. His other hand remains splayed over my belly, holding me against his body.

"Hush," he says. "Let me show you what an incubus can do."

The sinfully erotic tone of his voice makes my knees quiver and my tummy flutter. When he dips two fingers between my folds, my knees give out. His hands hold me up. Those fingers toy with my slick flesh, circling around my nub, stroking my folds, moving in slow motion yet driving me crazy with every deliberate movement. Little electric shocks fire through my sex. I moan and undulate my hips, desperate for more.

"Not yet," he says. "You won't come until I've devoured every last ounce of your pleasure."

He pulls his hand out of my shorts.

My breaths become sharp gasps.

"Look at me," he commands.

I twist my head around to see his face.

He raises his glistening fingers to his mouth and licks them, his tongue moving in sensuous sweeps, his eyes half-closed. "You taste better than anything I've ever had in my mouth."

"Please, Max."

"I do love it when you beg." He spreads his palm over my cheek. "First, I'm going to kiss you until you're on the edge of climax."

From a kiss? If any other man claimed he could do that, I'd laugh. Instinctively, I know he can make good on that promise.

And I want it.

He skates his lips over mine, the heat of his breaths teasing my skin. I moan, rubbing myself against him, loving the feel of his hard length pressed into my back. He crushes his mouth to mine, and a groan vibrates through his chest. When I open my mouth to him, he plunges his tongue deep inside and swirls it around mine in a delicate yet ravenous dance that leaves me breathless and moaning. I thrust my tongue into his mouth too, amazed by the heat of it and the taste of him, like the best dessert and the best booze combined with flavors I can't describe, the unique taste of him.

I'm drunk, drugged, hypnotized, and I don't care.

Something shifts in the atmosphere. I can't quite place it, but I sense it like the approach of a storm.

Max goes rigid.

I part my lids, though our mouths are still fused, and our gazes connect.

He eases his lips away from mine and mouths, "Don't move."

Out of the corner of my eye, I notice a silhouette darker than the shadows within which it hides near the door. A humanoid silhouette.

Max rotates his eyes in that direction. His mouth crimps.

I can't make out who's hiding in the shadows. A tall, slender figure is all I can see.

He whirls around, shielding me with his body while shifting one hand behind him to touch my hip in a protective gesture.

Our unwanted guest saunters out of the darkness into the edge of the cone of light from the lamp by the sofa.

The woman towers almost as tall as Max, her slender body filled out with just enough curves to give her that va-va-voom factor. Her silvery blue eyes almost glow in the lamplight, as does her white-blonde hair. It tumbles over her shoulders in lush waves. I would've taken her for a model except for her outfit. She wears a leather bustier held up by silver chains instead of straps, leather pants, and tall boots with stiletto heels.

"What are you doing here?" Max asks. He emphasizes the word you in a way that makes me wonder if he knows this woman.

She feigns a pout. "I haven't heard from you in ages, lover. Not since I left Hathor's temple."

"Because she booted you out. The goddess doesn't take kindly to a Valkyrie stealing her playthings."

Valkyrie? Well, she does have what sounds like a Scandinavian accent. First a vampire, now this. I didn't realize the Unseen realm housed so many beings from mortal mythology. Max might've been right when he called me clue-deficient. I have a lot to learn.

The Valkyrie tosses her head, flinging her hair over her shoulder. "Hathor was merely annoyed that she couldn't ensorcell me. It galls her to know Wodan's power supersedes hers."

"You pretended to be ensorcelled," Max says, "and enjoyed the company of everyone in Hathor's temple, often several at the same time. Is it any wonder she kicked you out?"

She wets her lips, eying Max with a hunger that literally burns in her eyes in the form of sapphire whorls. "I enjoyed you most of all. Forget the scrawny little mortal and come away with me."

"No thank you, Sigrun."

"Too bad." She sighs and raises her hand. A gleaming silver sword materializes in her grasp. "If I can't have you, I'll take the bounty."

"Why would Hathor give you a bounty? She despises you."

"The goddess wants you more than she hates me." Sigrun twirls her sword, and shards of light glint off its surface. "This will be easier if you surrender to me. Only shackles will be required then. But if you resist, I will be forced to damage you until you submit."

Damage him? Oh, like hell she will. My gaze flits to the bedroom doorway. My weapons and my battle outfit are in there, and I doubt this Nordic bitch will give me time to gear up. Max thinks I shouldn't be able to off an elemental, but I dealt with his vampire buddy.

No lopping off heads tonight. I have no weapons handy.

Max conjures a big sword, gripping it in one hand. "Back off, Sigrun. I will not go back to Hathor, and I'd prefer not to kill you."

"Kill me?" The Valkyrie laughs, the sound derisive rather than amused. "Your sword is not endued."

Max and Sigrun size each other up, swords at the ready, their eyes narrowed to slits.

I cower behind Max. Why the hell am I hiding? I've faced elementals before.

Glancing around, I search for something, anything, I might use as a weapon. The best option I see is a magazine on the table.

Max charges at Sigrun. Letting out an unholy roar, he slashes his sword at her throat.

Sigrun doesn't react fast enough. She takes the brunt of the blow to the side of her neck.

But her head does not drop to the floor. Max's sword leaves only a gash. Sure, blood pours from it, but the wound is far from fatal.

Max stares at her, incredulous.

Sigrun whacks him in the side of the head with the flat face of her sword.

He staggers, his gaze unfocused.

The Valkyrie produces a pair of shackles from thin air. "Time to go, Max. I'll take your mortal too and perhaps get an extra bounty for handing over a female you covet. Hathor will enjoy defiling her in every way imaginable."

Sigrun reaches for Max's wrist.

He shoots flames from his hands. They lash out at Sigrun, who bellows and scrambles away from him. The skin on her hands and arms has turned black and scaly.

"You will pay for this!" she shrieks, then poofs away.

Max staggers toward me. "We must go. If one hunter knows where you live, others will too. It's not safe here."

"I have nowhere else to go."

He palpates the side of his head, wincing, and his fingers come away blood-stained.

"You're hurt," I say. "You need a healing vortex."

"This wound will heal on its own." He snaps straight and rigid, his gaze going remote as if he stares into the void at the center of the universe. "We have to leave. Now."

He slings an arm around me and drags me into his body.

"Where are we going?" I ask.

"To the Unseen. We'll need to be quick about it because once I cross the veil, every hunter in the Unseen will sense my presence and come for me."

"No offense, but that sounds like a horrible plan. Why not go somewhere else in the mortal world? It might take a while before they find us again."

"Can't risk it." He rubs his eyes. "Sigrun saw you and sensed you belong to me. She will tell Hathor, or she'll tell someone else who will tell Hathor. I can't adequately protect you, not with the hunger clawing at me. The spell keeping me sane can't stop me from starving. I'm not as strong as I should be, and I'm no match for these hunters."

I don't bother pointing out I don't belong to him because we have bigger problems.

"We're going to the Unseen," he says. "My lair is warded and will be the safest place to hide you until I figure out what to do."

"You mean until *we* figure out what to do."

His mouth warps into an annoyed slant. "We can argue after I get you to safety."

Before I can respond, he whisks us away.

CHAPTER FOURTEEN

Max

THIS TIME I GET MY AIM RIGHT, AND WE LAND ON THE DIRT PATH THAT skirts the pool beneath the waterfall behind the rock shop. The wooden railing is still broken from when Harper stabbed me in the back and sent me plunging into the deep, frothing waters. A full moon glows in the sky above us, its light filtering down through the trees to glisten on the water. In this light, the falls seem to glow too, as if the cascading waters are lit from within.

I'm still clutching Harper to me with both arms. Releasing her, I take a step back.

She turns toward me. Her face almost glows like the water below and the moon above us. Her skin, always creamy, went paler back in her apartment. Now, the moonlight lends it a deeper pallor.

"Are you all right?" I ask. "Do you feel weak or nauseous?"

I've been through enough battles of late to know the signs of shock. I feel a bit off, but nothing I can't power through.

Harper clasps the back of her neck. "I'm okay. Are we back in Michigan? This place looks different in the dark, but it seems like the waterfall behind that rock shop."

"It is."

"Why are we here?"

"Because we need a portal, and this is the safest one I know of." I point at the rumbling cascade. "It's behind the falls."

"Yeah, I know."

How does she know? Mortals can't sense the portal, but then, she's no ordinary mortal. Besides, we don't have time for her to explain to me how she located it. I squint at the water cascading over the twenty-foot sandstone cliff and the ledge that leads into the hidden cavern behind the curtain of spray. "If you don't have a touch of the Unseen in you, crossing the veil will be fatal."

"I'll risk it."

The certainty in her voice sends a chill wriggling down my spine. Closing the distance between us, I spear her gaze with my own, praying she will understand, really understand, my words. "Listen to me. You might die. I'm not gifted with the ability to sense when someone has a touch of the Unseen, so I have no way of knowing if you can cross the veil. Violating the boundaries tears an elemental apart at the molecular level but breaching a portal will destroy a mortal in ways far more gruesome and horrific. First, your brain will melt inside your skull. Then, while you're still conscious, the energies will scald your skin, rip your flesh from your body, and crush your bones to dust. I've seen it happen before, and I will not watch you die that way."

A memory blasts through my mind. When Nevan was still the king of the sylphs, a gnome shoved him across a boundary. I'd been there, holding Lindsey back so she wouldn't leap in to try to save him and get disintegrated along with him. Watching Nevan's body be split apart, rent into minute particles, that had not been the worst of it. The way his body convulsed, the sheer agony on his face, and his unearthly screams… That was the worst by far.

But I've witnessed a mortal being destroyed by a portal too, and it's much, much worse.

I cannot let Harper suffer the same fate.

But how else can I protect her? My lair is the only safe place I know.

"Take me there," she says. "I accept the risk, and if I die, it won't be your fault."

She doesn't seem disturbed by the thought of dying. She severed a vampire's head from his body without flinching. I can't help wondering what transformed her into a battle-hardened warrior. What did the obsidian fae do to her?

"You protected me," she says, her voice rife with confusion. "Why did you do that? Why are you still trying to protect me? I threw a knife into your back. I've been nothing but mean to you."

That isn't true. She shared something of herself with me when she told me about the obsidian fae and her friend's death. She offered herself to me despite the way I'd behaved when we first met, here in this place where we now stand. Maybe we don't quite trust each other yet, but we aren't enemies either.

Gazing into her eyes tonight, I wonder. Might she be my fated mate? The thought winds a frigid coil around my soul. I don't deserve a mate. I don't deserve what this woman is offering me, but I must take it.

I back away from her until we stand a dozen feet apart. "I'm protecting you because I'm starved and you are my next meal."

"Then get us to the Unseen already."

A figure appears behind Harper.

Gunny lashes one arm around her torso and holds a knife to her throat with the other hand.

She doesn't move, doesn't fight. She keeps her focus squarely on me.

How the hell did Gunny get his head reattached? I've got no time to contemplate that because we have more pressing concerns.

Like the vampire holding a blade to Harper's throat.

"Come with me to Hathor's palace," Gunny demands. "Or I will slit this mortal's throat."

"Don't do it," Harper says. "I'm his leverage. He won't kill me until he gets his bounty."

Gunny nicks her skin with the blade, triggering a trickle of blood. "Perhaps that is true, but I can do worse than kill her." He bares his fangs. "I can feed on her."

My hands clench into fists. My shoulders bunch up as every muscle in my body tenses in anticipation of a fight. I rack my brain for something I can do. Conjure a weapon? Sure, but then I'll risk Harper getting hurt when I attack Gunny with that weapon. Could I conjure Harper into my arms? I've never attempted to do that with a mortal before, or with an elemental, and I have no sodding idea what might happen if I cock up the transfer.

My aim is off today. I'd gotten it right when I brought Harper here, but earlier I mucked it up and appeared inside Lindsey and Nevan's bedroom instead of their living room.

"Make your choice," Gunny snarls. "The mortal or your freedom."

I've been enslaved to Hathor's will before and survived it. I let a sorcerer trick me into a nasty bargain that enslaved me for centuries. If the price of saving Harper is my freedom, I'll pay it.

Assuming I can trust this slavering vampire.

Oh yes, he's actually drooling at the prospect of feeding on Harper. His saliva drips off his chin onto her shoulder.

She cringes slightly.

I open my mouth—to say what, I haven't a clue—but Harper beats me to it.

"Don't give him what he wants," she says. "I'd rather die than be the reason you get yourself ensorcelled again."

Her statement paralyzes me for the briefest moment. It almost sounds like she cares about me. If she does, that will be her worst mistake.

A vision assails me, of a pale face rent by pain and those bloodshot blue eyes beseeching me. Aurelia's voice echoes in my mind. *Please, Maximus, make me like you so we can be together forever.* My gut wrenches at the memory of what I'd done and how it all ended.

I destroy the things I love.

Just as I rouse from my paralysis, Harper leaps into action.

With her arms pinned to her body by Gunny's grip on her, she can't strike out at him with her fists. She slams one foot down on the top of his and clamps her hand around his genitals, squeezing and wrenching them so hard I wince.

Gunny roars.

His hold on her falters, and she runs to me.

I enfold her in my arms, intending to transport us onto the sandstone ledge beside the falls. We must pierce the cascade the old-fashioned way to reach the portal.

Harper squints at something past my shoulder.

"What is it?" I ask.

"Not sure. I feel…something."

Gunny raises his knife, about to charge us, but his attention veers to the same area behind me, and his eyes bulge. He hisses something in German.

And he vanishes.

What on earth can scare a vampire?

I try to whisk us away, but something blocks it. So I whirl us around, shoving Harper behind me, and conjure my sword.

A black shape hovers in the shadows beneath the trees, shadows made darker still by the night around us. The moonlight that trickles down between the boughs seems to get absorbed by the figure.

The thing shoots a black bolt of energy at us.

I duck sideways, knocking Harper down with me. The bolt lances across my side, setting off a firestorm of electric shocks that fan out over my skin and burrow beneath the surface.

The being raises its hand, clearly about to lob another bolt.

Harper wriggles out from under me and flings her body over mine. "Stop!"

And the being stops.

"Leave us alone," she demands. "Or I'll kill myself."

She grabs my sword from where I'd dropped it on the ground and lodges the tip against her own throat.

I try to move, to stop her, to do…anything. Every muscle in my body refuses to obey my commands. The pain sears through my flesh, sinking deeper every second, spreading out from where the black bolt of energy had struck me, threatening to consume my entire body.

The dark figure creeps out into the open area where we lie, emerging into the full moonlight. A skintight suit woven from the blackest fabric and tinged with silver conceals most of its body, exposing only its hands, feet, neck, and head. The creature's very presence seems to draw the light into its body, absorbing the glow amid glimmering shades of darkest purple and blue. Its eyes, as dark as its flesh, zero in on Harper.

It halts several feet away. The sapphire rings around its eyes spin, and the irises flame with obsidian fire. The being raises one finger to point it at Harper. "Do not harm yourself, for if you damage what we have worked so long to achieve, we will mete out retribution on anyone who has ever known you." The being swings his finger to me. "Beginning with him."

Harper glances at me and bites down on her lip.

She hasn't wanted me to be enslaved again. How can I let her surrender to the same fate?

I summon every last scrap of power I have left, everything this being's energy bolt hasn't yet depleted, and funnel it into my hand. With an effort that stabs agony through me straight down to my bones, I throw my hand out and hurl a fireball at the creature.

The ball strikes the fae flat on the chest. The flames spiral out to encompass the creature's body.

Until its skin soaks up the fire.

Though the thing isn't burned, its skin has paled half a shade.

"Soon," the creature hisses. "Soon we will come for you. But perhaps you need to simmer for a bit longer to improve the flavor of the magics."

With that, the being disappears.

Harper scrambles around to kneel beside me. She tears my shirt open to examine the wound, tenderly palpating it.

I wince and suck in a jagged breath. The wound is black, like the energy bolt that charred my skin. "Afraid it's more than a flesh wound."

"No shit." She looks into my eyes, hers glistening with the start of tears, though she sounds calm. "You don't look so hot."

I have a feeling that's a severe understatement. The cold spreading through me emanates from the wound but sinks deeper and deeper with every passing second. Electric shocks knife through me, spreading as swiftly as the arctic cold in my veins. An icy sweat dribbles down my scalp and temples, and every breath costs me a little more precious energy.

Harper cradles my face in her hands. "You need a healing vortex. I know there's one nearby, but I can't carry you. You're too heavy."

"I can't walk." Can't move at all, in fact, except for my eyes and my lungs that insist I haul in breath after agonizing breath. An endued weapon can't do this, and besides, that black bolt didn't seem to qualify as a weapon. Maybe it contained an endued poison, but it seems more likely the bolt is composed of dark magics. That realization triggers another, and I struggle to ask the question, my voice now as rough as sandpaper scraping on rock. "Was that an obsidian fae?"

She gnaws on her lip. "Yes."

"That thing wanted you."

"I know."

More questions surface in my mind, but trying to comprehend them stabs icy needles into my brain.

Harper shrugs out of her satin robe, balls it up, and presses the mass to my wound.

Pain rips through me anew, forcing a sharp cry out of me.

"Sorry," she says, her voice quavering. "It's all I could think to do."

"I'm not bleeding. I'm dying."

Or am I? The agony has begun to lessen, displaced by the bone-deep cold that has suffused my entire body. I still can't move, though.

"Please, Max, no." She sniffles, but her burgeoning tears don't flow. "You can't die. Who will annoy the hell out of me if you're not here?"

I almost laugh, but I don't have the energy for it. An odd sensation ripples through me, something like a chill except I'm far too cold to feel any chill. The wound throbs now. I gasp and choke on a breath. Hot fingers of magic slither out from the wound, unfurling through my body, carrying with them a dark and ravenous energy.

"Something's happening," I croak.

Harper bends over me. "What is it?"

"Not—not sure." I grit my teeth against the new agony as it... No, no, no. It's devouring the spells Ennea invested into me. The anti-stalking spell goes first, then the dark magics sink their fangs into the spell that masks my hunger. I seize Harper's wrist and shove her away, barely taking note of the fact I can move again. "Run."

"What? No, I will not leave you."

My breaths come heavier and faster. My flesh burns from the inside out, transforming my skin into a sheath of fire. The hunger rises inside me, scorching and powerful and unrepentant.

"Run," I snarl. "Quick. That black bolt eats magic, including the spell that's been keeping the hunger at bay. It's coming back, worse than ever."

She doesn't move, just sits there gaping at me.

"Fucking run!" I shout.

At the instant she leaps up and whirls away from me, the spell shatters—and so does my self-control. Hunger. Scorching, all-consuming hunger. A crimson veil descends over my vision, and the only thing I see is her. That skimpy outfit. Her nipples jutting under the fabric. Her bare legs, the slopes of her breasts, those delicious lips.

Hungry. Must eat—her.

I fly across the distance between us, whumping down inches in front of her.

Her eyes bulge.

I seize her and whisk us away.

CHAPTER FIFTEEN

Harper

WE MATERIALIZE ON THE LEDGE BESIDE THE FALLS, THE ROAR OF THE torrent drowning out all other sounds as it pummels the pool below us. He grabbed me around the midsection, but one hand has shifted up to clamp onto my breast. His fingers dig into my flesh, but the minor pain of his grip on me pales compared to the shock of how his appearance has changed. Before, his hair was black with maroon streaks, except when he was pretending to be a mortal. Now the streaks are gone, and his hair is fully black, almost obsidian like the fae's skin. His eyes are wild, burning a bright, swirling red with tiny sparks inside them. His chest heaves. The enormous bulge inside his pants scrapes against my backside. He growls and grunts like a demonic beast.

Everything about him screams danger.

And yet…I don't fear him. Yes, my pulse races, and I have trouble catching my breath. And yes, I tried to run from him—but only because he told me to do it. My first instinct was to stay with him, not run from him. *Crazy.* But that's the truth. I've called him a monster and a creature. The first time we met, he'd been like this, though to a lesser degree. He hadn't exaggerated when he told me it's much worse this time. I should grab his manly bits and wrench them like I'd done with the vampire. I should run.

I don't want to.

Maybe everyone has been right. I am crazy.

He leaps into the falls.

We whump down inside a little cavern behind the falls. The curtain of water conceals it from the outside. Despite the thundering cascade gushing past the cave's entrance mere feet from us, inside this sanctuary, the sound diminishes to a soft rumble. The floor seems level, though I can't see much in the gloom inside the cavern. When I feel around with my bare foot, I note pockmarks in the rock surface beneath me, each filled with cool water. At the rear of the space looms a darkness far deeper and blacker than the shadows around us. Whatever fills that area churns with varying shades of blackness that glitter with tiny flecks of star-like brilliance.

Max and I are both drenched, from our clothes to our dripping hair.

"What now?" I ask.

He growls softly, low in his throat, and releases my breast to raise his palm toward the menacing darkness at the cavern's rear. He closes his fist, then snaps his fingers straight.

A light that emanates from nowhere and everywhere fills the cavern with a gentle glow, giving me a clear view of what lies ahead of us. The inky blackness roils and writhes as if it's made of a thousand slender serpents with shimmering, iridescent skin in shades of blue, green, and purple. Those star-like lights pop and dissipate like paranormal sparklers inside the blackness.

Sparklers and serpents. How odd.

"This is the portal," I say, "isn't it?"

He grunts.

I realize that in his current state it's all he can do.

Max clutches me tight with both arms and jumps into the portal.

The seething blackness nips at my skin, but we rocket through it so fast I scarcely have time to notice the portal consists of a dark, eerie tunnel through a fathomless abyss. We touch down inside a clearing in a spooky forest lit by the glow of two moons, one large and one small. Water burbles out of a boulder and spills into a small pool, more like a puddle compared to the one we've just left in Michigan.

I glance around. "Where—"

He spirits us away again.

We land in the depths of the woods.

Max snarls in another language, clearly cursing, and whisks us away again.

This time, we reappear on a rocky shore.

He snarls more curses in that other language and takes off again.

Three more times we materialize in the wrong place, he curses, and we take off again. It's making me dizzy. I guess his current state of severe agitation has affected his teleportation targeting. He needs to calm down, or we'll spend all night bouncing around the Unseen.

By the umpteenth touch-down, I'm nauseous and sheathed in a cold sweat. At least this time, he pauses for a bit longer. I pull in slow, deep breaths to calm my pounding heart and to quell the nausea. When his posture changes minutely, I decide it means he's about to poof us away again. I might pass out if he keeps going like this.

"Stop, Max. You're making me sick."

He stiffens but does not teleport.

I try to turn around to face him, but he clamps his arms tighter around me and growls softly.

"No running," he rasps.

"Wasn't trying to get away. I need to look at you."

For several seconds, we stand there frozen. Then he loosens his hold a smidgen.

It's enough. I manage to wriggle around to face him, though I stay plastered to his body. His open shirt exposes his chest, and the heat of his skin scorches mine. Not enough to burn me. Not even enough to cause pain. Somehow, his skin can sizzle but not singe me. His body temperature shot up when the spell he'd mentioned shattered. His self-control weakened, but he clearly held on to a thick enough thread to keep himself from attacking me. For how long can he cling to that?

This is starvation. If I don't feed him soon, that last thread might snap.

A small voice in the back of my mind urges me to flee.

But I'm past the point of no return. If I abandon him when he's like this, he'll go insane and become the monster I'd labeled him as, the monster he fears becoming. "Run," he urged me back in that clearing. This man has protected me from a Valkyrie, a vampire, and an obsidian fae. He worked at a crummy fast-food restaurant just to spend time with me and prove he isn't a villain. He cares whether I truly want him or if it's his pheromones affecting me. He cares, period.

Monsters don't have empathy.

And that's why I cannot abandon him.

I lay my palms on his cheeks and stroke his skin with my fingertips. "You can't find wherever it is you want to take me because you're overwrought with hunger. Take a slow, deep breath and try again."

His eyes drift half-closed. He inhales a long, slow breath and lets it out gradually.

We zip away, surfacing inside an underground chamber hewn from pale rock. Its walls are smooth and carefully shaped. A bed nestles against one wall while a table and two chairs occupy its center, and a crimson chaise abuts the wall opposite the bed. And that is one large bed. It could fit all of Max and a few other people too. A fur blanket covers the mattress, though I can't tell what fills the mattress. It doesn't look like memory foam or springs or anything I've seen in the mortal world.

A gentle glow emanates from nowhere and everywhere.

Max stumbles backward a couple of steps and stares at me, wild-eyed and breathing hard. The tip of his erection pokes out of his waistband.

I reach for him.

He rushes at me, crushing me to his body, and flies us to the rock wall. Literally. My feet lift off the ground. My back slaps into the cool rock wall, and I slide down until my soles touch the floor. He pins my wrists to the wall at either side of my head and kicks my feet apart.

Shackles materialize around my wrists and ankles.

A shiver frosts through me. He has bound me to the wall. The short chains that connect the shackles to the stone allow me minimal movement.

Max backs away a few yards. He shoves his hands into his hair, whisking them back and forth, making his hair even wilder. His eyes are wide, the pupils as dark as the inky blackness of the portal, the rims churning with a red fire that burns with incandescent brilliance. His chest is heaving again, and his growls and grunts reverberate off the stone walls.

The black wound on his side has faded into a raised gray scar. Damn, he heals fast.

A scent I can't describe wafts around me, seeming to originate from him. It smells enticing in a way that affects my body, making my nipples pearl and my sex ache. Pheromones. It has to be. In his altered state, a slave to his sexual appetites, he must've started to exude more-powerful pheromones. Yes, those chemicals make me hot and bothered. But I'd wanted him long before this. I wanted him even when we spoke on the phone and I was nowhere near his pheromone-factory body.

I'd made my decision when I let him bring me here. Hell, if I'm totally honest with myself, I decided to have sex with him days ago. I've needed time to come to terms with my desire for him and what might happen once I surrender myself to an incubus. Still have no idea, really. Will I want him and only him from now on? I don't care. Not anymore.

Max begins to pace in front of me, his arms hanging at his sides while he fists and unfists his hands in an erratic rhythm. Between grunts and low growls, he grumbles words I can't understand. They might be another language, or they might be nonsense. Maybe he's so far gone that he's lost the capacity for comprehensible speech.

His grumbling grows louder with each circuit until I can finally make out the words.

"Need. Hungry. Need. Starving." A wolf-like growl snarls out between his bared teeth. "Must feed. Must eat." He swerves his fiery gaze to me. "Must feed—on you."

I swallow hard, unsure what affects me most—the worry he might utterly lose control and attack me, or the desire that burns hotter inside me every moment. He won't hurt me. I believe that, though I can't explain why. But he might become so agitated he hurts us both without intending to do it.

Max paces faster, fisting and unfisting his hands faster, muttering faster.

I muster my sternest voice and say, "Stop, Max."

He freezes midway through another circuit, breathing hard, but keeps his focus on the floor.

"Look at me," I command. When he simply scrunches his brows and continues staring at the floor, I make my voice more forceful. "Look at me, Max."

With his head down, he swivels his eyes in my direction. His shaft stiffens in the few seconds during which we regard each other, the bulge in his pants enlarging and the tip protruding above his waistband even more.

My tummy flutters, and an electric tingle of anticipation spreads through me.

"Come closer," I say, softening my tone now that I have his attention. "Come to me, Max. Walk this way."

He shuffles around to face me. His gaze rakes over me from head to toe and back again, zeroing in on my eyes. Now fully aroused, he takes careful steps toward me as if the hard-on in his pants pains him. An arm's length away, he halts.

Even from a few feet away, he towers over me. His body consumes my view, giving me no choice but to admire his chest, trace every curve of the muscles, track them down his torso until I find the trail of fine, dark hairs that taper down to his hip-hugging waistband and the reddened tip of his erection. My sex aches with an emptiness only he can fill. My breathing becomes labored. When I meet his gaze again, the fire swirling within them transfixes me. The depth of his hunger, of his lust for my body, bears down on me. I clench the chains that bind me, my fingers closing around them where they link with the handcuffs.

I understand what he needs, but I have to calm him down first. I know of one way to ease his hunger without letting him ravage me. My pulse speeds up at the words I need to say next.

"Kiss me, Max."

His eyes go so wide the whites seem to glow, then they narrow to slits. "Why?"

"I said kiss me, Max. I want you so badly, and I need to feel your mouth on mine." I lean in as much as I can with the shackles restraining me. "Come over here and kiss me."

For an agonizing moment, he stares at me.

With a harsh growl, he surges toward me and cages my body with his own. His hands pin my wrists to the wall, just below the metal cuffs of the shackles. The full length of his body is pasted to mine, his skin blazing hot even through his clothes. His erection, though caught inside his leather pants, presses into me as a hard and impossibly thick line. When I imagine taking that girth inside me, I suck in a ragged breath.

"Kiss me," I breathe.

He mashes his mouth to mine in a brutal kiss that unleashes a tidal wave of need inside me. His teeth scrape on my lips while he grinds his rock-hard shaft into me, and I moan, opening my mouth in a silent plea for more. He thrusts his tongue deep. I gasp into his mouth while he ravages me with wild strokes of his tongue, spurring me to respond with equal hunger, desperate to take inside me any part of him I can, to become one with him and satisfy this all-consuming thirst only he can slake.

I struggle to grab on to some part of him, with my arms or my legs, but the shackles and his body prevent it. I grunt and moan, no longer caring if I sound like a pathetic fool. I want him. Need him inside me. Crave everything ounce of pleasure he once vowed to give me.

He tears his mouth away from mine but keeps his body pasted to mine. The chaotic swirling in his eyes has lessened, almost back to his normal whirlpool gaze. The rims of crimson fire still whirl, though less wildly. He swallows hard, his Adam's apple bouncing. While he fights to catch his breath, he swipes his tongue over his lips.

"Starving," he says, his voice strained but no longer feral. "I need— need to—"

"I know what you need. Do it, Max. Take me, I'm yours."

He peels himself away from me but lingers close enough that the heat of him still radiates over me. A few inches separate us. He glances down at my body and winces. "Not naked."

Though I've calmed him, I realize he still has trouble expressing himself as eloquently as usual. He also seems to have trouble forming complete, coherent thoughts. Otherwise, he would've made my clothing disappear. I told him to take me, after all. I gave my permission.

"Get rid of my clothes," I say. "Hurry, I can't wait any longer."

He scuffles backward another half a foot and frowns at my black satin shorts and top. His tongue slides across his lower lip, the movement slow and sensuous, as his gaze lands on my stiff nipples where they just against the silky fabric.

God, how long is he planning to devour me with his gaze before he devours *me*?

With a sharp snarl, he seizes the neckline of my top and yanks downward.

My top splits in two.

He jerks the fabric away and tosses it over his shoulder, then grabs hold of the waistband on my shorts. With another swift yank, he rips those apart too and tosses them away.

The air, while temperate inside this space, cools my skin. I shiver from the faint draft that kisses my nipples.

Max rushes forward, half-kneeling to place his head in front of my breasts. He growls as he studies one nipple. His tongue darts out to slide across the aching peak and trace circles around it.

I gasp and arch my back. "Oh yes, Max."

He seals his mouth around my nipple, suckling with fervid intensity, his cheeks caving in. Pleasure ricochets through me from my breast straight down to my core, where I ache more and more with every greedy tug of his teeth and mouth while his tongue torments my peak.

I throw my head back, not caring that I bang it on the hard rock of the wall, and let out a long, throaty moan. "Oh God, Max, please."

A zing of magic pierces me, like the light prick of a pin. Somewhere in the recesses of my mind where I hold on to the tatters of my will-power, I understand I've just indebted myself to him in a minuscule way. I don't care. Can't care. With his mouth driving me wild, with the lust I've repressed for so long rising inside me, I wouldn't have cared if I'd vowed to be his sex slave for the rest of my life and sealed it with a magical bargain.

He drops into a crouch.

My breast, damp from his mouth, feels deliciously cool.

With two fingers, he parts my folds and stares at the most intimate part of me.

I open my mouth to complain, to order him to hurry the hell up, but I don't get the chance.

He pushes his head between my legs and scrapes his tongue up and down my cleft, then laps at every millimeter of my slick flesh that he can reach. While I writhe and cry out, he dives his tongue into my entrance, swirling it to tease places no man has ever touched before, making me thrash against my restraints, desperate with the need to have him inside me. The tip of his tongue isn't enough. I crave all of him, the entire length of that thick erection buried inside me to the hilt.

A voracious rumble in his throat vibrates into my sex, and he latches on to my taut nub. With his tongue and his lips and his teeth, he torments my flesh and whips me into a frenzy of need. The mark on my back prickles, but the sensation only heightens my desire.

I come like a wild thing, thrashing and shouting and bucking my hips. Oh God, I've never experienced a climax like this. When it reaches its zenith, the sheer power of the pleasure stuns me breathless. My mouth gapes on a silent scream, and choked gasps are the only sounds that emerge.

Max sits back on his haunches and wipes his mouth with the back of his hand. He gazes up at me, his breaths coming so hard and fast he seems unable to speak. The look on his face tells me everything I need to know. He's as shocked as I am by what just happened.

"That's not all, is it?" I ask. "Don't get me wrong, that was beyond mind-blowing, but I kind of thought we'd, you know, go all the way."

He smirks. "Yes, *dulcisssime*, I am going to fuck you. No way out of it now. You begged me to take you."

"Don't want out." I consider him for a moment, noting the change in his demeanor. He's much more relaxed, though no less aroused. "You seem better."

"I feel better."

"Glad to hear it." I rattle my chains. "Um, why am I shackled to the wall?"

"So you won't run."

I want to lay a hand on his cheek but can't. "You don't need to restrain me. I don't want to get away from you. I'm here because I choose to be with you, because I want you. I don't know where the door is, anyway."

"There is no door." He rises, unfurling that impossibly tall, impossibly muscular body, and inches closer to brace his hands at either side of my head between the shackles. "I don't want to hurt you, but I can't promise I won't. Though the hunger has lessened, it is still powerful."

"You won't hurt me." With his body brushing against mine and his breaths teasing my mouth, I have trouble thinking. "I trust you."

His mouth opens, then closes."Why?"

"Let's talk later. Right now, I need you inside me. Don't make me beg again."

"I don't want you to beg. Debts, even small ones, are dangerous in this world." He moves his hands to my arms and glides them up until his palms cover mine. His breaths grow uneven and harsh. "Can't wait any longer."

The shackles vanish.

He grasps my thigh and lifts it, pushing inside me inch by exquisite inch, groaning and closing his eyes while his expression transforms into one of sheer relief and intense pleasure. The thickness of him penetrates me with such exquisite slowness that the sensation robs me of breath and anticipation of what's to come shudders through me and excites my skin. Every fine hair on my body lifts and stiffens. I latch my arms around him, my head alongside his neck. When he's sunk himself in to the hilt, filling me completely, he pauses there.

I suck in a breath.

Bending his head, he whispers into my ear, "Ready?"

"Yes," I say. "Oh God, yes, I'm ready."

With another long groan, he pulls his hips back and thrusts into me again, gently at first, but soon escalating into a relentless pounding that nails me to the wall and has me clutching him tighter with my arms and my leg even as I throw my head back and let out wordless cries of ecstasy. The mark on my back prickles harder and hotter, but the sensation only intensifies the pleasure, intensifies my lust.

Suddenly, we lie on the bed with the fur blanket beneath us and Max on top of me.

Though I register the change, I can't care. I'm too consumed by the sensation of his cock pummeling me. The new position makes it easier for me to wrap myself around him, clinging on like I'll fly away without him holding me down. His hips jerk back with every withdrawal, and his length consumes me with every powerful thrust. The heat and hardness of his shaft match that of his body, a delicious sizzle that seems to infuse my skin and sink deeper to claim every part of me down to my very soul. This is more than earth-shattering sex. Something shifted between us the moment I admitted I trust him.

And I do. That's the most terrifying part.

He straightens his arms, his hands braced above my head, pushing up to hover over me even while his length plows into me even faster, even harder.

My climax explodes inside me. My whole body goes rigid, my back flattens into the bed, and my head snaps forward. My legs become fastened around him like a vise as he keeps thrusting and strangled cries erupt out of me. He swings his hips back, pulling out until only his crown nudges my opening.

Still gripped by my own orgasm, I whimper and sink my nails into his biceps.

He slams into me so hard the bed bounces and thumps and scrapes across the floor. His shaft throbs as it unleashes the searing jet of his release.

I come harder, the pleasure so intense it rips a scream out of me that echoes off the walls.

Max collapses on top of me, his breaths harsh and heavy. Seconds pass, maybe minutes. I lose track of the time, too stunned by the ferocity of my double orgasm to speak or move. The weight of him is considerable, but I relish it.

Lying here with him, I recognize the truth. I like him, and I want to tell him about everything, including my vendetta and my plan to destroy the Unseen. Somehow, the thought of confessing scares me less than another problem. Destroying the Unseen will mean destroying every being in it.

A chill whispers over my skin. It will mean destroying Max.

CHAPTER SIXTEEN

Max

I ROLL OFF HARPER TO LIE ON MY SIDE. RAISED ON ONE ELBOW, I GAZE down at her with rapt wonder, overcome by the intimacy of what we've done. Sex is just sex for me, always. But with her, it's become something more. She tamed the beast within me. Even after seeing me at my worst and knowing the danger, she wanted to be with me. It makes no sense.

"Why did you let me do that?" I ask. "I turned into the monster you think I am."

"I shouldn't have called you that. You're not a monster."

"But I'd still like to know. Why let me ravage you?"

She laughs, though it comes out breathless. "Why do you think? I knew you'd give me mind-blowing sex, but this was…" She fans her face with one hand. "Whew. There's no word strong enough to describe how amazing that was. I've never had two orgasms in a row, like wham-bam, but I came again before the first one had really ended."

"That's because of my, ah…" I duck my head, unwilling to meet her gaze. Talking about sex in graphic detail has never bothered me before, but now, I can't manage to get the words out to explain. "That's because of my…fluid. It's imbued with chemicals only an incubus has and invested with innate magic to enhance the pleasure for my partner."

Her lips twitch as if she struggles not to smile. "Fluid? You mean you have magic semen."

"Ah…yes. I suppose so." I paint twirling lines on her belly with my fingertip, my focus centered on the movements so I can avoid looking at her. Why does my explanation sound moronic? On other occasions when I've explained the nature of my emissions, the women thought it was erotic and sexy. Telling Harper about it makes me feel…uncomfortable. When she called it magic

92

semen, I felt utterly ridiculous. "You could have gotten away from me if you'd wanted. I wasn't in my right mind, and you managed to subdue a vampire who was at his full strength. Why did you stay with me?"

"Because I like you, okay? When you're not annoying the hell out of me, that is, like you are right now."

"I'll accept that explanation. I like you too, when you're not calling me a creature or a monster." I rise onto my hands and knees to straddle her body, my face hovering over hers. "I wasn't in top form the first time. We should do that again, so I can prove to you I can do better."

"Oh lord, if you do any better, I might pass out. You were incredible."

"I know."

She covers her face with her hands, makes an odd noise, then pulls her hands away. "No one's ever made me feel that way. Other guys are just—oh, there's no comparison."

"I know."

"You're so..." Her eyes roll back in her head for a second. "Good. No, that's not right. Beyond good."

"I know."

She contorts her mouth into a slanted smirk. "You're not humble, are you?"

"No." I bend my arms, bringing my face to within millimeters of hers. "I'm an incubus, darling. I was forged into the perfect sex machine. Of course I'm the best you've ever had, and of course I know it. Would you have me pretend to be humble?"

"That wasn't a complaint. It was a rhetorical question, which is one that doesn't need a response." She wrinkles her nose. "What do you mean you were forged? I remember you saying that word before, but you wouldn't explain."

"Let's talk later." I drag my tongue up her skin from her collarbone to her throat and all the way to her earlobe. When I tease the lobe with my tongue, her gasp makes me go hard in an instant. "Let's have another go. I want to show you everything I can do when I take it slow."

"Uh-huh." She wags her finger at me. "We don't have time for more sex. We've both got crazy evil people after us, and we need to figure out what to do about that. It's time we told each other the truth, all of it, no holds barred."

The naked truth? The only person, human or elemental, to whom I've told the whole truth was Lindsey O'Rourke. Even Aurelia hadn't known everything.

Please, Maximus, I want to stay with you forever.

My throat thickens as her words from literal lifetimes ago echo in my mind.

Harper's palm on my cheek rouses me from the memory.

"Whatever it is," she says, "you can tell me. I'm not as rigid and unforgiving as I might seem to be. You haven't caught me at my best, but here and now I'm feeling very relaxed and amenable."

"Amenable? You don't speak like other humans I've met, except for Lindsey. How old are you, in mortal years?"

"What are immortal years?"

I move to sit near her feet, my back against the wall and my feet hanging off the bed's edge. A weary sigh rushes out of me. "Immortal years are the ones I've endured. Eternity sounds like a wonderful bargain in exchange for your mortal life, but after two thousand years, it grows tiresome."

She sits up, folding her legs in the manner humans call cross-legged. "You're two thousand years old. That's what you said before."

"A little more than that. One tends to lose count after a few centuries."

"Tell me what 'forged' means."

I bend my knee to rest my arm on it and gaze into the empty space in front of me. "The forging is a process that transforms a dying mortal into an elemental being. The magics involved are powerful and unforgiving. Your body is ripped apart at the most basic level, what humans call molecules, and reconstituted into a vastly different form. A forged elemental might resemble his mortal self, but he will be changed in ways both visible and hidden deep inside."

Harper regards me for a moment.

Peripherally, I notice her doing it. I feel her gaze on me too.

"Sounds like it's painful," she says.

"The agony is indescribable."

"Was this forging thing forced on you? Like in a bad bargain?"

"I volunteered for it. To be fair, I was bleeding to death at the time and only half-conscious. Still, when a being appeared to me and offered eternal life in exchange for everything that made me human, I agreed without hesitation. That being was an incubus." A harsh laugh grunts out of me. "My savior neglected to mention the horrors of the forging process and the downsides of being an immortal incubus."

"What an asshat. I hope you reamed him good for that."

This time, my laughter stems from genuine amusement. I can't help it. Many of the terms mortals use sound ridiculous. "Asshat? I suppose he was that. I never saw him again after the forging, so I had no chance to ream him."

She clasps her hands over her knees. "What happened to you after the forging? Did you find an elemental brothel where you could feed to your heart's content?"

"It's not my heart that savors sex." I tip my head back until it meets the wall. "But no, I could not feed for weeks after, though I was hungry. The post-forging is almost as agonizing as the transformation itself. I remained in the mortal realm since I had no bloody clue how to get to the Unseen. I crawled into a bear's den, and apparently, my glowing red eyes and snarling terrified the beast so much it gave up its home. I slept there for weeks, gradually becoming stronger. Once I'd reached the point where I could walk and talk again, I went out hunting for sex. Luckily, the forging didn't leave me in a starved state. I was very hungry but in no danger of assaulting anyone."

"Did you find a way into the Unseen?"

"Not immediately. I tried to seduce the first mortal female I came upon, but my appearance terrified her." I study the ceiling, anything to avoid looking at her. "Fortunately, a succubus had sniffed me out and—" I can't stop the self-satisfied smile that tightens my lips. "We had bloody fantastic sex for a month, nearly nonstop."

"Nonstop sex?"

The shock in Harper's voice spurs me to look at her.

Her mouth has fallen open, and her eyes are large. It's adorable.

And it makes me want to shag her again.

"Yes, *dulcissime*," I say, "we screwed each other in every way imaginable and some I'm quite sure we invented. She fed my hunger, and I fed hers. It was a symbiotic relationship."

"Why aren't you still with her?"

"Because it also turned into an unhealthy relationship, at least for me." I consider how much to reveal to Harper, but she did ask me for total honesty. "Dhara slowly revealed her sadomasochistic tendencies. She enjoyed sexual torture, and I don't mean the rather tame version mortals today sometimes engage in. Dhara craved pain with her pleasure. She wanted me to torture her mercilessly and vice versa."

"You weren't into that."

"No. I still am not."

Harper nods. "I really don't see you as the BDSM type."

"It's your turn." I lean forward until I've captured her gaze. "I think it's time you told me why you were so hell-bent on getting into the Unseen."

She wriggles, her lips pinched, and her gaze shies away from mine.

"Come on," I say. "I shared my past. Time to share yours. Why did you want to get into my world?"

"Because—" She puckers her lips, then squashes them between her teeth, before she squares her shoulders and aims her blue gaze straight at me. "I was going to destroy the Unseen realm."

For a moment, I'm sure I've misheard her. I sit still and silent while the truth of it seeps into me little by little and I come to terms with the fact she means it. Harper is not making a joke. No, she's telling the bald truth.

I throw my head back and laugh so loud it reverberates off the walls.

The irony of her statement is perversely hilarious. My fated mate wants to destroy my world with me in it. Not that I believe in fate, not for myself at least. Lindsey and Nevan had been destined for each other in ways I still don't fully understand. Time itself couldn't keep them apart, not even when a harpy tried to rewrite it. Those two deserved to find each other. They fought valiantly to save two worlds three times and had been willing to sacrifice everything, even each other, to accomplish those feats.

What have I done? As a mortal and as an elemental, I made bloody awful decisions out of weakness and selfishness. I don't deserve a fated mate. I don't deserve Harper's understanding or affection.

My laughter dies away.

Harper watches me with her brows knit together. "What's so funny? I just admitted I planned on destroying the Unseen."

The past tense in her statement suddenly catches my attention. She said she "was going to" and "had planned to" destroy this world.

"You've given up your plot to destroy my world?" I say.

"Maybe. I don't know." She hunches her shoulders. "I was absolutely sure of what I needed to do—until I met you. Everything seems different now, like I'm finally seeing the whole picture of this world and realizing maybe I shouldn't destroy it."

"Purely for the sake of curiosity, by what means did you plan to annihilate the Unseen?"

"I don't know."

"Brilliant. How's that plan working out for you?"

She grabs the pillow off the bed and lobs it at me. "Jackass."

I catch the pillow. "You're the one who desperately wanted into this world so you could destroy it but who has no idea how to do that. Don't blame me for your lack of preparation."

Harper pulls her bottom lip into her mouth, staring into space with her brows wrinkled.

I toss the pillow into the air and catch it, three times, while she cogitates.

She touches a hand to her chest, her head shaking faintly. "I—I never had a plan. Get to the Unseen, destroy it, and then..."

"What?"

She flaps her head. "Nothing. That was it. I had this mantra in my head for all these years, telling me to find a portal and destroy the Unseen. I was obsessed with fulfilling that mission, but it was almost like..."

"The thought wasn't yours." I stop tossing the pillow and crush it in my hands. "You were programmed."

"What?"

"Someone enthralled or ensorcelled you to do their bidding. You're a pawn, Harper." I turn to face her. "Someone else controls you."

CHAPTER SEVENTEEN

Harper

SOMEONE ELSE CONTROLS YOU, MAX SAID. I CAN'T EXPLAIN WHY I've been obsessed with finding a portal, why for more than a decade I searched for a way into the Unseen, but when I finally found it, I hadn't known what to do. Destroy an entire world? How exactly was I going to pull that off? All I knew was that I had to do it.

For Kelsey, that's what I'd told myself throughout the years. I was doing this for her, to avenge her death and prevent anyone else from falling victim to the obsidian fae.

If I want to kill every one of the obsidian fae, why did my mental mantra urge me to destroy an entire world? Is Max right? Am I programmed by magic? If I am, I have no idea why or to what purpose.

Those red-hot pins and needles start to prickle on the back of my shoulder.

Nausea swells inside me, pushing up into my throat. I'm a pawn. My stomach roils, the nausea rising higher and higher. The acrid taste of bile seeps into my mouth.

"Are you all right?" Max asks.

My pulse races as I swing my feet off the bed, but they don't touch the floor. I gulp against the nausea, gripping the bed's edge, and squeeze my eyes shut.

The need to vomit passes, but I keep my eyes closed.

"What the bloody hell is that?"

Max's question, and the shock in his voice, make me glance back at him. "What's what?"

"That." He points at my shoulder. "You have a tattoo on your back, and it's…moving."

I try to twist around in a way that might let me see my back, but I'm not a contortionist. "You're crazy, I don't have a tattoo. It's just a scar."

Then why does it burn?

"Scars aren't black," he says. "And they don't wriggle around like they're alive."

"It's not black. It's a white scar."

"Not anymore." Max conjures a handheld mirror and holds it so I can see my shoulder. "Look at it."

The scar has morphed into a black tattoo. Its twisting lines move almost like snakes writhing. While I stare at the image in the mirror, the burning prickle begins to intensify.

"What the hell is that?" I ask, my voice hushed and panicked at the same time.

"Not sure." Max rasps his tongue over the tattoo and grimaces. "Tastes bloody awful."

"And that means what?"

"Dark magics." He licks it again. "Very dark. Very powerful. Light magics taste sweet and savory, but dark spells are bitter with a metallic tang."

"How do I get rid of it?"

Max sets down the mirror and scrutinizes my back, his expression curious and fascinated. He touches the tattoo, and the spot where he touched it burns less for a split second.

But when he drags his tongue over it again, the discomfort lessens considerably.

I peek at him over my shoulder. "When you lick the mark, it stops hurting for a few seconds."

"The tattoo causes you pain?"

"Yeah. Not always, just sometimes. It burns, and at its worst, it can feel like pins and needles."

"Lie on your stomach."

I stretch out on the huge bed.

Max crouches over me and dips his head to lave the tattoo with his tongue. He traces its sinuous lines with the tip of his tongue, over and over, his hot breaths teasing my skin. The trail of moisture he leaves behind cools my flesh, and his velvety tongue does more than eradicate the prickling. My body responds to his ministrations by warming and tingling in a completely different way, his every touch arousing me more and more. I grow damp between my thighs again. Damp and achy.

"You should stop," I say. "I'm liking this way too much, and we don't have time for more sex."

"There's always time for sex." He places his open mouth on my skin, swirling his tongue over the tattoo while dragging his lips over my skin. Just when my breaths begin to shorten, and that delicious tingle in my core spreads to my clit, he kisses my shoulder and withdraws his mouth. "The mark is gone."

He sounds surprised.

I glance back at him. "You licked it away?"

"For now. I would expect it to come back. Dark magics aren't that easy to get rid of." He nuzzles my neck, and his stiff shaft brushes my ass. "I want you, Harper. One more time. Then we'll venture out there and search for answers. But let me have you one more time first. Maybe it will keep the magics in that tattoo at bay a bit longer."

His lips on my neck have me so turned on I feel lightheaded. The thought of more whopping-huge climaxes, delivered by a scorching incubus who exudes magic pleasure-heightening fluid...

I want to say yes, but I have to say, "We can't. No time to waste, what with enemies hunting for us."

The fact I'm breathing hard, almost panting, from the way he licked my tattoo probably makes my statement sound less convincing.

Max slides his tongue over the spot where the black design had been. "I do quick and earth shattering better than anyone. So we do have time—"

"No, no, no. I need to focus, and everything you do to me has the exact opposite effect."

"All right. If you insist on abstaining..."

"I do. For now."

He lies down beside me, on his back.

The two of us stay like that for several minutes, I guess, though I have no measure of time in this sanctuary. I need time to recover from what we just did, and I suspect he does too. At last, Max slides over to sit on the bed's edge, his feet on the floor. Even when I swing my legs over the edge, I can't reach the stone surface even if I stretch my toes out as far as possible. The bed is made for someone large and nonhuman.

"Where are my clothes?" I ask, then I spot the remnants of my satin shorts and top on the floor by the wall where he'd chained me up. I aim a playful smile at Max. "Oh, that's right. Somebody shredded them."

"You ordered me to get your clothes off."

"I kind of assumed you would make them disappear."

He hikes up one shoulder. "What does it matter? I'll conjure you new clothes."

"Let me guess," I say, sliding off the bed, "I'll wind up looking like a reject from a BDSM club."

"You mortal women are so fussy. I'll conjure you whatever your little heart desires. Say the word, and it's yours."

"Just like that?" I glance sideways at him. "This whole conjuring business is a little creepy. I know you said you won't take clothing from a corpse, but I still don't understand where the stuff comes from."

"As I told you before, I don't get receipts for the bloody things. I think of what I want, and it appears." He waves a hand in a dismissive gesture. "They're abandoned property, or some such thing, for the most part. Only on occasion do I nick something, and only from those I know well."

"But—"

"Do you want the ruddy clothes or not?"

"Sure, yeah. But maybe you could conjure stuff from my apartment."

He flicks his gaze up toward the ceiling and sighs. "You're jolly good fun when we're shagging, but you're downright tiresome any other time."

"Max, plea—"

He zooms to me so fast he becomes a blur and slaps his palm over my mouth. "No P-word. No T-word. No gratitude of any kind. Your life depends on your ability to restrain yourself. Understand?"

I nod.

Max pulls his hand away. "All right. I will get some clothing for you, from your apartment. Though honestly, I think you look quite fine as you are."

"Come on. I can't walk around naked all the time."

"Why not? I do."

"That's different. You're—I don't know. It's just different." I scrub my hands over my face and groan. "Why can't we go back to my apartment? I could pick my own clothes that way."

"Unless you want to be abducted by parties who won't treat you as nicely as I have, you cannot go back there."

"You mean, like, ever?"

"Correct."

"The obsidian fae are after me or waiting for me to ripen or whatever." I rub my arms, afflicted with a chill when I remember my nightmare. "I dreamed that an obsidian fae attacked us and told me I need to simmer for a while. Then it actually happened."

He opens his mouth but doesn't say anything.

"What do you think it means?" I ask.

"That you are connected to the obsidian fae. Your tattoo proves that." Max exhales a long, groaning sigh. "They're after you, and Hathor is after me. If she finds us together, she'll either kill you or capture you along with me."

"You mentioned Hathor before. She's obsessed with you." I give him a playful smile. "And now I understand why."

"I don't want you anywhere near her. She ensorcells everyone who enters her temple."

"Stay away from Hathor's temple. Got it."

"No, you don't have it." He grasps my shoulders. "She's been sending bounty hunters after me. That's who attacked us in your apartment. While you're inside this lair, you are protected by the wards, which means magical force fields. Hathor and her minions won't find you here. Out there"—he nods toward the wall—"no one can protect you, not even me."

"I get that, but I have to find out what the obsidian fae did to me." I glance at my shoulder and instinctively rub the mark there. "Max, I need your help. You know this world, I don't. Help me, p—Just help me, okay?"

At least I hadn't said the P-word. Jeez, this world is complicated.

"I will help you," Max says. "But we need advice and assistance from someone who knows more about magic than either of us."

"Who's that?"

"A friend. The fae witch Ennea."

"Let's go."

Max eyes me up and down, his lips kicking up at one corner. "You don't want clothes anymore, then? It's fine with me—"

"I want clothes. If you don't mind."

"Nice avoidance of the P-word. I shall conjure my lady her clothing."

Smirking, he bows deeply and flourishes his wrist.

Clothes materialize on my body. My clothes. I've got leather pants, a blouse, boots, and all my weapons—plus an extra one. The small sword I used yesterday to lop off the vampire's head.

I pull the sword free of its scabbard, waving it in the air in faux strikes, and grin. "Now this is more like it."

"Unfortunately, it's not endued," he says. "But it does have the uncanny ability to behead elementals, or one vampire at least."

I hop up on my toes to kiss him. "You really do know exactly what I want."

He studies me for a moment, his lips twisting this way and that. "Where did you get that sword?"

"I found it. When I was eighteen, I stumbled into a ditch, literally, and the sword was just lying there. Filthy, but intact."

"As if it were waiting for you."

"Sure, I guess." A wave of ice crackles through my veins. "You don't think it actually was waiting for me, do you? In my dream, the fae said they gave me a weapon that could kill you—and other elementals, I assume."

Max rubs his jaw. "But your sword did not destroy Gundisalvus, the vampire."

"Hathor might've somehow saved him from destruction with those dark magics you think she's been using."

"I suppose." He shoves his hands through his hair and sighs. "I should go out there and reconnoiter before I even consider taking you outside the wards."

"Reconnoiter?" I say with a laugh. "That sounds strange coming from a naked incubus."

"I'll be right back."

He disappears, leaving me alone.

CHAPTER EIGHTEEN

Max

I JUMP FROM PLACE TO PLACE, TRYING TO SENSE THE BOUNTY HUNTERS and the obsidian fae, but I have no idea how to do that. Sensing Harper, that I can pull off with my eyes closed and my powers bound. But finding our enemies proves much more challenging. There's a reason I'm having trouble, and it has nothing to do with hunger or my lack of adequate talent. Elementals have an innate instinct to shield ourselves, and the Great Bargain granted us additional protection. It also protects mortals from being abused by our kind via treacherous bargains and debts.

So now, when I need to track my fellow elementals, I can't. They're concealing themselves.

"*Di te perduint*," I curse, and then I wonder why I've reverted to Latin. I've been doing that a lot lately, ever since I met Harper Goode. Who am I demanding the gods damn with that curse? Everyone, I suppose. But I switch to a different Latin profanity for added impact. "*Merda.*"

Yes, "shit" seems much more appropriate. Not that I think the gods, or anyone, are listening. Still, I keep muttering that to myself while I blip here, there, and everywhere in the Unseen.

Now I'm thinking the word blip as I travel instead of saying…nothing, actually. Elementals don't have a word for the way we travel. "Blip" is Lindsey's word for it, along with "zip" and "whisk" and "poof." Harper had used a similar term. Why do mortal females insist on coming up with ludicrous descriptions of the way I live and travel?

Thinking the word blip reminds me of Lindsey, so I cross the veil to check on her and Nevan. They're fine, and I don't speak to them or let them see me.

What the bloody sodding hell am I doing? Teleporting all over both worlds. Why? This isn't helping me keep Harper safe. Then again, if I waste days "whisking" myself to every corner of the Unseen and the mortal realm, perhaps Hathor and the obsidian fae will get bored and find a new hobby.

Not likely.

At least I'm now at full power, fueled by the cracking great sex Harper gave me. No one else, human or elemental, has ever fed me as well as she does. Maybe that means she is my fated mate, but I still can't accept that idea isn't pure rubbish.

Lindsey's voice echoes in my mind, a memory of months ago when she'd told me, "You deserve love, Max, and you will find it. I believe that with all my heart." Immediately after that, she'd called me a "sweet, sweet salamander," so maybe I shouldn't worry about the things she says. Lindsey is barmy. A kind, generous, brave, and selfless person but still barmy.

She knows what I did to Aurelia. The abridged version, at any rate. How can she believe I deserve anything good?

I've taken a break from blipping about like a stone skipping across a pond to sit in a clearing with my back against a thick tree. Resting my head on the trunk, I close my eyes and invite the memories to torment me. That's what I deserve, to be tormented, to be punished.

So long ago…

Aurelia lay on a chaise when I entered the palace, her body stretched out along the length of it, a spray of golden-red hair framing her head. A long, flowing white tunic covered her body, but I knew what beauty lay beneath the clothing. Aurelia had the most beautiful body of any woman I'd ever taken to bed.

She leaped off the chaise, racing up to me and throwing her arms around my neck. While she showered kisses on my throat, I wrapped my arms around her waist and hoisted her off the floor. She smelled wonderful and felt even better.

"I have missed you, Maximus," she said, then planted a firm kiss on my mouth. "These campaigns to defeat the barbarians are tiresome. You have been gone far too long."

"Yes, I know." I slid my hands down to her rump. "I need to penetrate your lovely body before I lose my mind."

She giggled. "Yes, my Maximus needs a great deal of coitus."

"How have you been?" I asked. "Has the emperor, ah…"

Aurelia bowed her head. "No. My father has distracted Caligula from his plans for me, but I do not think that will protect me for much longer."

I crooked a finger under her chin, urging her to look at me. "I will take you away from here soon. We can run away to Gaul, or even to Britannia, or to Egypt."

"To the lands of barbarians who despise Rome? How would we ever survive?"

"We will find a way." I kissed her forehead. "You have my vow, Aurelia. I want you as my wife, even if that means abandoning everything we have ever known."

"I will go anywhere with you."

On that day, I'd made love to Aurelia for hours, so desperate to be inside her after months away that I couldn't let go of her. I'd loved Aurelia. Deeply. But fate did not look kindly on our love, and I would have her in my life for only sixteen months. Then my legion was dispatched to Gaul to subdue those barbarians. I wanted to flee with Aurelia instead, but she insisted we wait until after this final conflict was done. After all, my brothers and her half-brother belonged to the same legion. I'd promised to watch over all of them.

But I fell in battle along the banks of the River Rhine. Any natural water feature is always a portal to the Unseen. I knew nothing about other worlds or elemental beings until the day I lay bleeding to death on the riverbank, on my back, my head buoyed by the lapping waters. My blood trickled into the river, and that was all it took.

A copper-skinned being rose from the depths of the river and knelt beside me.

"You are dying, mortal," he said. "The life essence drains out of you more every moment and will be extinguished soon."

Half-dead already, I could do nothing more than gaze at the strange being through a haze of blood and sweat.

"I can offer you another way," the being said. "Imagine living on but never again fearing death or injury. You will become as a god, omnipotent and immortal, stronger and faster and more cunning than you ever have been as a mere mortal."

When I tried to speak, I achieved nothing more than to hack up blood.

"Listen to me," the being said, leaning over me with his face inches away. "The one you love is in danger. Caligula has become far more depraved in your absence, and he covets Aurelia. Imagine what he will do to her. The pain, the shame, the violation. You want to save her, do you not?"

Somehow I managed to say, "Yes."

Aurelia. My sweet, loving Aurelia. If the emperor got his hands on her, he would defile her body in ways even I couldn't imagine. Though I'd witnessed his depravity first-hand, I had also heard rumors of far worse things.

"If you become like me," the being said, "you can save her and destroy the emperor."

Save Aurelia. Yes, I must do that. At any cost.

Maybe my mind had been too damaged, my will too weak, for me to realize this creature wanted something from me and cared nothing about the woman I loved. I had too little blood left in my veins to clear my thoughts. The world had become a hazy mural, something distant and disconnected from me.

All I could think about was Aurelia and what Caligula might do to her.

"Yes," the being said, his voice hushed but imbued with intensity. "You know what you must do. Become like me, become as a god, and spare your love. All you need do is blink your eyes twice, and I will grant you the freedom and power you deserve."

So cold. From my skin down to my bones and deeper to my soul. The ice consumed me, swallowing up everything that made me human. I would slip into the darkness soon, and my soul would travel to the underworld. Aurelia would be alone.

I blinked twice, my lids seeming to have become lead curtains that required an enormous effort to move.

"The choice is made," the being said. "Now the forging begins."

My savior rose to his full height, looming over me, and now I saw that he wore no clothing. His naked, tanned body glistened with a coppery sheen, and his eyes burned with swirling shades of molten metal. He raised his hands to the heavens and began to chant in another language.

The words, so strange and disquieting, sent a chill skittering down my spine.

Glowing, glittering orbs materialized around us, spinning and twirling, finally swarming around my body. They nipped at my skin, their light transforming into a blanket of blinding white energy. The searing, prickling pain intensified with every passing second until it became a shroud of blistering agony that tore at my flesh.

I screamed.

The energy consumed me from the outside in, rending every last shred of flesh from my skeleton, shattering those bones and disintegrating them. The agony went on and on and on, a never-ending torture that transformed me into...nothing. I ceased to exist for a moment, maybe for an eternity, I had no conception of time. *Please let me die*, I prayed to the gods I had once believed in without reservation.

They ignored my silent plea.

But the worst was yet to come. The forging didn't simply destroy my body, it rebuilt me from scratch, taking every molecule that had once formed my body and transmuting it into something new and, yes, far more powerful. I've learned since that power isn't everything. It can't save your soul.

Did I save Aurelia?

As it turned out, no.

For years after my forging, I struggled with the transition from mortal to elemental. I battled the hunger, but more than that, I fought to comprehend what I had done out of a selfish desire to live on and become the hero who saved Aurelia. The incubus who created me had vanished as soon as the forging ended. I later learned that none of my kind cares about the so-called children they create via the forging. They do it to keep our race alive, nothing more. They deem pregnancy and childbirth to be unseemly, degrading, unworthy of ones as high as we, the sex demons, are.

When I'd met Lindsey, she jokingly called me a sex demon. I bristled at her description, insisting I'm not like that. But since then, I've become the beast I never wanted to be. I am a sex demon.

Look at what I've done to Harper.

Why in the multiverse had she let me do that to her? I'd turned into a ravenous maniac. Yet she calmed the beast within me and showed me how to tame the hunger. I don't deserve her any more than I did Aurelia.

I need to get back to Harper.

And I pray I can protect her better than I had done with Aurelia.

CHAPTER NINETEEN

Harper

WHILE I WAIT FOR MAX TO COME BACK, I EXPLORE HIS LAIR. THE bathroom has a waterfall in it. Seriously. His shower is a waterfall. I think about bathing but decide I don't have time for that right now. Max ought to be back any minute. So instead, I wander into the kitchen. My tummy has started grumbling, but I can't figure out where the food is in this kitchen.

The counter consists of smooth rock that has no seams as if the entire room has been carved out of the mountain itself. I see no fridge, no oven, no cabinets. Where does Max get his food? Does he even eat? Well, he has a kitchen, so I assume he does eat something sometime.

An even better question occurs to me. Does every incubus have jaw-dropping abs? Seeing Max's ripped torso makes my jaw crash to the floor for sure.

I lean against the stone island, gazing at the wall in front of me, my back to the doorway. God, I need food. How can I fight the bad guys on an empty stomach? I can't remember when I last ate. This morning? Yesterday? Damned if I know.

"Whoa."

That syllable, spoken by an unfamiliar voice, makes me jump and spin around, brandishing my sword.

A huge man hovers in the doorway. His skin has the same coloring as Max's, his hair is the same deep-brown shade that's almost black, and he boasts a similar physique—meaning outrageously large muscles and a height that lets him tower over me. He isn't naked like Max, though. This incubus sports blue jeans and a white shirt with all the buttons undone.

I assume my self-defense posture, stance wide, knees bent, hunched over a little while I wield my sword at the stranger. "Who are you? What do you want?"

"Looking for Max," he says in a Texas twang. "I'm Travis. Who are you?"

"Maybe I'll tell you that later, if I decide not to kill you."

"Hey, I ain't looking for trouble." He raises his hands, palms out. "Just wanted to talk to Max. He's kinda my…adviser."

"Uh-huh." Whatever Max does with this creature has nothing to do with me.

Travis's eyes begin to swirl, slowly at first, speeding up the longer he looks at me. At my body. My upper body. Mostly, at my tits.

Oh great. Is this another sex-starved incubus? Why can't these guys get any? Jeez, I thought they all had seduction superpowers.

"My face is up here," I say, pointing at my head. Once Travis shifts his gaze up to my face, I ask, "What does Max advise you on?"

"How to be"—he gestures at himself—"like this. I ain't been an incubus for very long, and I'm not too good at it yet. I mean, I feed regularly, but, uh…"

"I get it. You can stop explaining." Because I really do not need to hear the details of this guy's sex life. Deciding Travis isn't an immediate threat, I relax and sheath my sword. "Max will be back any minute."

Travis tips his head left and right, then sniffs the air. He groans deeply, his eyes going hooded.

And the bulge in his jeans gets bigger.

Fabulous. Just what I need, a newbie incubus who gets turned on by whatever he smelled in the air. I set my hand on my sword's hilt, ready to whip it out if this guy turns ravenous on me.

"Damn," he says, his voice rougher. "I can smell it. Max did the nasty with you a few minutes ago, didn't he? An hour ago at most."

I open my mouth to tell him to mind his own business, but I don't get the chance.

"Travis, what the bloody hell are you doing here?"

Only by leaning sideways can I see Max behind Travis, though all I can make out are his huge biceps and his hair. I recognize that voice, though, and it triggers a fluttery sensation in my chest as my breaths quicken and my pulse kicks up a few notches. Okay, more than a few. Max's presence always does this to me.

Travis moves to the side, out of the doorway, and rotates halfway toward Max. "I needed some, uh, advice. About that…stuff. Ya know."

"I don't have time to be your elemental counselor today." Max looms on the threshold, fists clenched, jaw tight. "You'd better not be lusting after my woman."

His woman? Like hell. Having sex—awesome, incredible, world-altering sex—doesn't make me his.

Barring my arms over my chest, I glare at Max. "I am not your property."

"Yes, you are." He storms past Travis and straight to me, latching his hand around my arm. "If you don't like being my property, you shouldn't have gifted me with your body."

Travis warps his mouth into an expression of discomfort. "Okay, think I'd better skedaddle. Nice to meet you, uh…whoever you are."

"My name is Harper," I say, blatantly ignoring Max's furious expression. "Nice to meet you too, Travis."

The other incubus blinks out.

I shake off Max's hand. "You are acting like a caveman."

"This lair is a cave."

"But I am not a Stone Age chick you kidnapped and forced to become your mate." I slam my palms onto his chest and shove, which has little to no effect on him. "You don't get to be jealous because I'm having a conversation with someone else. Isn't Travis your friend, anyway?"

"Travis is…a long story."

I hop up onto the stone island, my feet dangling over the edge. "I'm in the mood for a long story. And I'm starving. Don't you have any actual food?"

"We have problems—"

"And I don't do well with solving problems when I'm about to pass out from hunger."

Max sighs, his shoulders flagging. "Yes, all right. Here's your food."

He flourishes his hand.

And a plate of food appears beside me on the island. A glass of dark liquid too.

"Your meal," he says. "All the things you seem to like. A hamburger with ketchup and cheese, French fries, apple pie with ice cream, and root beer to drink."

He carefully enunciates the words root beer and ketchup like he's not sure how to pronounce them. Well, maybe he's never tried to pronounce them before. Do elementals eat burgers and fries? Probably not.

"Do you eat food?" I ask. "I mean, I know you devour sexual energy, but I was wondering—"

"I do not need to consume food, but I often do for the pleasure of it."

"Uh-huh. We mere mortals have no choice." I pick up my burger, which looks way spiffier than any I've had before. Eying the burger, I turn it this way and that. "Where did you get this food? Please tell me you didn't steal it from a little old lady or something."

"No," he says with a huff. "I procured it from a restaurant. Not the one where you and I used to work. A good one."

"You mean an expensive one." I sniff the burger. "When you say you 'procured' it, do you mean you bought it? Paid for it with mortal money?"

"No, I—" He scrunches up his face, then blusters out a sigh. "I nicked it from the restaurant kitchen. Technically, it didn't belong to anyone yet since the order hadn't been served to the customer."

"That's a clever little fine line you drew yourself there."

"I'm glad you appreciate my cleverness."

The look on his face suggests he knows I was being sarcastic.

While I take a bite of my burger, I ask him a question with my mouth full. I'm too hungry to care about manners. "So, mind telling me more about your mortal life?"

"Why? It's the distant past."

"I'll tell you mine if you tell me yours."

He studies me with narrowed eyes, tilting his head to the side and folding his arms over his impressive chest. He's not naked, though. He popped into the kitchen wearing those black leather pants and that white shirt, untucked. As hot as he looks au naturel, I like the way those pants cling to his thighs and the way that shirt, half unbuttoned, gives me a tantalizing glimpse of his chest.

Max is hot, period.

Often literally.

"All right," he says after a moment. He drops his arms to his sides and leans back against the island an arm's length from me. "What do you want to know?"

"What kind of life did you have in ye olden days? Were you a blacksmith? A gigolo? A schoolteacher?"

He snorts, grasping the island's edge with both hands. "Do I look like a ruddy schoolteacher?"

"Not now, but you looked different back then. Right?"

"Yes. I looked human, which is bloody boring if you ask me."

"Once again, you're being evasive." I shove several fries into my mouth. "Tell me about yourself, Max. I'd say the P-word, but you wouldn't like that." I swallow my mouthful of mushed-up fried potatoes, then I get an idea. "Hmm, what if I threaten to use the P-word? Oh Max, would you pl—"

He slaps a hand over my mouth. "Do not do that."

I mumble against his palm.

Frowning, he pulls his hand away. Then he moves closer, leaning in like he's about to kiss me.

Can't help it. I part my lips for the kiss I crave.

He shoves a handful of fries into my mouth. "That ought to prevent you from saying the words you aren't meant to say on this side of the veil."

While I chew, I mumble, "Jackass."

"Better a jackass than a cloud of disintegrated flesh."

"How does telling me about your past doom you to destruction? You're being silly about this."

Max plucks a single fry from the plate and pops it into his mouth. Once he's eaten it, he gazes down at the floor. "You won't like what you hear, take my word on that."

"I can handle it."

He huffs again. "I rather doubt that."

Though I've already picked up my burger, ready to take a bite, I hesitate with the food inches from my mouth. "I've been through stuff as bad as anything you might've gone through, trust me."

Sometimes I've wished I could forget all that stuff. Often, I wished with all my might that I'd never told anyone what really happened to me and Kelsey. Would my life be different now if I'd stayed silent?

The mark on my back suggests the answer is no.

Max is leaning back against the island again, but he swivels his head to look at me. His eyes swirl, but not with heated shades. They've morphed into muted hues of blue laced with copper. His voice is subdued too and filled with tenderness. "What did the obsidian fae do to you?"

I set down my burger, suddenly not hungry at all. Hunching my shoulders, I rub my arms to ward off a chill that has nothing to do with the air temperature. "They tortured us."

"Did they…" He fidgets, his face pinched. "Ah, did they hurt you in a…sexual way?"

"No, thank God." I hug myself. "They used old-fashioned physical torture plus the magical kind. I had horrible hallucinations that caused real, down-to-earth pain. For three days, they did everything they could to terrify us, hurt us, make us scream and sob and beg for death."

"Christ, Harper…"

"They murdered Kelsey. I watched it happen, and I couldn't do anything about it." I suck in a ragged breath, my head bowed. "The obsidian fae said Kelsey didn't have what they needed, so her life served no purpose—except to prepare me for my destiny." Tears burn in my eyes, and I sniffle, helpless to stem the imminent flow. "I watched them run a black sword through her heart. She was looking at me when it happened. Crying. Pleading for mercy. They didn't give a shit about that or us or anyone except themselves and whatever it is they want. Why couldn't I save her? It's my fault she died, because I wanted to go for a walk that day."

Max sidles closer, his hip nudging my leg. "It's not your fault. You couldn't have known what would happen."

I can't believe that, no matter how many years go by. The guilt eats away at me.

"After they killed Kelsey," I say, "they put the brand on me. The scar. The tattoo, whatever. I couldn't see how they did it, but it felt like a red-hot branding iron with needles attached to it. The pain was…indescribable. Once they'd done that, they dumped me back in the mortal world, at the same waterfall where they'd abducted us. They dumped Kelsey's body there too."

Max slips an arm around me, tugging me into his body.

I rest my head on his shoulder. "No one believed me when I told them what happened. Obsidian fae, magically induced hallucinations, a portal to another world, it all sounded like the ravings of a diseased mind. The cops went to the waterfall but didn't see anything except Kelsey's body."

"The portal would only have opened for an elemental. To mortals, it would seem like nothing more than water and stone."

"Yeah, I know that now. At the time, I couldn't understand why the portal was gone."

He glides his hand up and down my arm in a gesture that soothes me more than I would've expected. "What did you do? If no one believed your story…"

"They decided the trauma of being abducted by a child molester and seeing my friend murdered had made me crack. I told them I hadn't been sexually abused, but they refused to believe anything I said." I snuggle closer to Max, letting the heat of him chase away my chill. "My parents threatened to have me committed to a mental institution, so I learned to shut up and let them believe what they wanted."

"You don't seem like the sort who shuts up for long."

"No, I'm not. For three years, the mark on my back would sometimes itch, but that was about it. Then, when I was fifteen, it started to change." I absently reach for the mark on my shoulder, but Max's arm is in the way. "The itching became a prickling sensation. And I started having these compulsions to hunt down the obsidian fae and destroy the Unseen realm. I didn't know what this world was called at first or how to find it, but I knew I had to get there."

"And destroy us all."

"Yeah. I became kind of a problem child, so my parents threatened to send me to a rehab clinic for troubled teens. When I put my foot down and said no way, they kicked me out of the house. Told me never to come back. I learned to take care of myself and trust no one."

"I assume you stumbled onto a few elementals along the way since you have some knowledge of our world."

"The mark led me to them." I inhale deeply, letting the delicious scent of him suffuse my senses. "I never questioned why or what I was doing. I followed the instinct, the compulsion. That's how I found you. Nobody else from the Unseen would take me through a portal."

"It's time you found out what the obsidian fae want with you."

"Yeah, it is time." I hop off the island and face him. "But first, you need to tell me about your past."

"After you've eaten." He offers me the plate. "I strongly request that you finish your meal."

"Strongly request? Wow, you really do have fine lines down to an art."

I take the plate and gobble up my meal, partly because I'm starving, but mostly because I want to hear his story. Once I've guzzled my root beer, I wipe my hands on my pants and say, "Your turn, Max. Here's a question to get you started. What was your original, mortal name?"

He juts his chin out, his lips ticking upward in a smug little smile. "Mentula Maximus."

Because he's smirking, I get the idea that's not his actual name. But I have to ask, "What's that mean in English?"

"The largest penis."

I try not to laugh, but it splutters out of me anyway. "Your name is the Biggest Dick? In my world, that's not usually a compliment. It means you're a jerk."

He scrunches up his lips.

"Come on," I say, "you were lying, so tell me your real name."

"If you insist." He looks none too happy about sharing his life story with me. "My name is Quintus Salonius Maximus. My parents called me Salonius when I was a boy, but I always preferred Maximus. Satisfied?"

Chapter Twenty

Max

YOU HAVEN'T CHANGED YOUR NAME SINCE ANCIENT ROME?" HARPER asks. She raises her brows and waits for me to answer.

"No." I scratch my arms, evading her gaze. "Elementals usually do take a new name after the forging, but I didn't."

"Why not?"

"Because I didn't feel like it."

She clucks her tongue. "Not a good enough answer, Max. I told you things about myself that I wasn't super comfortable sharing, so you can't chicken out on me now."

"Chicken out? Are you hungry again? I can conjure you a plate of fried chicken. It's actually rather tasty."

"Nice evasion, but I'm sure you know what I mean. So spill, Max." She walks up to me, so close that the intoxicating scent of her surrounds me. A sexy smile curves her lips. "And by 'spill' I mean confess. I'm not begging you to come inside me again."

Why did she have to mention that? The words come and spill are enough to make me hard again. But it doesn't do that. Probably because I'm distracted by scratching a phantom itch and avoiding answering Harper's questions.

Perhaps I should stop avoiding it and just tell her.

But I can't look at her while I do that.

Head down, I say, "I didn't choose a new name after my forging because I thought—I felt that I didn't deserve to forget my past as a mortal. I had done things that should never be forgotten or forgiven."

"Like what?"

"Terrible things."

"You're trying to convince me you're evil, aren't you? Well, I've seen you at your worst, and I'm still here."

I'm staring at her feet, at the leather boots that cover them, because I refuse to see her expression. She must understand what I've been, what I've done, so she will stop feeling…whatever it is she thinks she feels for me. She said she likes me.

She should not do that.

Harper lays a hand on my chest. "Tell me, Max."

"You want to know everything?" I snarl, because nothing short of becoming a beast again seems likely to dissuade her. "I was a soldier in the Roman legions. Do you think I rescued kittens from trees for a living?"

"No, I don't think that." She sounds offended, but that's exactly what I need her to feel.

And I will not look at her.

"I was a centurion," I tell her. "That means I was the leader of a small group within the legion to which I belonged. My men followed my orders, but I answered to the Primus Pilus, the leader of the cohort to which my century, my unit, belonged. If the Primus Pilus ordered us to raze a village, we did it. If he commanded us to rape and pillage, we did that too. And torture? Of course we tortured our enemies, for they were savages unworthy of mercy."

"Did you…rape anyone?"

Her voice is quieter now, and tight with anxiety.

I scratch my arms, so vigorously that I might be drawing blood, but I don't glance at my skin to find out. "No, I have never forced myself on any woman or man. But I participated in everything else. I murdered innocent people because the emperor commanded it and everyone in the legions carried out the imperial command."

"Did you kill children?"

"I didn't, but others in my century did."

"And did you enjoy killing?"

"No. But don't excuse my behavior because I hated doing it." I turn away from her, stalking to the other side of the island. "I was not a good man by any measure. I loved women. I loved sex. I took part in orgies of wine, drugs, and fornication. All I cared about was physical pleasure—until I met Aurelia. She taught me that being strong means being good and making sacrifices for the ones you love."

"Aurelia? She was your girlfriend?"

I flatten my hands on the island, shutting my eyes briefly. "I loved her. I wanted to marry her, but our stations wouldn't permit it. I was a soldier, a plebeian, and she was the daughter of an aristocrat. I begged her to run away with me, but she feared leaving the only home she'd ever known. By the time she finally agreed to leave with me, it was too late. I'd been called to battle again, and I had to go. My century—my garrison, I suppose mortals would call it—included Aurelia's half-brother and my two brothers. So I promised her I would participate in one last campaign for the emperor, to protect our families, then we would run away together."

"Something happened to her, didn't it?"

"Eventually, yes." I risk glancing up, moving only my eyes. The look of empathy on Harper's face tightens my chest. "I was slain in battle along the banks of the River Rhine. A salamander came to me, offering eternal life and untold power. I agreed to be forged because I selfishly believed I could save Aurelia if I only had more power. You see, the emperor Caligula had set his sights on her, and her father's attempts to shield her wouldn't work for much longer. I had first-hand knowledge of Caligula's depravity."

"How is saving the woman you love a selfish act?"

"Because I wanted to be the hero. I cared about my own glory."

"That's bullshit, Max." She leans over the island but can't get close to me, a fire burning in her eyes—though not literally. "You loved Aurelia. Wanting to protect her makes you a good man, not a bastard."

"But I didn't protect her," I snap. "I took off on another campaign to glorify myself by impressing the emperor, instead of taking Aurelia away to somewhere safer. I abandoned her. And after my forging, I needed a long time to adjust to being an incubus. I did not even check in on Aurelia for ten years. And when I finally did check, she was dying of a disease the emperor gave her when he violated her body for his own pleasure."

Harper bites her upper lip as if she's preventing herself from speaking by doing that.

"She could see what I'd become," I say, "since I hadn't yet learned how to hide my natural appearance with a glamour. She wasn't frightened, though. She asked me how I became a salamander, and I told her about the forging. She begged me to make her like me so we could be together forever."

"Did you do it?"

I fist my hands on the island, my jaw tight. "The transition was far more difficult for her than it had been for me. She couldn't handle the hunger. Aurelia had been a light in my darkness, the best living soul I'd ever known, but the forging corrupted that light. She went mad. Did things…even I couldn't stomach. Ensorcelling men and women alike to force them to want her, torturing them for pleasure, murdering them in the most vicious and agonizing ways. She wasn't Aurelia anymore. She was a ravenous, wild monster that craved more and more sexual energy at any cost."

"Oh God, Max. What happened to her?"

"I destroyed her."

Harper's eyes glisten with a hint of tears.

And I focus on the island, on my hands still splayed on the stone surface. I'm shaking, just a touch, and the tremors infect my voice. "I entered into a bargain with a dark sorcerer. In exchange for being provided with an endued weapon, I agreed to become the sorcerer's slave. You must understand that magical slavery is absolute. There is no escape without an even greater magical intervention. A bargain is unbreakable by any other means. I knew this, and still, I consented. To save Aurelia from herself. From what I'd turned her into."

"I'm so sorry, Max."

"Three young mortal women died last year because of that bargain, because of what the sorcerer forced me to do."

"How did you get away from him?"

"I didn't. A mortal saved me." I set my elbows on the island and cradle my face in my hands. "Lindsey Astrid Porter freed me from the bargain. She saved me, in every way. I owe her my life and my soul, but nothing will ever erase what I did, all the horrific mistakes I made that brought me to the sorcerer."

Her footsteps clap on the stone floor, but I don't realize how close she's come until she loops her arms around my waist and rests her chin on my shoulder.

"What are you doing?" I ask. "After what I've told you—"

"Yeah, I get it. You expect me to hate you, but I don't. I know what it's like to be haunted by the past and wish you could change it. We can't do that. What's done is done, and all that matters now is what we do to make things right."

"I can't make it right. Aurelia is gone. Those mortal girls are dead."

"This Lindsey you keep mentioning, I thought her last name was O'Rourke."

"Now it is. She married Nevan, the former king of the sylphs who became a mortal, and she took his new surname. When I met her, she was Lindsey Porter."

Harper kisses my cheek.

"What was that for?" I ask.

"That was appreciation. You told me your story, and I know it wasn't easy to do that."

I straighten and slip my arm around her waist. "We've wasted enough time on the past. We need answers to our present problems."

Before she can speak, I whisk us away.

We emerge in the clearing at the base of the mountain inside of which my lair hides. I don't like this, but I have no choice. I would've preferred to leave Harper safely inside the wards, out of Hathor's reach, but she's right. We both need answers and assistance. I can't protect her, that much has been demonstrated for me with shattering clarity.

And I will not fail her the way I failed Aurelia.

My need to consume sexual energy makes me a liability. That obsidian fae bastard stripped away Ennea's spell as easily as the wind blows away smoke. Harper needs an ally who has no weaknesses. But since that seems unlikely, I have no choice but to do the best I can for her.

What is that ruddy tattoo? I've never seen anything like it.

"Is this it?" Harper asks. "Are we there?"

"No, we're just outside my lair. I need a moment to, ah, gather my thoughts."

"Time is kind of essential at the moment."

"I know," I snap. She doesn't need to remind me of that. "Now we're there."

The world shifts in the blink of an eye—less than that, in fact. Our journey through the rift takes a nanosecond, according to mortal ways of measuring such things.

We stand inside Ennea's cave.

The wavering light of oil lamps lessens the gloom inside the cavern and flickers on the coarse stone walls. Like my lair, this chamber is nestled inside a large hill to conceal it from prying eyes and make it more difficult to penetrate. It's also warded, naturally.

Ennea hunches over a table, peering down at a piece of paper like she's trying to read whatever words it contains but having trouble deciphering it. She glances up and straightens when she notices us.

"Hey, Max," she says. "You brought a friend this time. Or is she more than a friend?" Ennea switches her attention to Harper. "I know you're a friendly and not a hostile because Max brought you, and because my wards detect your intentions."

"Detect intentions?" Harper says.

"Sure." Ennea waggles her fingers in the air. "It's freaky woo-woo magic, ya know."

The fae witch smiles and winks.

Harper offers a halfhearted smile in return.

I can't blame her for not feeling terribly cheerful.

"We need your help," I say to Ennea. "Hathor sent a ruddy vampire after me, but it was the obsidian fae who annihilated the hunger-dampening spell you gave me."

"Obsidian fae? They're supposed to be a myth."

"They are real." I take Harper's hand in both of mine. "This is Harper Goode. She's, ah, my, um… Well, we're shagging."

Why was that hard for me to say? I'm an incubus, for pity's sake. Sex is my favorite topic. It used to be, at any rate, before I met Lindsey and started to feel uncomfortable discussing the subject. Since I met Harper, I get…anxious about it.

"Good for you, Max," Ennea says. "About time you found your fated mate."

"She is not my fated anything."

Harper flutters her lashes like she's having trouble focusing or has grit in her eyes. "Fated what?"

"Never mind. It's bollocks anyway."

Ennea laughs. "Still in denial, eh?"

"*Merda*," I growl. "We don't have time to talk about that nonsense. The obsidian fae put some sort of tattoo on her Harper's back that's infused with dark magics. We need to know what it does."

"Better tell me the whole story."

Harper relates everything she told me about the obsidian fae, her abduction, and the mark on her back. Once she finishes, Ennea has her sit on a stool at one of the many tables in this laboratory of magic. The witch retrieves a large, round slab of convex glass or crystal and holds it between her palms.

For a minute. Or two. Or fifty thousand.

"Time is an issue," I tell her, and even I note the edge in my voice. "How many centuries is this going to take? You're just standing there with a glass lens between your hands."

"Gotta warm it up first." Ennea shakes one finger at me while still cupping the lens. "Getting grumpy with me won't speed up the process."

I grumble.

"Do you need to feed?" Ennea asks. "I can throw out a cloaking spell, so I won't see or hear you and Harper getting busy in the corner."

"No, I bloody do not need to bloody feed."

"Oh look," Harper says. "He's blushing. Isn't that adorable?"

And she's grinning at me. Grinning and trembling from laughter she's trying to suppress. Tears brim in her eyes too, brought on by that same withheld laughter.

"Sure is cute," Ennea agrees, "the way his copper cheeks are pink now."

I grumble for the second time and collapse onto a chair so hard it thumps and grates across the floor. "Just get it done with, would you?"

Ennea blows on the lens, and the glass shimmers silver. "It's ready. Better get undressed, Harper. Gotta see the tattoo before I can suss out what it was."

Harper strips off her coat and her shirt, leaving only her bra. She slides one strap off her shoulder to expose the entire black tattoo.

And her skin. Creamy, soft, luscious skin.

Don't think about sex, you idiot.

I focus on what Ennea is doing.

She holds the lens close to Harper's skin and peers through it at the mark. "Hmm."

"What does 'hmm' mean?" I ask. All right, I might have barked that question.

"Kinda stressed, aren't ya, Max? What I'm seeing is dark magic, but it's the blackest I've ever come across." She moves her lens further from Harper's skin, then closer again, over and over while she studies the tattoo. "Ain't never seen nothing like this before. It's almost like it's...alive."

"Can you get rid of it?" I ask.

"Sorry, no can do. It's too deeply embedded, and besides, I can't defeat a kind of magic I don't understand." She sets down the lens. "You need to talk to an oracle."

"Fine. Let's do that."

Ennea winces. "There's a slight problem. The oracle won't let an incubus into his lair."

"Bob likes me. I spoke to him last week."

"There's more than one oracle, ya know. The one you need to see specializes in dark magics and how they'll evolve. But Ken doesn't like salamanders."

"Harper is not visiting an oracle on her own."

"I can handle it," Harper says. "I managed all by myself for a long time before I ever met you."

"Not in the Unseen, you didn't."

Ennea touches Harper's shoulder. "You can put your shirt back on, hon. We're finished here." The witch fixes her stern gaze on me. "And you need to either trust Harper to do this alone or come up with an alternative plan. Kennisowalloshavitz will never permit a salamander to enter his lair."

Harper starts pulling her clothes back on.

"Why do oracles always have such ridiculous names?" I ask. "Since they want to be called Bob or Ken, they shouldn't bother with all those extraneous syllables."

Ennea rolls her eyes at me. "Bobanzhistilanovitz is very proud of his oracle name. Ken feels the same way about his. Does anybody tell you to get rid of your extraneous syllables, Quintus Salonius Maximus?"

I grumble. Again.

Why had I ever shared my full name with Ennea, Tris, and the others?

The witch taps her chin. "Maybe you could get into Ken's lair, if you can finagle a way to sidestep his wards. Didn't you do something like that when you and Lindsey jumped into the time stream together?"

Harper has just slipped her jacket on, and she glances between me and Ennea. "Time stream?"

I wave a dismissive hand. "It's a long story."

"And we're in a hurry. Yeah, that's always your excuse for not explaining things."

With a snarl, I leap out of the chair and fly straight to Harper, latching my arms around her, then I transport us out of Ennea's lab. As we zip away, I hear the witch call out, "You could at least say adios, Max. Sheesh, you're a grouch these days."

Harper and I materialize in the woods not far from the lair of the oracle Ken. Finding oracles isn't that difficult. It's getting inside their lairs that can be deadly.

She scowls at me. "That was rude."

"We don't have time for the niceties." I step back a few paces. "I'll need to ride in your bra."

"Excuse me?"

"That's how I got into the time stream with Lindsey. Only the Janusite was allowed to enter it since she had dominion over time itself." I roll my shoulders back and lift my chin. "As her familiar, I could go with her as long as I was on her person."

"How does that equate to you in my bra?" She gestures at her bosom and then at my body. "You're slightly larger than my boobs."

"At the moment. We need to try this, Harper." I can't stop myself from admiring her breasts, since she mentioned them. "I've seen your 'boobs' before, so you can't be shy about it. And I'll be considerably smaller in my alternate form."

She sags her shoulders and blusters out a breath. "Go on. Do it."

I shift into salamander form amid a flare of flames. Then I run over to her and skitter up her leg to her chest. She holds her shirt away from her body while I crawl inside her bra.

Ahhh, it's lovely in here. The scent of her envelops me while I snuggle between those voluptuous mounds.

She giggles. "Stop moving around, will you? It tickles."

I would chuckle if I could. Now I know a secret place where she's ticklish, and I will take full advantage of that knowledge later. When we're naked. And alone. And not being hunted.

"How do I know where to go?" she asks.

Reluctantly, I crawl out from under her breast and place my tiny red paws on the front of her bra so I can point in the right direction with one finger. A trail is just visible in the gloom of the forest.

"Okay," Harper says, squaring her shoulders. "Thataway."

She giggles when I scurry under her breast again.

Then she heads for the trail.

Chapter Twenty-One

Harper

I TROMP DOWN A NARROW TRAIL THROUGH A DARK AND FORBIDDING forest full of black trees and black grass and black…everything. Instead of leaves, or even the moss-like stuff I'd seen on other trees in the Unseen, the forest here has oozing black gunk that clings to the trees like droopy leaves and exudes goo that drips onto the ground.

Yeah, it's the creepiest thing I've ever seen.

The trees smell too, and not in a good way. This whole forest stinks of motor oil or something like that. Underneath that smell, I detect an even worse stench, like acid and decaying flesh.

I really hope Max knows where the hell we're going.

The trail gradually widens and, after a length of time I can't gauge, the path ends at a small mound-like hill that hunkers a hair taller than my head. If this is the oracle's lair, I see no way Max will fit inside it. I might not even fit.

Peeking into my bra, I ask the salamander, "Are you sure this is it? Doesn't look like much."

He nods his cute little salamander head.

Dang, he's adorable in this form.

"Okay," I say, then I approach the mound.

What should I do? Knock on the dirt? Scream the oracle's name?

I'm about to try both of those when the side of the hill opens up, revealing a set of steps that lead down to a recessed door. One I can fit through without walking hunched over. Thank goodness.

Max fidgets inside my bra, making me giggle.

Jeez, I never giggle. Never. But the sensation of his cute little salamander tail twitching against my boobs and his cute little salamander feet scooting around makes me do that.

"Hold still," I whisper to him. "You're distracting me."

When I glance into my bra, he raises his tiny hands and mouths with his cute little salamander lips, "Okay."

At least I think that's what he mouths. Those lips are so tiny it's hard to tell for sure.

I descend the steps to the door.

And it swings open for me.

So I walk through it, into a hallway with smooth rock walls and a barrel ceiling. Light from nowhere and everywhere illuminates the corridor, and at its far end, I spy another doorway. That one is made of shiny, bronze-colored metal.

I make my way down the corridor until I reach the inner door.

This one opens automatically too.

Which is kind of creepy.

I tiptoe into the darker chamber beyond the doorway, though I'm not sure why I tiptoe. Something about this place makes me feel like I'm intruding on a sacred space. Maybe I am since this is the lair of an oracle. The inner chamber stands empty except for a large metal bowl seated on a low stand, the legs of which resemble that of a lion or a tiger. The metal bowl shimmers bronze in the flickering light of oil lamps.

Here, the walls have not been smoothed out. They're rough and natural, almost primal, like I've entered the home of a prehistoric caveman—except for the fancy metal thingy in the middle of the chamber.

I approach the big bronze bowl and halt there. Now what?

"Hello?" I call out.

My voice echoes inside the chamber, though it doesn't seem large enough to produce echoes. Well, I am inside the lair of a supernatural being within a world that teems with supernatural energy. If the cave behind the falls in Michigan can dampen the roar of the water, then this chamber could certainly enhance echoes.

A figure appears on the other side of the bronze bowl.

The being stands at least a foot shorter than I am, and he wears an old-style leisure suit with the jacket half unzipped, revealing the tank top he wears underneath it. His skin looks faintly golden with a smattering of dark hairs on it. The hair on his head is dark too, as well as long and super curly.

He studies me with his eerie yellow eyes. "You are Harper Goode."

"Yes. And you must be Ken the oracle."

"I am." He runs his gaze over me again, from head to toe. "I've always loved a woman in leather. Makes me horny."

What on earth should I say in response to that? I kind of expected an oracle to speak in big, fancy words and with a booming voice. Instead, Ken has a reedy voice and tells me my clothes make him horny.

Max sneezes, and it's the cutest little salamander sneeze.

Ken's gaze jerks to my chest, and he narrows his eyes. "You've brought a hitchhiker."

"Um, yeah. Sor—" Cripes. I stopped myself a fraction short of saying I'm sorry. "Didn't mean to offend you."

"Smaller elementals are harder for me to detect." He sniffs the air, and his lip curls. "Smells like a salamander."

"I've heard you don't like them, but Max is a real sweetie." The salamander in question nips my boob with his tiny teeth. "Ouch! Cut that out, Max. If you don't behave, Ken will kick us out of his lair. Or home. Or whatever."

One side of the oracle's mouth kicks up. "It's my office."

Sure, that makes sense. This creepy cavern looks like an office—in Hell. But I can roll with it.

Ken sighs and gestures toward my chest. "He might as well come out. What I have to say involves both of you."

How does he know what to say to us? I haven't told him anything or asked any questions.

The guy's an oracle. That means he knows things without asking. *Duh, Harper.*

I pluck Max out of my bra and set him on the rough stone floor.

Flames erupt, and Max appears.

Naked, of course.

Ken's lip curls again. "Why do you salamanders insist on prancing around naked? Some of us don't appreciate it."

Max snorts. "And some of *us* don't appreciate your sorry excuse for clothing."

I grab Max's arm and drag him toward me, close enough that I can whisper to him. "Stop being a smart-ass. We want this guy's help, remember?"

Max grunts.

"Why did you bite me, anyway?"

"You called me a sweetie." He says that like I called him a dickhead instead of the nice thing I did call him.

Okay, maybe he's got a complex about receiving compliments. He does feel guilty over things that happened so long ago that nobody remembers it, except for him. That might make him shy about having nice things said about him.

Whatever. Bigger fish to fry and all that.

"It was only a love bite," he says with a smirk. "You'd like it if we were both naked when I did it."

"Maybe." I face the oracle. "Since you seem to know everything already, what can you tell us that might be helpful? We're kind of in deep shit, like up to our eyeballs."

"Yes, I know," Ken says. "You two really are clueless, aren't you?"

"Could you try informing us instead of insulting our intelligence?"

"You're a spitfire, eh? Females like you make me horny."

Oh jeez, everything makes this guy horny.

And I really, really hope he doesn't expect me to screw him to get whatever info he might have.

"Why are you making advances toward my mate?" Max snarls through his gritted teeth.

"Your what?" I say, lodging my hands on my hips. "I've told you before, I don't belong to you or anyone."

Max opens his mouth—to complain, no doubt—but he doesn't get the chance.

"But you do belong to someone," Ken announces. "You belong to the obsidian fae."

I jerk my head back, chin tucked. "No, I do not."

"Afraid you do, dear. The tattoo on your back is the mark of the obsidian fae, and the magics imbued into it bind you to them." He gives me a pitying look, shaking his head slowly. "Why else do you think you would do their bidding without realizing it? Your search for portals to the Unseen. Your quest to find an elemental who would bring you into this world. Your hatred of all things elemental. Have you really not grasped the implications?"

"Well—" I glance at Max, but he looks as confused as I feel. "We figured out the tattoo contains black magics, but we haven't figured out what it does."

Ken bends forward from the waist and levels his glowing yellow gaze straight at me. "The magics bind you to the obsidian fae. You are theirs. They can find you anywhere you go, and they will come for you soon."

"One of them told me I needed to simmer a little longer."

"The darkness without will soon consume the light within. Once that happens, you will cease to exist as a mortal with free will. They will command you like a marionette."

I clutch my stomach as nausea churns inside it and crawls its way up toward my throat. A frigid chill invades every cell in my body, making my teeth chatter the tiniest bit. The light within me will be consumed by darkness? I would rather die than become a puppet for the obsidian fae, forced to do whatever they order me to do.

Max slips an arm around my shoulders and tugs me against his side. His heat chases away the chill little by little, and I know that's why he pulled me into him. My teeth chattering probably alerted him to my freaked-out state.

"Why me?" I ask in a small voice. It's all I can muster.

"You were destined for this before you were even conceived in your mother's womb. Nothing can stop what must happen next."

"That's rot," Max says. "You can't tell her that, like she has no choice but to give up. We will fight those bastards with or without your help, and we will win. I won't let them have her."

I know from the intensity in his voice that he means it. He will fight until his own destruction, maybe even beyond that, to save me from the obsidian fae.

But I can't let him die for me.

"Here's what I can tell you," Ken says. "What must happen will happen, but the outcome is yours to affect."

Max scoffs. "What sort of bollocks is that? If it's fate, then we can't change it. Isn't that the way it works? I've been told it is, and I've seen fate's hand at work in the lives of others."

"You are so young, salamander, and so innocent in the ways of destiny." Ken hovers a hand over the bronze bowl. Flames shoot up from its center, writhing and licking at his palm, shimmering with shades of pale green, amber, and gold. "I wish I could divert your shared path from the direction in which it must lead you, but I cannot."

"Can't you remove the tattoo?" Max asks. "Remove the spell or whatever it is?"

"No." Ken twitches his fingers, and the flames twitch in unison with them. "This destiny was born in ages past. What must be done will be done."

Max steps away from me and flaps his arms. "What was the point of coming here, then? Ennea said we needed to speak to you, but all you've got to say is that we're screwed upside down, sideways, and everywhere in between."

"Don't assume you understand my words. The truth will be revealed in due time." Ken shrugs. "I regret what you both must endure, but I have faith the necessary outcome will occur. Remember, darkness and light are two sides of the same coin, like Janus himself. You've never quite understood that, have you, Max?"

"What the bloody hell does that mean?"

I lay a hand on Max's arm. "It's okay. Let's go, huh? I don't think Ken has much else to tell us."

The oracle pulls his hand away from the writhing flames. "You're correct, dear. Good luck."

"What about Hathor?" Max asks. "Can you at least help us with that problem?"

"Two halves of the same coin, salamander."

Max throws his arms up and huffs.

I take his hand. "We appreciate your insight, Ken, but I think we should go now."

As I lead—okay, half drag—Max toward the doorway, the oracle calls out to us.

"Seek the light, but do not fear the dark. Sometimes the truth lies within it."

His voice reverberates through the cavern with unnatural power and clarity.

A shiver rattles through me. I can feel the meaning of everything he said hovering just beyond my reach, taunting me with what I need to know but can't quite grasp yet.

Max and I exit the oracle's lair, and the hill swallows up the opening.

"Let's travel the faster way this time," Max says, and he scoops me up in his arms to teleport us away.

We touch down in the clearing around the portal that accesses the mortal realm. Water bubbles out of the boulder, spilling down into the little pool. Everything seems as it was before, but a creepy-crawly sensation on my skin warns me of something.

"It's too quiet," I say. "I heard weird bird songs before, and the trees rustling. But nothing is moving now, except for the water."

"We need to get through the portal. Fast."

Max moves toward the portal, his hand around mine, pulling me with him.

An arrow slams into his back.

He jerks, freezes for a split second, and crumples to the ground.

I whirl around, searching for the source of the attack. My heart pounds so hard and fast that I can't catch my breath and my ears ring.

A figure saunters out of the trees.

The vampire Gundisalvus sneers at me. "I brought friends this time. So you, mortal whore, shall not escape us."

I reach for my sword, but I don't get the chance.

Another being pops in behind me and wraps her powerful arms around my midsection, pinning my arms to my sides. Sigrun ducks her head to whisper in my ear, "The bounty will be mine, little human. And you will be Hathor's newest toy."

Sigrun is taller and stronger than I am, powered by elemental strength and magics. I kick at her legs but can't get enough leverage to even annoy her.

Max lies on the ground, facedown, unmoving. Blood streams from his wound.

"Oh, don't worry," Sigrun says. "That's not an endued arrow, though it is tipped with a tranquilizing potion. Hathor wants her plaything alive."

"Max is not a toy for that crazy bitch goddess to play with."

"Doesn't matter what you think." She tells Gundisalvus, "You bring Max. I'll take care of his sweet little mortal."

The vampire rushes over to bind Max's hands with metal manacles that glisten in eerie shades of dark green.

Max jolts like he's rousing from the tranquilizing potion.

Gundisalvus seizes the chain that links the manacles, hauling Max to his feet.

Sigrun locks the same kind of manacles around my wrists, triggering a zing of magic that makes me wince. The manacles must be enchanted or bespelled or whatever to prevent us from getting free—or at least to prevent Max from getting out of them. Sigrun might've shackled me just for the hell of it.

The Valkyrie mashes her lips to my ear. "Time to meet your new mistress."

And the world vanishes.

Chapter Twenty-Two

Max

Gunny the repugnant vampire keeps shoving me in the back with his taloned hand, pushing me forward with a suddenness that has me tripping and cursing. Normally, I don't trip. I have the agility of a seasoned elemental. But the enchantment in these bloody manacles has turned me into a bumbling idiot with awful balance and no strength to even kick the bastard in the shin. I hate magic when it's used against me. The rest of the time, I love it. Yes, I have a double standard. Only I and my allies should have supernatural abilities. The rest of the elementals can piss off.

We had popped out of the rift into a dense forest that looks nothing like the forests I've visited in other parts of the Unseen, but I know this one all too well. The trees and the deep gloom they create form a buffer zone around Hathor's temple. The sickly yellow slime that oozes from the tree trunks, coupled with the vile stench in the air and a variety of eerie animal noises, engender a sense of foreboding and unease in most visitors. Not me. I've been here too many times before.

Never shackled, though. This is new, and a sign of Hathor's determination to get me in her clutches again.

Harper has her nose wrinkled and her face cinched up in a tight expression.

At least Gunny and his cohort have let me walk alongside Harper so I can keep an eye on her. I manage to sidle a touch closer to ask her, "Are you all right? Did Sigrun hurt you?"

"No, I'm fine. I want to smack that bitch five ways from Sunday, but I'm not hurt." Harper rotates her eyes to look at me. "What about you? Sigrun said the arrow had a tranquilizer potion in it."

"Yes, I was dazed for a moment there. All right now, though."

"Can't you, like, break these damn manacles and get us out of here?"

"Oh yes, wouldn't it be brilliant if I could do that? But no, I can't. These bindings are imbued with magics that sap my strength."

She curses under her breath. "Why didn't they zip us straight to Hathor?"

"This forest is a protective barrier to discourage anyone from attempting to breach Hathor's temple compound." I roll my eyes this way and that to indicate our surroundings. "The entire forest is swimming in dark magics."

"Ew. I didn't need to know that."

"Actually, you *do* need to know. Everything. You can't protect yourself if you have no idea what's going on around you."

Gunny shoves me again. "Keep moving, salamander."

I *am* still moving, and the arsehole knows that. He enjoys harassing me, probably because he's jealous. I have a body women love, while he looks every bit the rotting corpse who feeds on blood. Thinking about vampires and their blood lust is enough to make me want to say "ew."

"Listen to me," I tell Harper. "Hathor ensorcells everyone who enters her temple. It is going to happen." I glance at Gunny, then dare to slant closer to Harper to deliver my hushed words straight into her ear. "Fight it with everything you have and pray your tattoo will protect you."

Gunny punches me in the back of the head. "Move away from the woman."

Merda, my head hurts. I move away from Harper, but I'm plotting the most horrendous ways to punish my mate Gunny once I get free.

But I can't get free. I'm too weak.

The forest spreads its arms to reveal the open, grassy area that encircles Hathor's temple. A white wall with enormous wooden gates encompasses the compound, but inside the walls, white towers rise toward the sky. Those towers form the upper portion of the temple, and like the main structure, they feature brightly painted murals of the goddess.

I clench my fists and my jaw. We have arrived.

Gunny and Sigrun march us across the field to the gates of the compound, which slowly swing open as we approach. The sounds of revelry—music, singing, laughter—emanate from within the walls. Yes, it's always a blasted party inside Hathor's domain. The ancient Egyptians in the mortal realm worshiped her as the goddess of intoxication, revelry, and sex. Hathor still loves to embody those concepts, even though the civilization that revered her is long gone.

Maybe she ensorcelled the Egyptians to adore her. She's masterful at doing that.

I glance sideways at Harper. Whatever I must do to stop it, I cannot let Hathor get her claws into Harper. Whatever it takes, I must fight the ensorcellment.

Right, because I've had cracking great luck doing that in the past.

Once we've trudged through the gates, they ease shut behind us.

Locked in. I grit my teeth harder.

Magic swirls around us, but the ensorcellment won't happen out here in the courtyard. Hathor likes to make a grand show of it in her throne room.

Gunny and Sigrun herd us into the temple and down a long, wide corridor. Everywhere the walls display ancient Egyptian motifs and color schemes, including papyrus-shaped columns and murals of Hathor's minions bowing down to her, washing her feet, kissing her feet, raising their hands in supplication.

I hate this rotten temple.

We're taken straight to the throne room, and its wooden doors close behind us. Here, an opening in the roof lets sunshine blaze down on us, seeming to gild the entire room with its light. Harper looks even more beautiful with her skin painted a golden shade by the sun's rays.

Gunny and Sigrun bring us to a halt just in front of the stepped dais that holds the throne—a solid-gold chair decorated with more images of the goddess and of the sun, the god Ra, enfolding her in his arms that are composed of rays of sunlight.

I wonder if Ra knows she depicts him that way in her temple, as if she is more powerful and important than the sun god himself. I've never met Ra and have no idea if he actually exists, but since Hathor does, I assume he must as well. After all, ancient mortals got their ideas about the gods from elementals.

"Kneel," Gunny barks, and he punches me in the back. "Show deference to the exalted goddess who honors you with her presence."

"She's not here yet, so she can't honor me with anything."

He slugs me again, right in the spine. "Kneel. Both of you."

I glower at him but drop to my knees. Glancing at Harper, I nod for her to do the same. The last thing I want is for Sigrun or Gunny to punch Harper. Besides, there's little use in fighting the inevitable.

Harper kneels, though she doesn't look pleased about it.

The blaring of horns resonates through the room.

A pair of doors behind the throne swing open, and Hathor saunters out.

I despise the abominable goddess, but I can't deny she is lovely. Her beauty disguises the rotted soul underneath. She has skin as pale as alabaster, eyes as yellow as a feline's, and a slender body with breasts that are neither too small nor too large. Her glistening raven hair drapes halfway down her back, the loose waves dancing as she struts past the throne and descends the steps to halt an arm's length from me.

Any minute now she'll cast her spell and strip away my free will.

Her clothing consists of a gold-trimmed, white linen bra with gold straps and a scarab amulet affixed to it right between her breasts. Scarab beetles aren't a standard motif for Hathor in ancient Egyptian artwork, but she's always loved them. The only other items she has on her body are a leather belt with a long, ornately decorated strap that hangs down in front of her body, a gold headdress with a cobra's head rearing up on the front, and some jewelry. A wide, elaborate necklace encircles her throat, while huge gold hoops hang from her ears.

"Maximus," she coos in her bizarrely American accent, "isn't it joyous to be home again? I have ordered a lavish feast to welcome you back into the fold, but first, we must get reacquainted."

Her sultry tone leaves no doubt about what she means by getting "reacquainted," but I would have known what she meant without the overdone sensuality in her voice. To Hathor, renewing an acquaintance requires an orgy. Sex, drugs, and music.

Elementals don't need to snort or swallow actual drugs, though. We have magic for that.

Hathor bends over, grasps my face, and kisses me—with tongue. "Now, you absolutely must introduce me to your new friend. I want to get acquainted with her too."

She casts her sultry gaze at Harper.

Futuo, I wish I could murder Hathor right here and now.

The hag of a goddess moves in front of Harper, skimming her gaze over all of Harper's body while dragging her tongue across her bottom lip. "Mm, I can't wait to induct you into the fold. I can see why Maximus has been spending so much time with you. A body like yours is made for the kind of fun I excel at. Now, tell me your name, *neferet*."

She just called Harper "beautiful" in ancient Egyptian.

No point in dragging this out. Sighing, I tell Hathor, "Her name is Harper Goode. She's a mortal, so take it easy with her, would you?"

I don't expect she'll do anything of the sort, but I had to try.

"Oh, I know she's human," Hathor says like I'm an idiot for pointing that out. "But mortals can be the most exciting to play with. They're so…responsive."

Just ensorcell us and have done with it, you crackbrained shrew.

Hathor claps her hands above her head. "It's time for the induction ceremony. Gundisalvus and Sigrun, you may leave us."

The bounty hunters exit the room, leaving me and Harper alone with the goddess.

"You first, Maximus," Hathor says.

She steps in front of me, forcing me to stare at her groin.

I grimace. That thin leather strap does nothing to conceal her pubic hair. "Purely out curiosity, how did you get Gunny's head back on?"

"Gunny?" Her brows furrow while she squints at me for a few seconds, then she shrugs and smiles. "Oh, I assume you mean Gundisalvus. His head dissolved into a puddle on the floor at my feet, so I had to reconstitute it from scratch."

His head dissolved? What in the worlds does Harper's sword have in it?

"No more chatting," Hathor says.

She holds her hand above my head and begins to chant softly in a language that might be ancient Egyptian, but I've never figured that out for sure. Since I've seen her do this before, I know what to expect. Her palms exude golden streams of glittering light that fan out around my head, and their energy nips at my skin. I wait for the magics to enthrall me, but nothing seems to be happening. Is Hathor off her game? I can't imagine that's true, but I also can't imagine how else I wouldn't be feeling the effects of the ensorcellment.

She finishes, falling silent, and watches me. Her fingers twitch. She slants in a touch, drilling her unblinking gaze into mine.

I know what she's waiting for—me to fall down at her feet in supplication. But I feel no different. Why, I have no idea. She clearly thinks her magics have done their job, and if I don't give her what she expects, she'll know I'm not in her thrall.

So I fall down before her, my head between her golden-sandaled feet. "Hathor, my goddess, my love. May I wash your feet with my tongue?"

Yes, she genuinely expects her minions to do that. And yes, I've done it. Not because I wanted to, but because she forced me to want to do anything she suggested. Ensorcellment is the most malignant magic.

"You may tongue-wash my feet later," Hathor says, "when you and Harper can do that together."

I turn my head to the side, just a hair, pretending I'm inhaling the beauteous scent of her foot when I'm actually hoping to get Harper's attention.

She is looking at me, her mouth open and her upper lip curled.

Now that I have her attention, I mouth, "Fake it."

Her brows crinkle, but the rest of her face goes slack.

"Fake it," I mouth again. I hope she understands this time, because if the ensorcellment doesn't work on her either and she lets on that it hasn't, we are both buggered.

"Rise, Maximus," Hathor says in her most imperious voice.

I get to my feet and affect an expression of dazed adoration—or at least that's my aim. I can't tell for sure if I've succeeded, though Hathor seems enormously pleased with herself, so I gather she believes my act.

"My queen," I say, "how may I serve you?"

"By standing there looking pretty." She steps in front of Harper, hovering her palm over Harper's head. "Your new friend needs to be initiated."

Those golden streams of energy swirl between the goddess's hand and Harper's scalp.

Don't work, it can't work, don't let it ensorcell her. Oversoul protect her, please.

I don't know if thinking the word please will indebt me to the Oversoul, but I rather doubt, whatever the Oversoul is, the entity cares about having me in its debt. And I will gladly incur any obligation to spare Harper from ensorcellment. How many times had Hathor forced me into her thrall? More than I can count. I remember everything she made me do while I was her helpless puppet, all the twisted acts she dreamed up to humiliate me.

Harper's brows crinkle again, but then her expression mutates into the sort of rapt adoration I've been faking. I pray she's pretending too.

The goddess backs away to the edge of the stepped dais, clasps her hands in front of her, and smiles haughtily at us. "Welcome to the fold, my children. You are now bathed in the golden light of submission, and soon you will serve me in the most pleasurable ways possible. Rise, Harper."

Without the slightest hesitation, and without letting her enthralled expression falter one bit, Harper rises.

I hope she's faking it.

"We will have plenty of time to play later," Hathor says. "But first, you need to be properly clothed. I prefer Maximus in the nude, but the rest of my thralls must wear the appropriate uniform until we enter the orgy chamber. Today, perhaps he should too."

Harper betrays no shock when Hathor mentions the orgy chamber. Either she's a brilliant actor or she's ensorcelled. Or maybe the idea of an orgy doesn't disgust her.

The goddess waves her hand.

A kilt appears around my hips, white linen with gold threads interwoven.

I bloody hate the things she makes me wear. And these ruddy kilts are always so tight they stick to my skin like wet paper.

Hathor nods, satisfied with my attire, but then clucks her tongue. "Harper, *neferet*, your drab ensemble is depressing me."

I love Harper in those leather trousers. She looks good enough to devour.

But the barmy goddess has her own ideas about Harper's clothing. When she flourishes her hand, a baggy white-linen robe materializes around Harper's body. It's so baggy, in fact, that it seems about four sizes too large for her. The linen trash bag passing for clothes hides her luscious figure, and I'm certain that was Hathor's intention. She must have noticed that I lust for Harper's body. Even if I were ensorcelled, I'd still crave her. I know that without any doubts.

And the goddess envies Harper because of it.

"Maximus," Hathor says, "you will go to the orgy chamber and help make it ready. I will join you there in a few moments once I've escorted my new toy to her private quarters."

I grind my teeth, though I doubt anyone else will notice. I know what "private quarters" means. Hathor plans to abuse Harper in private where no one can see or object to what she does with a mortal whose body can't handle the goddess's depravity.

The manacles around our wrists vanish.

But I know the magics that run through every inch of this temple will prevent me from doing anything to stop Hathor. I feel the power in the air—and the weakness in my body. I'm no stronger than the average mortal.

I have no choice but to watch as Hathor leads Harper away.

The only consolation I have is that Hathor said she'll only escort Harper to those private quarters and then come to the orgy chamber. At least that might give me time to come up with an escape plan.

But the wretched temple is warded. I can't simply grab Harper and spirit us both away from this place. No one leaves Hathor's palace without her express, and magical, permission.

I will destroy that bitch, somehow, some way. She will never get her filthy, degenerate hands on my mate.

CHAPTER TWENTY-THREE

Harper

THE GODDESS HATHOR ACCOMPANIES ME DOWN A LONG HALLWAY UN-til we reach a T-intersection, then she guides me down another corridor to the door at the end. Well, doors. Two big wooden ones decorated with stripes of what looks like real gold. Not that I'm an expert on precious metals. But I have a feeling Hathor wants everything to be the most luxurious version available.

"Here you are, *neferet*," she says, spreading an arm out toward the doors.

They swing open.

"Let me give you the grand tour," Hathor says as she leads me into the large bedroom. "This is your new home, complete with an attached bathroom and a full wardrobe."

The bed is huge. Long enough to fit Max and wide enough to host, like, ten of him. Four white, fluted posts hold up a golden canopy over the bed.

Hathor ambles over to an intricately carved armoire and flings its doors open. She moves aside, spreading an arm again to indicate the armoire's contents. "Your new wardrobe. And your old one too, though I would pre-fer you don't wear that depressing thing. You wouldn't want to make me unhappy, would you?"

"No, my queen, I want to please you in every way." I might vomit any second if I have to keep spouting crap like that, but I guessed from what Max mouthed to me—"fake it"—that this crazy chick with outrageous powers believes she has ensorcelled us. We aren't ensorcelled, though, and I have no clue why.

My tattoo had burned like crazy while Hathor used her rancid magics to try to get me in her thrall. It burned so much that tears stung my eyes, but I fought the impulse to grimace or cry or do anything else that might draw her attention to the tattoo.

Did the obsidian fae's magic overpower a goddess's?

I do not want to think about what it means if that's true. And how could my tattoo affect Max?

Hathor pulls my little sword out of its sheath and saunters up to me holding it in her palm. "Here, you may keep this. It's not endued, and besides, no weapon known to mortal kind or elemental kind can destroy me. But I might enjoy watching you hack at my thralls. Most of them are elementals and so will heal from even the most grievous wounds."

She offers me the sword.

I take it. This is the sword that let me chop off a vampire's head, even though it's not endued. This must be the weapon the obsidian fae told me to use to kill Max. I'm never going to do that, but maybe this blade holds the power to stop a goddess.

Later, maybe I'll get the chance to test that theory. For now, I haven't got one shred of an idea about how to escape from this place—and I won't do it without Max.

"You are so generous," I say in my fake-thrall voice. "I'm blessed to feel the warmth of your light, my queen. I will serve you in any way you wish."

I will lop off my own head with this sword before I do one damn thing this monster wants me to do, but she doesn't need to know that. Max knows more about Hathor and her temple than I do. He must be formulating a plan. All I can do is wait for him.

I hate waiting. After being alone for so long, I'm not used to needing anyone's help.

Hathor kisses my cheek. "We'll see each other in a little while, when you join me in the orgy chamber."

Yeah, I will absolutely lop off my own head before that happens.

The goddess flounces out of my private room, and the doors swing shut behind her.

I press my ear to one of the doors, listening until her footsteps fade away.

And then I try to open the door.

Naturally, it's locked or barred or magically sealed or something. I can't get it open. *Rats.* I had to try, but I didn't really expect I could just let myself out.

For the next I-don't-know-how-many minutes or hours, I pace back and forth across the width of the chamber, ignoring the gorgeous murals on the walls and the huge, gorgeous bed in the center of the room. Where is Max? What is Hathor doing to him? He seemed fine after the goddess attempted to ensorcell us. What if she tried again, using more powerful magics, and it worked?

Even worse, what if the ensorcellment had worked the first time after all? He would lie about it, wouldn't he? Pretend he's not under her spell? Anything to protect his mistress.

I flop onto the bed on my back and stare up at the golden canopy with its flower-shaped center. Seconds drag by, followed by minutes, followed by so much time that I stop trying to figure out how long it's been. I have no windows in this room, so I can't judge by the sun's progress. Since I'm in another world with a different sun, it probably behaves in ways I can't fathom.

Jumping off the bed, I wander into the bathroom.

It houses an enormous, round tub with a showerhead positioned over it. There's a sink too, and a doorless cabinet full of toiletries. And yeah, there's an actual toilet too.

Exiting the bathroom, I start pacing again near the foot of the bed where I can keep my eye on the doors.

Time drips by. Drip. Drip. Drip.

Movement draws my attention to the doorway. A small red salamander squeezes through the gap under the doors, stopping a few feet inside the room.

Is that... No, it can't be. Can it? There must be other salamanders besides Max in residence here, and Hathor probably sent one of them to seduce me.

Flames erupt from the little lizard, forming a man-shaped column of red fire. The flames snuff out, revealing Max.

My heart skips a beat.

He's wearing a kilt in the ancient Egyptian style, off-white with gold trim and gold threads woven through the fabric. It molds to his hips and thighs, highlighting the bulge of his dick.

My mouth waters just looking at him.

I might think that means I'm ensorcelled, but I always get lustful when I gaze upon his sizzling-hot body. I glance down at my own clothing and huff. "Hey, how come you and everyone else in this palace-temple whatsit get to dress sexy and I'm stuck wearing a tent?"

"Hathor is envious of you." Max drinks in the sight of me like I'm the best meal he's ever seen. "Doesn't matter what you wear. You are more desirable than anyone, even Hathor, even Aphrodite herself."

I want to thank him, but I cannot do that in this world. His words and his tone of voice have shivered a steamy thrill through me. "Are you okay? How did you get away without Hathor noticing?"

"She's preoccupied with an orgy, I made certain of that. It may be hours or even days before she notices I've left her vicinity."

"Oh. Good. Have you found a way out?"

"No." He stalks toward me with all the masculine grace and feral hunger of a panther stalking its prey and halts inches away from me. "I'm feeling peckish."

My body revs up at the idea of sex with Max, but I don't want to do it if he's on Hathor's side now.

"Um..." I tip my head side to side to examine him, but I can't tell if Max is Max or if he's under the goddess's thrall while pretending not to be. "Are you, um, yourself?"

"Yes, *dulcissime*, I am."

"How do I know you aren't faking not being ensorcelled?"

"You'll know it for certain when I'm taking your body."

"I don't know. Maybe we shouldn't. I mean, we're trapped in a crazy goddess's temple of orgies and—"

"Please stop speaking and let me have you."

A touch of magic zings through me but then it fizzles out. "Did you just indebt yourself to me?"

"No. You said the P-word to me earlier, so my use of it canceled out your debt to me."

"Oh." I swallow hard, my throat dry even while my sex gets wetter and hotter and tinglier. "Should we be wasting time on sex when—"

"It's not a waste of time. I need a great deal more power to get us out of this hellhole, and you are the only one who can feed me."

"Getting shot in the back with an arrow must've sapped your energy, huh?"

Why am I trying to talk him out of screwing me? And why am I making inane small talk? It's pathetic—and pointless, because I want him like crazy. Even here, on Hathor's home turf.

Max moves a little closer, the heat of him radiating over me. "No more talking. You know what I need to hear, and I know you want to say it. So go on, *dulcissime*, say it."

I suck in a quivering breath, my skin alive with an electric current of need. And I say it. "Fuck me, Max."

Chapter Twenty-Four

Max

I WALK FORWARD, FORCING HARPER TO BACK AWAY FROM ME. OUR gazes are bound to each other, and I feel something, some sort of energy or magic, pulsing between us as we inch our way to the bed. Yes, we need to find a way out of here. But I hadn't lied to her. I do need to feed, to replenish my energy stores, if we're going to have any hope of circumventing the wards and the innate magics of this place to escape. I've done it before, but only on my own. Having Harper with me might make escape more difficult, but I can't pretend I'm not glad she's here.

Not that I wanted Hathor to capture her. But I do like having her with me. More than I expected.

Harper's legs bump into the foot of the bed, halting her backward progress.

"You know what I'm after," I say, fingering the edge of her awful robe, where it opens a touch in a V-shape near her throat. I can see her pulse throbbing in her neck. "Get rid of this thing you're wearing, or I'll rip it off for you."

"I loved it when you did that before."

"Yes, *dulcissime*, I know." Sliding my finger along that edge, I graze my fingertip down her skin. Her shiver makes my rod so stiff it feels like the bloody kilt will split open any second. "Do it now, love. Show me your delectable body."

She unties the robe's belt and lets it slide off her shoulders. The fabric pools around her feet, but I'm not looking at that.

Her body. That's all I can focus on. Her lovely, delicious body.

I reach for the gold clasp that holds my kilt up.

She stays my hand with her own. "Let me do it."

"Go on, then."

Harper unhooks the clasp and drops it on the floor, but she's holding on to the kilt with one hand. She kneels in front of me and releases the kilt.

It falls to the floor.

And her mouth is inches from my cock.

She closes her hand around it, leans in, and opens her mouth.

I stop her with a hand on her shoulder. "You shouldn't do that. My, ah, fluids are very potent. Swallowing them will make you come for hours, maybe days. Off and on, but frequent nonetheless."

And I'd love to watch that happening, but it will be impossible to sneak her out of here if she's writhing and screaming in ecstasy.

"But I want to eat you up," she says, her voice hushed and ravenous at the same time. "I want to do this. Desperately."

"And I'd love for you to do it, but we can't. Not today." I grasp her shoulders and urge her to stand. "Let me make love to you, Harper. Right now. Before whatever plan we concoct goes tits-up, and we're fighting for our lives again."

"Glad you're keeping a positive outlook."

"No more talking." I pick her up. "Only screaming from now on. These walls are magically soundproofed, so you can scream my name as loud as you like."

I toss her onto the bed.

She bounces, but instead of looking shocked or irritated, she grins at me. "Come and get me, Max."

This woman is wonderful.

I crawl up the bed until I'm straddling her on all fours. "You have the most beautiful body I've ever seen in any world. I'm going to worship you so thoroughly you'll never want anyone else to touch you."

"Already feel that way." She curls her fingers around my length again. "I'm ready for that worshiping to start."

"Then unhand my cock if you don't mind. I'll need it."

With a lovely, sexy smile, she releases me. "Mm, hurry up, Max."

I dip my head to take hold of her nipple, suckling and licking it, grazing my teeth over the tip, laving it with my tongue so I can blow air across that delicious little bud until she gasps and fists her hands in the sheets. I know I can make her come by doing only this, but I don't want her to jump off that cliff until I can go with her.

Every iota of her desire feeds the beast in me.

I drag my lips up her skin, over her collarbone, traveling up the slender column of her throat while I tease her with light flicks of my tongue. Her breathing grows labored, her breasts rising and falling with each inhalation, her mouth open while she struggles to haul in enough oxygen. The scent of her need envelops and intoxicates me, but more than that, it feeds energy into me like she's injecting the most addictive drug in the multiverse straight into my veins. I can't catch my breath either, and I can't stop touching her.

My hands trace a path up her side while my lips reach her ear. I tug the lobe into my mouth, swirling my tongue around it, while I slide one hand up to cradle her breast.

"Oh Max," she moans.

The stream of sexual energy flowing into me strengthens, pulsing faster and hotter.

I push her thighs apart with my knee and drive into her.

She arches her back, crying out and clutching my biceps.

Her lust, her need, it courses through me like a powerful current of electricity. And it consumes me. I pump into her again and again, trying to take it slowly so I can relish every second of this, but the strength of her desire strains my self-control, strains my erection that's throbbing with the need to let go and come inside her body, branding her in the only way an incubus can. She feels so good, and every time she cries out, the sound is louder and wilder.

"More, Max," she cries out. "Please, don't hold back."

"*Futuo*!" I shout, thrusting so hard and so fast that the bed bounces and thumps, the sound reverberating through the room.

I shove my arms under her body and hoist her up while I rise onto my knees, still pounding into her. She lashes her legs around my waist and her arms around my neck, her head thrown back as she cries out my name. Every time I lunge upward into her, the force of it thrusts her up high enough that only the head of my cock is inside her, then she slams back down onto me with a strangled cry. She's squeezing her eyes shut, her face wrenched by the need to climax.

And I need it too. Fuck, do I need it.

Claim her, a part of my mind demands. *Make her yours forever.*

Harper's entire body goes rigid. Her cries are silenced because she's stopped breathing, even while she keeps pistoning on my shaft.

An irresistible impulse seizes me, and I clamp my mouth down on her shoulder, my teeth sinking into her flesh. A trickle of blood oozes onto my tongue. The flavor of it—sweet, metallic, tangy, and rich—crackles through me with drugging potency. The sensation is nothing like what I get from sex, but I have no idea what that means.

No time to think about it because Harper comes.

It's like a bomb has gone off inside her. The breath explodes out of her lungs, detonating a scream so loud that it vibrates my eardrums. Her body clenches me like a steel vise, over and over, demanding I give her everything I have. And I do. I can't stop it. My release erupts inside her, making her come even harder, scream even louder, her voice hoarse from the power of her cries. Her nails dig into the back of my neck, but I don't give a toss about that or anything, except the unbridled pleasure and the intense energy she's giving me.

Once it's over, I lay her down on the bed and settle in beside her. "Are you all right?"

She lies there, not moving, struggling to regain her breath. "Gimme...a minute."

Have I done her in? What if I've shagged her so ferociously that it's taxed her mortal body to the breaking point? That's never happened to me, but then, I've never done to any other woman what I've just done to Harper.

Claim her, something inside me had urged. Helpless to resist the call, I'd sunk my teeth into her shoulder. Why? What the bloody hell had that been about? I look at her shoulder, but the wound is already healing. It no longer bleeds, and the puncture marks are sealing up, even beginning to fade.

Harper is fanning herself with one hand.

Unwilling to leave her, I conjure a glass of water and hand it to her.

She lifts only her head to gulp down the contents.

"Are you all right?" I ask again.

"Yes, Max, I'm okay." She holds the glass out to me. "I don't need this anymore, but you're so sweet to get it for me."

"Since I'm responsible for the state you're in, it was the least I could do." I peel away the hairs that have been plastered to her forehead and cheeks by the sweat that still glistens on her body. "You need a shower and a massage."

Harper laughs, though it's light and affectionate. "Honestly, I'm fine. Never realized you're such a worrywart."

"I have never suffered from warts of any kind. Mortals contract them by worrying too much?"

She laughs again. "No, Max, they don't. 'Worrywart' is a term for somebody who's constantly anxious."

"Oh. I see." Though I don't really understand, I've learned from my recent experiences with mortals that it doesn't pay to admit I'm confused. Their explanations often confuse me even more.

"What was that word you said? Sounded like *futuo*." She struggles to pronounce the unfamiliar word.

"It's a Latin obscenity that means fuck."

"Guess I shouldn't be surprised you speak Latin, since you are an ancient Roman." She touches her shoulder where I bit her. Instead of grimacing, though, she smiles. "That was hands-down the hottest, most mind-blowing sex ever. I don't think even an actual god could give me pleasure like that."

"You haven't met Eros." I grunt. "And I'll make sure you never do."

"Not interested in anybody but you." She blows out a breath. "I loved it when you bit me. Never thought I'd like that kind of thing, but wow, it was unbelievably hot."

"Didn't it hurt?" I don't see how it couldn't have. "I—drew blood. Like a ruddy vampire."

If vampires experience anything like what I felt when I sank my teeth into Harper, then I finally understand the appeal of drinking blood.

Oh no. I'm like Gunny now.

Peeling my lips back, I point at my teeth. "Do I have fangs?"

"No, your teeth are normal." She sits up, braced with one straight arm. "Um, why did you bite me? Is that a normal incubus thing to do? I mean, you didn't do that the first time we got it on."

"As far as I know, drinking blood is not an incubus trait."

She raises her brows. "You actually drank my blood?"

"Well, ah…" I scratch the back of my neck. "It was more like I lapped up the blood that seeped out of your wounds. I never imagined I'd do anything of the sort, especially since I despise those ruddy vampires."

"Yeah, the one I've met is one hundred percent icky." She slides a hand along my thigh, her voice turning sensual. "But I loved the way you did that. Can't believe I did, but damn, when you bit me, I came even harder."

"I know." I regard her for a moment since I still can't accept that she not only isn't revolted by what I did but that she enjoyed it. "I don't plan to ever do that again."

"What if I want you to?"

Now I sit up, facing her. "Why on earth would you want that? I lost control and ravaged you."

She spreads a hand over my cheek, gently caressing me with her fingers. "You could've ravaged me if you wanted, but you didn't. That bite was hot and in no way life-threatening. You broke the skin, but you never ripped my flesh or sucked my blood. You said so yourself. You lapped up the blood that oozed out."

I stare down at the sheets.

"You're really anxious about this, aren't you?" she asks. "Did something else happen that I didn't notice?"

She really is far too perceptive.

But if she already suspects I have another reason for feeling disquieted, I might as well tell her. "I, ah, also had a strange thought right before I bit you."

"What kind of thought?"

"It was like something inside me was commanding me to—" I swallow hard. "Claim her, that's what it said."

"Claim me? What does that mean?" She grasps my chin and lifts, forcing me to meet her gaze. "Does this have anything to do with what you and Ennea were talking about? She asked if I'm your fated mate, but you said it's bollocks."

"Because it is. It must be."

"Look, I've read enough werewolf romance novels to know what a fated mate is. You tried to claim me by biting me, right?"

"What do you mean I tried? I did it, and now you're mine." Why am I banging on about this? It's rubbish, and I don't believe a word of anything anyone says about fated mates.

Have I claimed her? What does that even mean?

"You don't own me," Harper says, her voice sharper now. "Nobody does. Not you, not the obsidian fae, nobody. So whatever it is you think you claimed with that little stunt, it has nothing to do with me."

"If it's fate, I don't think either of us has a choice in the matter."

"Bullshit. I make my own decisions."

She really does not want to be joined to me in any way other than sex. I can't blame her. I am a sex demon after all, and apparently, a ruddy neck-biter.

I say the only thing I can say. "You're right, it's bollocks. I lost my head for a moment."

Telling her that shoots a stabbing pain through my chest. How I feel doesn't matter. She wants me only for sex and to help her solve the mystery of her black tattoo. What do I feel, anyway? No idea.

"Never mind," she says. "Let's forget it ever happened."

"All right." I take a slow breath. "We have other, more pressing matters to discuss. Like the fact that the ensorcellment didn't work on either of us."

"Guess Hathor's magics are defective."

"She's a goddess. Her magics are never defective. It was more like something blocked them, though she clearly thought they worked."

"What could do that?"

I nod toward her back. "Maybe it was your tattoo."

"Do you really think that's possible?"

"You're in the Unseen, Harper. Almost anything is possible here."

"Right. I forgot where I was for a minute. I also forgot about the obsidian fae and Hathor, but it's all crashing back into me now."

I wish I could make it all go away for good, for her.

Our gazes intersect, and we stay like that for a long moment while something indefinable passes between us. That pain in my chest returns, softer than before, and I wonder what it means that I want her to want to stay with me for more than sex and supernatural detective work. Hearing her say she doesn't want that… Christ, I've never felt so defeated. Not even when I was literally defeated in battle.

I never want to lose her.

"Do you have enough power to get us out of here yet?" Harper asks.

"Yes, I think so. Won't know for certain until I try to breach the wards." But she just fed me the most intense sexual pleasure I've ever received. I think I might be able to crumble a mountain with my bare hands right now. Instead of attempting that, I conjure her clothes onto her body, leather trousers and all.

The doors blast inward, slamming into the walls and sticking there.

Hathor storms into the room.

Before I can even try to whisk us away, a magical force the likes of which I have never experienced plows into me and cinches itself as tight as a steel jacket around my entire body. I can't move or teleport. The magic is too strong.

"You tricked me," Hathor says, halting at the foot of the bed. "Why aren't you two ensorcelled? The magics were potent. I felt it. But you…" She veers her searing glare to Harper. "You repelled it. How? Tell me now, or I will tear Maximus apart piece by piece."

The irony of that statement makes me chuckle with no mirth whatsoever. Harper had issued the same threat on the day we met.

Of course she doesn't want me. I'm a monster. Harper told me so countless times.

Harper nails her flinty gaze to the goddess. "I have no idea why your disgusting ensorcellment failed. Maybe you're not as all-powerful as you think, you nasty piece of garbage."

Hathor opens her mouth, about to speak.

An explosion rocks the palace, the concussive power of it jolting through me. The walls tremble. The floor trembles. The bed jumps, almost knocking into Hathor.

Her eyes go wide, and she scuttles backward. "What—"

Another explosion detonates through the palace, more powerful than the first. Bits crumble off the walls and ceiling, raining down on us.

The spell that's keeping me bound shatters.

I grab Harper and whisk us out of the palace.

We ricochet off the wards that enclose the temple compound.

Harper flies out of my arms, landing in a heap on the grass.

I roll across the ground like a sideways top spinning and spinning and spinning. When I crash into a tree, I finally stop. My head is still spinning, though, making it hard for me to decipher anything around me.

With a blinding flash and a thud, the wards fall.

"Max!"

Harper's cry jolts me out of my confusion. I leap to my feet, staggering toward her.

A dark-skinned being clad in an obsidian bodysuit has its arm around her midsection and holds a long, black knife to her throat.

I stumble but catch myself, staggering onward. "Let her go, you sodding bastard."

"You have lost," the obsidian fae hisses, "and we have won. Your need to fornicate with her has made this mortal ripe for the plucking. Congratulations on a job well done, salamander."

They both vanish.

I throw my head back and roar.

Chapter Twenty-Five

Harper

THE OBSIDIAN FAE AND I ROCKET THROUGH THE ABYSMAL TUNNEL, AND unlike the times when Max teleported me, the abyss fights back. It claws and gnashes at me, stinging and burning my skin. The void comes alive to struggle against our flight, and it screams with a fury that deafens me. If I could slap my hands over my ears, I would. But I don't have hands anymore, or a body, as far as I can tell.

We tumble out of the tunnel into a space so gloomy that my eyes need time to adjust. Blinded by the darkness, I stand there frozen as the fae releases me and, I sense, moves away from me.

"You are well simmered," the creature says. "Talos will be pleased and anxious to meet you. We have long waited for your time to arrive."

Yeah, everything he says sounds…ew. Simmered? I'm not food. Though I've heard this creep or another like him speak those words before, I still don't like it. Nobody simmered me or stewed me or any other icky cooking metaphors.

A knife-sharp chill slices through me. What if that's their plan? To eat me?

Nausea surges up in my stomach, and I gulp against the urge to dry heave. They can't be cannibals, can they? Then again, I'm not a fae. Maybe to them dining on human flesh doesn't count as cannibalism.

But still…yech.

A sniffing sound near my left ear suggests the fae is smelling me. "Fornicating with the salamander has sped up the simmering. Perhaps Talos will reward him for his unwitting service by killing him swiftly instead of torturing him for eons. Talos does love a good torture session, and an elemental can survive an eternity of that. Only endued weapons can end their lives."

I'm getting so sick of this creature and its hushed, smarmy voice telling me creepy things.

So I ram my elbow backward, having no idea where to aim. My elbow punches into soft flesh, so I'm guessing I hit its abdomen.

The fae grunts and hisses like a snake. "You little bitch."

A puff of air flutters my hair.

Somehow, I sense the fae has left.

I'm alone, in the dark, in an unknown place with unknown beings who have an unknown agenda. The only things I know are that the obsidian fae want me, they let me "simmer" for thirteen years, and now they have captured me.

What did that creature mean when it said Max sped up the simmering? The fae had claimed "fornicating" with Max had done it. Sure, we enjoyed amazing sex, but I have no idea how that helps the obsidian fae with whatever they have planned for me. This particular fae also mentioned Max had unwittingly helped them.

At least he didn't do it on purpose. The idea of Max betraying me makes me queasy again, but only for a moment because I know he did not do that. Even if the fae hadn't told me so, I would know. Max would never betray me.

Yet I had betrayed him, in a way.

I told him I am not his fated mate and that he does not own me, despite the fact I don't believe he wants to own me. He seemed as disturbed by the idea of having a fated mate as I was by the idea I might be his. What I said had been a knee-jerk reaction. I don't like the idea that anyone or anything might have power over my destiny. No one else decides the course of my life. Only I control my fate.

Except the obsidian fae have chosen my path for me since the day they let me go. I've been hunting for the Unseen, determined to destroy it, because they programmed me to do it. Is that program still working? I haven't even thought about destroying the Unseen in days. When I told Max that had been my plan, I'd felt weird about speaking those words.

I don't want to do it anymore.

My eyes have started to adjust to the gloom, and I examine my surroundings without moving. The fae who brought me here has left me inside a cramped, windowless room hewn from black stone. Obsidian? I assume so. According to Max, the obsidian fae bound themselves to their namesake stone to acquire more dark power, so I guess it makes sense they would fashion their headquarters from the same material.

Is this a building? Or a single underground chamber?

The faint glow inside the space seems to come from everywhere and nowhere, like the much homier, warmer glow inside Max's lair.

With nothing else to do, I wander around the perimeter of the room while absently dragging my finger along the wall as I go, and I let my thoughts take me where they will. Memories flit through my mind, but a single memory seizes control and forces me to relive that one moment.

Max. His face contorted with anger and grief. Roaring and shaking his fists in the air.

Because the fae had me. Because I was whisked away from him.

The queasiness returns, and I clutch my hands to my belly, swallowing hard. What happened to Max after I was torn away from him? Does Hathor have him again? Maybe she can ensorcell him now that I'm gone. If my tattoo protected us, like Max suggested, then he will be vulnerable again. Ensorcelled again.

I don't want that to happen to him.

Slumping against the wall, I sniffle and swipe at my eyes. Tears burn in them and threaten to stream down my cheeks. No, I will *not* cry. But why does the thought of Hathor getting Max in her thrall again upset me this much? The answer slams through me with such force that I gasp.

I want to be with Max.

He means something to me, something more than a guy I screwed a few times. I can't lose him. I *won't* lose him. Somehow, I will get out of here and find him. Whatever I have to do to break Hathor's ensorcellment of him, I will do it. No more losses. Maybe I couldn't save Kelsey, but I will save Max.

Decision made, I push away from the wall and straighten my shoulders.

Um, how am I going to save him?

I've got some kind of magic whatsit inside me, inside the tattoo on the back of my shoulder. Maybe I can tap into that. "Simmering" apparently means this tattoo has been gathering magics. Dark magics. Do I really want to tap into that?

The words of Ken the oracle replay in mind.

Darkness and light are two sides of the same coin, like Janus himself.

Why does everyone have to be so damn cryptic? Would it kill them to say, "Here's what you need to do step by step"? Ugh. Instead, everybody's got to cryptify things. The oracle, the obsidian fae, even Max sometimes does that.

Oh Max. Please hold on for me.

Ken had also told us that "what must happen will happen, but the outcome is yours to affect." Awesome. I can affect the outcome.

Uh, how?

Think, Harper. You've got a brain, so use it.

Darkness and light. The same coin. Darkness. Light.

There is no light without the darkness and vice versa. I suppose that's what Ken meant, but it still doesn't help me.

I pace across the center of the room, steepling my fingers under my chin and humming tunelessly. No darkness without light. No light without darkness. One can't exist without the other, so maybe...

A revelation hits me, and I halt mid-step.

Maybe I can tap into good magics via the dark magics infused into my tattoo. If the two sides of the magic coin depend on each other, then why can't I convert one into the other?

Great question, but it leads me back to… Uh, how do I do that?

I start pacing again, tapping my steepled fingers.

A grinding noise stops me, and I pivot toward the sound. It seems to emanate from the wall, but one particular section of it. That section is inching backward, away from the room itself. Within a minute, maybe less, the door-size block of obsidian has pulled free of the wall and slid off to the side, out of sight.

Now I see a dimly lit corridor outside the doorway.

A fae, possibly the same one who brought me here, steps in front of the opening and makes a come-hither gesture with one scrawny finger. "Lord Talos awaits you."

I'm meeting a lord. Maybe I'd feel more impressed by that fact if I didn't know Lord Talos is going to look a lot like the grotesque creature who's summoning me to meet the head honcho of the obsidian fae. He'll have shimmering skin the same color as their namesake stone, and he'll creep me out and annoy me simultaneously.

Since I still haven't worked out an actual plan to escape and find Max, I have no choice. I follow the fae.

He leads me down the longest corridor I have ever seen, for what feels like hours but has probably been ten minutes. I've got no sense of time, here in this palace of obsidian. If there are other doors along this corridor, they're as well concealed as the one to my cell. Eventually, we round a corner and start down another, identical corridor.

I could hit this obsidian-skinned twerp with a scissor kick, but I have a feeling that won't do much. Elementals are immortal and virtually unkillable. A slithery sensation in my gut warns me that this variety of fae might prove even harder to wound, much less kill. All those dark, oily magics…

My little sword, the one I found by what I'm suddenly sure must've been the obsidian fae's plan, it can sever an elemental's head clean off the body. Hathor had needed to "reconstitute" Gundisalvus's head. If I had that sword, maybe I could sever Talos's head, so it won't ever grow back.

Sure, no problem. I'll just conjure that up right now, like I'm ordering a supernatural pizza.

Max could do that.

I can't.

Or can I? When Max and I had sex right before all hell broke loose, it had felt different. More intense, for sure. But also more…connected. Like he and I had bonded in a new and powerful way. I'd even liked it—okay, loved it—when he bit me and licked up the blood. Plus, I'd just happened to stumble onto him in the woods the day we met. I also just happened to have the ability to tame his inner beast when the hunger consumed him.

Aw, shit. I *am* his fated mate.

That fact shocks and disturbs me for about two seconds, then a tingling wave of excitement rushes through me. I like knowing Max and I are inextricably connected. In fact, I love it.

Does that mean I love—No, I will not finish that thought. If I do, it will distract me from plotting how to harness the dark magics in my tattoo and convert them into light magics.

Hold on, Max, I'm working on it.

My fae guard stops where the corridor dead-ends, waves a palm at chest level, and waits.

The grinding noise of another doorway opening reverberates through my skull and vibrates into every part of my body.

Once the doorway is open, my guard waves for me to enter. "Lord Talos is anxious to meet you."

"Yeah, I'm super excited to meet him too." And lop his head clean off his neck if I can figure out how to summon my sword.

"Enter the throne room," my guard says.

Why do all these nutjobs have throne rooms? Probably because they all think they're the coolest thing in history, the baddest baddie ever, the most amazing godlike whatever, blah, blah, blah.

I walk into the frigging throne room.

The walls are obsidian here too, but rippling waves of rainbow colors coruscate through it in slow motion, casting multicolored light throughout the large chamber. A long, narrow, silvery gray rug forms a path to the throne itself, which squats atop a dais crafted from the same rainbow-like stone as the walls. The throne is a chair hewn from what looks like one solid slab of regular obsidian.

A fae occupies that throne, one elbow resting on the chair's arm, his raised hand bracing his chin. Unlike the others of his tribe that I've seen, he doesn't wear a silver-tinged bodysuit. He's taller too, and his skin mimics the color of deepest obsidian but with streaks of amber curling through it. And his eyes. They're a golden-red shade that shimmers and swirls like ripples on a pond, with rims of silver off of which the rainbow light glints. His body is so emaciated I can see the bones, but incongruously, I notice thick muscles strapped to his skeleton.

I recognize this creature. The memory barrels through me, stealing my breath for a precious few seconds. Talos is the one who plunged a sword into Kelsey's heart.

Talos rubs his chin with one long, bony finger. "You are Harper Goode."

"Yes." Duh. Shouldn't he have already known that? I mean, it must've been *his* diabolical plan to have me simmer for thirteen years.

The lord of the obsidian fae unfurls his tall body from the throne and saunters down the steps to halt a few feet from me. He stretches out one hand to coil a lock of my hair around his finger. "I've waited a long time to meet you, Harper. Welcome to the lair of the obsidian fae, where you will live out the remainder of your life—with me, in my palace, as my wife."

His what? Oh, hell no.

Talos chuckles. "Yes, human, that is your fate."

No, my fate is to be with Max, but I won't tell Talos that. Not yet.

"Come," he says, taking hold of my arm, "I will show you to your bridal chamber. Our union will take place during the new moon, tonight."

I jerk my arm free of his grip. "Screw you, asshole. I am not your wife-to-be, and if you expect me to have sex with you, think again. Never going to happen."

"But you will submit to me. And you'll enjoy it. Fucking an obsidian fae, especially a fae lord, is the best sex you shall ever experience."

No, Max gave me the best sex ever. Not this creepy, shiny-skinned freak who's probably overflowing with dark magics.

"Never going to happen," I repeat, making sure my lip movements make my point. "I'll kill myself before I let you touch me."

He seizes my shoulders, hauling me into his body, and hisses, "You are mine, Harper Goode. No one can take you away from me, certainly not that repulsive salamander."

I lift my chin. "Go to hell."

"No, that's where *you* are going. A hell made of obsidian fire."

Chapter Twenty-Six

Max

WHY AM I STANDING IN THE CAVE BEHIND THE WATERFALL STARING at the cascade like a moron? Because I have nothing else to do. I tried to help all those people in Hathor's temple, but I couldn't get in there. She didn't pull up the wards again. No, something much worse than Hathor had been at work. The structure crumbled before my eyes, but magics I'd never experienced in all my existence had prevented me from getting back inside—and the immense power of those magics destroyed every being in Hathor's domain.

Their annihilation shuddered through the fabric of the Unseen, like a chorus of death screams with no sound.

And Harper...

I've searched the Unseen for her, but I can't find her. My hope that she is my fated mate and therefore I have some sort of connection with her has been shattered. Why should I be allowed to have that connection? I don't deserve it, and I don't deserve her either. I couldn't save Aurelia from the emperor, and I failed to save Harper from the obsidian fae.

Knowing we had enemies pursuing us, what did I do? Waste time shagging Harper. Yes, wasn't that a brilliant idea? And as my excuse, I convinced myself I needed more power from her sexual energy.

All right, I do have more power now. I feel stronger than ever, but it hasn't helped me one bloody bit.

When the fae took her, I had roared and thrown myself at the pair of them. Wasted energy, wasn't it? They vanished just as I hurled my body at them. I doubt Harper even saw me do that. She probably thinks I'm ensorcelled by the sodding goddess and has given up on me. Not that she ever wanted me in her life to begin with. I'd forced my way in and tried to convince her it's fate that brought us together, that she belongs to me, that she is fated to be mine.

A load of stinking rubbish. I don't get a fated mate.

"*Merda*," I snarl, and pound my fists on the cave wall. "What a bloody useless wanker you are, Quintus Salonius ruddy Maximus."

I grunt and smash my fist into the wall again. The two times I'd helped stop an apocalypse had clearly been a fluke made possible by the Janusite-familiar bond. I am impotent on my own.

At least I hadn't been ensorcelled again. Hathor never got a second chance to try that. Has she been destroyed along with her thralls? I would say no, except that the magics I sensed in the disintegrating temple had been like nothing else in this world.

None of that explains where I am now. What am I doing in this cave?

Oh, I know the answer to that. Admitting to the truth means I'm a pathetic fool, but I see no point in fighting the impulse. I step through the cascade and transport myself into the rock garden where I sense no one is around. Then I hurry down the hill to the rear door of the shop, rushing through it.

I stop at the sales counter.

Lindsey is standing there, one hand on her large belly, murmuring to the unborn child in her womb.

Why do mortals do that? They think I'm bizarre, yet they speak to minuscule fetuses.

Lindsey's head pops up, and she smiles at me. "Maxie, I'm so glad to see—What's wrong?"

Yes, I must look as frazzled as I feel. Countless hours spent hunting for Harper, for the obsidian fae, for any being in existence who might be able to help me. I'd met with Ennea, but she had no advice to give and no spells or potions that might do the trick. I attempted to venture into the woods that surround Ken's lair, but the wards prevented it.

The oracle let Harper inside, but I'm forbidden from entering.

Of course I am. Why should anyone help me?

Lindsey walks out from behind the counter and takes my hands in hers. "Tell me what's happened, Max."

"I lost her."

"Who?"

Squeezing my eyes shut, I take a sharp, shallow breath. Then I look at Lindsey. "I lost Harper, the woman I've been trying to… Bollocks. I don't know what I was trying to do. For a moment there, I thought she might be—well, could potentially be—"

I throw my hands up and growl.

Lindsey touches my arm. "You thought she was your fated mate."

"You know I never believed in that nonsense." I scrub a hand over my mouth. "But yes, I sort of allowed myself to consider the possibility. But she's clearly not anything of the sort. The obsidian fae took her, and I can't find her anywhere. Shouldn't a fated mate be able to find his, uh, fated whatever?"

Lindsey snorts, trying not to laugh.

I'm having a severe problem, and she's laughing at me.

"You need to calm down, Max," she says. "Getting upset only makes problems seem worse and more impossible to solve. Trust me, I used to be the queen of denial and self-recrimination."

"I know. You were very uptight when we first met."

"Now you're the one who needs to relax." She brackets my face with her hands. "If you believe Harper is your fated mate, then she is. You're one of the smartest people I know."

"I'm not a person, Lindsey. I'm a salamander."

"You're a person to me." She pats my cheeks. "Now, tell me all about the problem."

She leads me behind the counter where I sit down on a stool, at her command, and she takes a folding canvas chair.

And I tell her everything.

Well, all right, I leave out the sex bits. Talking to a pregnant woman about that seems, as Lindsey might say, icky to the extreme. It's irrelevant, anyway. My problem is how to find Harper and save her from the obsidian fae, not how to shag her mindless. I already know how to do that quite well.

Once I've finished explaining all of it, Lindsey gets that squinty-eyed look I've come to know means she's considering the issue.

"You said this tribe of fae is bound to obsidian," she says, her hands linked over her belly and the fingers of one hand tapping. "The actual stone, not some freaky elemental version of it. Real obsidian rock."

"Haven't I said that fifty times already? Yes, they're bound to obsidian, the way leprechauns are bound to copper. Except in a much less useful and far more unfriendly way."

"I'm sure it's useful to them. But yeah, I get your point." She slaps her hands down on the chair's arms and struggles to push herself up.

"What are you doing?" I leap up and set her on her feet. "You should be resting, not working."

"I don't do much. Nevan won't let me." She sighs. "I'd rather hang out here than at home by myself. Now, about your problem…"

She ambles around the counter and starts down one of the aisles that contain bins of polished rocks.

I follow her, though I have no idea what we're doing. I'd hoped for concrete advice, not a stroll through the aisles of a rock shop.

Lindsey stops at a bin full of black stones. "This is obsidian."

"Yes, I know." Maybe I sound a touch irritable. "I admit I'm a complete moron, but I do recognize black stones."

"Don't be so grouchy." She runs her fingers over the stones in the bin. "There's something I know about obsidian, but it's stuck in the back of my mind. I thought looking at the rocks might help."

She puckers her lips, staring down at the bin.

"Obviously, it's not working," I say, trying not to sound grouchy anymore. "I should go. This is pointless."

"No, it's not." Lindsey whips her head around as if she's searching for something or someone. "Nevan! Come here, honey."

Her husband, who was restocking the bins on the other side of the store, hurries over to her. "What is it, darlin'?"

"Max has a problem with the obsidian fae."

"I thought they were a myth."

"No," I say, getting a bit testy again. Why can't anyone just tell me what to do? This discuss-and-assess nonsense is driving me insane. "One of those obsidian bastards tried to kill me, and now he's taken Harper."

"Who is Harper?" Nevan asks.

Lindsey pats his chest. "She's Max's fated mate."

I open my mouth to proclaim she is not, but what's the point? No one believes me. Not even I believe me.

"His fated mate?" Nevan says, grinning. "That's wonderful news."

Why is he so damn cheerful about it? Nevan and I have become sort of, grudgingly, friends. To make Lindsey happy. But he's always thought I'm an interloper, trying to seduce Lindsey away from him. All right, maybe I did try it on once. She wouldn't have any of it. Lindsey is my friend, and that's all.

"Yes, isn't it bloody wonderful," I say with enough sarcasm that even a deaf gnome couldn't fail to recognize it. "Harper Goode is my fated mate, so naturally, I lost her to the obsidian fae. Let's all have a right good laugh about it."

"Oh Maxie," Lindsey says, giving me a quick hug. "We both want to help you. So shut up and let us talk."

No other being in the multiverse could get away with hugging me and then ordering me to shut up. She says it with affection, so that softens her statement a bit. Still, it's embarrassing to be treated like a child. In public. With her husband, a former elemental king, smirking about it.

Lindsey snuggles up to Nevan, her arm around his waist. "There's something about obsidian, something that reminds me of Max, but I can't quite put my finger on it. I think I saw it in a catalog or a magazine."

"Hmm." Nevan gazes down at the bin of black stones for a moment that feels like a bloody eternity. "Could it be fire obsidian?"

"Yes!" Lindsey grins and claps. "Fire obsidian."

I rub my forehead and groan. "How does that help me? Another type of sodding black rock. Yes, all my troubles are over."

Lindsey gives me a look I know well, the one that implies I'm being an idiot. "You are bound to an element just like every other being in the

Unseen. Except for the gods, apparently. Well, you know what I mean." She leans forward, keeping her arm around Nevan, and stares straight into my eyes. "You are bound to fire, Max. And there's a rock called fire obsidian. Get it?"

Not one little bit.

I must look baffled because she says, "Fire. You burst into flames. And there's a type of obsidian that looks kind of like fire. You, fire. Rock, fire. You, rock, fire."

"Yes, I grasped your meaning before you spoke to me like I'm a little baby salamander who only understands simple, one-syllable words."

"I wasn't being condescending. I was pointing out the synchronicity." She moves closer, halfway between me and Nevan. "You command fire. Maybe that means you can also command fire obsidian. It's worth a shot, isn't it?"

"There's a flaw in your plan. I don't have any of that rock."

Nevan smirks again. "But we've got some in the back room. Lindsey ordered it from a catalog the other day and paid for overnight delivery. She had an intuition it might come in handy sometime."

I should've guessed as much. Lindsey still has uncanny instincts, even if she's no longer the Janusite. I remember the other day when I'd come here to talk to Lindsey and she had picked up a catalog of rocks. She must have ordered the fire obsidian then. Had my presence spurred her to open that catalog? I'll never know for certain, but I've learned never to doubt Lindsey's intuition.

"Well, I, ah," I begin with such eloquence. "Maybe I should try that. Got no bloody idea what to do with the stone, but I'll…figure something out. Can you get it for me?"

Nevan jogs off toward the rear of the shop, past the sales counter. He returns a moment later, holding up a stone. "Here it is. Lindsey kept it where we could easily find it again. My wife is very clever."

"That she is," I say, accepting the rock when he offers it to me. The stone is the size of my palm and polished to a high shine. It's black, naturally, but it has swirling ribbons of other colors inside it—salmon, amber, azure, and much more. "Thank you, Nevan. And thank you, Lindsey. I don't know what I would do without you."

"Oh, you don't need me," she says. "You're very smart, and you would've figured something out on your own." She kisses my cheek. "But I'm glad we could help."

"I'd better get back to the Unseen and…do something with this rock."

"Good luck, Max. And if you need anything else—"

"He will stay away from you," Nevan announces. "If these obsidian fae are as powerful as he says, you shouldn't be anywhere near them or near him until he deals with the problem."

Lindsey starts to protest.

"He's right," I tell her. Then I say to Nevan, "Keep her safe."

I rush out the back door. As I'm crossing the threshold, an odd shiver chases over my skin. I don't get cold. My body is far too hot for that. But this chill felt more like... I don't know. Like an elemental spirit passed through me. Like a warning of some sort.

Which is nonsense.

But I halt a few feet outside the door and lean through it to shout to Nevan, "Keep Lindsey away from water. You know what I mean."

He nods. "We'll let our employees run the store for a day or so."

"Good idea."

We're talking about the boundaries that prevent elementals from penetrating more than one mile into the mortal world. One mile from any natural water feature. The house where Lindsey and Nevan live sits well outside any boundary.

But Gunny and Sigrun got past the limits.

No, I can't think about that. Nevan will look after Lindsey. I'll never do what needs to be done if I'm distracted by worrying about her.

I will find Harper, no matter what I must do to make that happen. And I will destroy any obsidian fae that gets in my way.

How will I do that? It's simple.

Waving my hand, I conjure Harper's little sword, the one that sliced Gunny's head off. Yes, this will do just fine. In my other hand, I still hold the fire obsidian stone. I don't know how it might help me, but I have the strangest feeling it will.

CHAPTER TWENTY-SEVEN

Harper

WELL, AT LEAST I'M NOW IMPRISONED IN A MUCH NICER CELL, ONE with a large bed and a sofa, plus a few chairs. Talos expects me to marry him, so I guess he's trying to butter me up for that. Why bother? I'm sure he can force me into this so-called marriage whether I want it or not. Oh, wouldn't my parents love to hear I've gotten married—and to a lord, no less. Sure, he has a skeletal figure and skin that's like polished lava rock, and he often sounds like a snake when he talks, but so what? I got me a high-class fiancé.

Ugh. Good thing I don't give a shit what my family thinks of me anymore.

I've been stuck in this room forever. Okay, it's probably been an hour or two. It feels like an eternity, though. At least the lighting in here is brighter, though the walls are made of obsidian like everywhere else I've seen in this palace.

And yeah, for as long as I've been stuck in this room, I've kept trying to harness the dark magics in my tattoo. No luck so far. Maybe I'm too anxious for it to work. Instead of trying to access those magics, maybe I should focus on contacting Max.

Right. That's so much easier.

Do I even have that kind of power? One way to find out.

I lie down on the bed, on my back, and close my eyes. How should I do this? Think Max's name? Picture him? Sheesh, I have no idea. So I'll start by picturing him. That tall, impossibly muscular body. The coppery sheen of his well-tanned skin. His dark hair with those maroon streaks. His lips, the ones I've kissed so many times. His eyes, the way they swirl and burn and draw me down into the most delicious whirlpool of warm desire. The way his hands feel on my body, the sensation of his tongue teasing every part of me, and the fullness of his shaft inside me.

He calls me *dulcissime*. I still don't know what that means, but the last time he'd called me that, his voice had conveyed a depth of emotion that made my chest ache. I focus on the image of his face—of the way he smirks in that confident, sensual way right before he takes my body.

Max, where are you?

I sense something, like a thread inside me is unwinding and snaking out through the ether, questing for Max. I keep picturing him, remembering our time together. That thread stretches out farther and farther, seeking, seeking, seeking.

Suddenly, it stops.

And heat rushes through me, the most beautiful, sweet sizzle I've ever experienced. It feels like Max. I almost cry when that sensation hits me because I know what it means.

I've found him.

Can I speak to him in my mind? I have no idea, but I need to try. So I do my best to kind of beam thoughts into his brain. *Max, can you hear me? Can you feel me?*

No response, but that heat continues to penetrate me down to my soul. I beam those thoughts in his direction again. And again. And again. Still nothing. I sit up and let my shoulders sag. Damn, he can't hear me.

Harper?

That single word whispers in my mind—in Max's sensual voice with that sexy British accent.

Is that you? he asks. *Or am I hallucinating?*

No, Max, it's me.

Where are you?

Trapped in the palace of Talos, lord of the obsidian fae. Where are you?

I swear I hear him huff. *In the ruddy woods trying to find you.*

Maybe I can send you a beacon or…something.

Brilliant. Do you have any clue how to do that?

The answer is no, not so much. But I had no clue how to contact him, and I've done it. How hard can it be to create a beacon, like a supernatural lighthouse in my mind that only Max can see?

I flop back down on the bed and moan pitifully.

You've got no bloody idea, Max says. *Am I right?*

Now I growl like he often does. *Yeah-yeah, you're right. Try being helpful instead of sarcastic. Not like I've ever had telepathic powers before.*

Let's try focusing on each other, he says, *at the same time. Maybe that will intensify this bond or whatever you've created.*

Sure. Do we need a countdown?

Yes. Counting down from three. You start.

I take a deep breath and exhale it slowly, then I start the countdown. *Three, two, one…*

Nothing happens.

Are you actually trying, Max?

Yes, I bloody am. Let's give it another go, and I'll do the counting, start-ing at five.

Be my guest.

After a brief pause, he starts counting down. *Five, four—*

His enticing voice lulls and arouses me at the same time, which seems odd considering this is all in my head. But I listen to his countdown and let his voice penetrate my mind and ripple warmth through my entire body, from my head down to my toes.

Three, two—

Max. Hot, sweet, incredible Max.

One.

The instant he transmits that one-syllable thought, a bolt of electricity fires out of me straight down the telepathic phone line between us. I sense it happening and feel the moment when that bolt strikes Max and the line between us connects.

Is this a permanent thing? Because I'm not sure I want his erotic voice rumbling inside my head all the time, like when I'm sitting on the toilet or in a library. I can practically orgasm just listening to him talk, so yeah, I might be imprisoned again after I escape from the obsidian fae. I'll get ar-rested for indecency.

But I love the warmth and safety of this connection.

I think it worked, Max says. *I can't describe this feeling, but I know I can find you.*

Good. Now get your naked ass in gear and storm this damn obsidian palace.

I'm wearing trousers at the moment.

Who cares? Get a move on.

Yes, yes, I'm working on it.

The door to my lovely little prison cell bursts open, and Talos saunters inside followed by two other fae who I assume are guards.

Sorry, Max, gotta go. Lord Talos is here.

He snarls something in my mind, but I can't understand the words. Then I sense he's not listening to me anymore, though that line between us stays connected. He needs to concentrate on finding me.

"Get up," Talos commands. "It is time for our handfasting."

I've heard of that. I think it's like a wedding.

While I scramble off the bed, I ask, "Don't I get a dress or a veil or anything?"

"Dress?" Talos hisses. "You will be nude during the handfasting so that I may consummate our union whilst the mage speaks the vows."

"You mean we don't say them ourselves?"

"Why bother? You have no choice, which means you need not speak at all. Once I have copulated with you, all the power we've simmered inside you for so long will become mine." He waves a hand toward one of the guards. "Bind her."

The guards both stalk up to me. One grasps my shoulders to hold me in place while the other secures shackles around my wrists and ankles.

When that's done, our lord and master flicks his wrist.

My clothes evaporate.

Oh yeah, this is exactly how I pictured my wedding day. Naked, in chains, about to be violated by an asshole who won't let me speak during our sham of a wedding. What a dream come true.

If Max wanted to marry me, I'd volunteer to do it naked.

Talos leads the way as his guards shepherd me out of the room, down corridor after corridor, until we've returned to the throne room. The lord of the obsidian fae doesn't march up the dais to his throne. Instead, he stands at the base where a pale-faced man with a bald head stands dressed in flowing black robes. His eyes are so dark that it's impossible to distinguish the pupils from the irises. Or maybe he doesn't have either of those. I don't know what kind of creature he is, so I have no idea if his appearance is normal or not.

I glance down at my chained wrists and feet. Will Max get here in time? I can't wait and hope. The pale man in front of me must be the mage who's about to marry me to Talos.

"What do you want?" I ask the fae lord. Yeah, I'm hoping this delaying tactic will work. "I mean, bad guys always have goals. Do I at least get to know why this is happening to me?"

Talos sighs. "Does it matter? You will serve me either way."

"How can I be impressed by your cunning if you don't share your end-game with me?"

Talos lifts one brow. He watches me for a moment, then shrugs. "Why not? If you know, perhaps you'll give up fighting me."

"Maybe." No way in hell, but I'm not dumb enough to say that out loud.

He leans toward me and speaks in a hushed tone. "I am going to seize control of the entire Unseen, destroy the Great Bargain and thus eliminate the boundaries in the mortal realm, and become lord of two worlds. Slaves of every ilk at my disposal, worshiping me."

Oh jeez. I'd been hoping for something more original. But nope, it's the old world-domination plan.

"Won't the gods be, um, annoyed by that?" I ask.

"I will become more powerful than any being, even gods." His lips slide into a creepy smile. "Even the Oversoul."

Though I have no idea who or what the Oversoul is, I don't need to fake being terrified by Talos's plan. The total subjugation of two worlds gives me plenty of reasons to feel afraid.

Not to mention the fact I'm about to get copulated on by a repulsive, evil bastard.

"You have no conception of what obsidian truly is, do you?" Talos asks. "It is the essence of evil, dark magics condensed down to their purest, most potent form. The power within the obsidian lies dormant until it's activated. In this case, by the power I've invested into you and nurtured with your suffering."

Gee, thanks a lot, you asshat freak.

But he's not done bragging yet. "I imbued into you an overpowering need to find the Unseen. To find me. And here you are, following my orders."

"I came here to destroy the Unseen, you moron."

"That's what you believe?" He harrumphs. "But you haven't done it, have you? Because that rage is simply a construct of your mind, created to encourage you to find me. Your puny mortal brain needed a stronger impetus, that's all."

Max had already figured out I'd been programmed. Even if Talos had done that to me, he doesn't control my mind anymore.

Wait… If the magics in my tattoo will give Talos the power to control two worlds, they must give me incredible power too. Now I just have to figure out how to harness it.

The mage raises his hands and begins to chant in a language I don't understand.

That old pins-and-needles sensation ramps up in my tattoo. Any second, I'll be frigging married to a frigging lunatic.

Like hell.

I concentrate on my tattoo, shutting my eyes so I can better visualize the magics roiling within those black lines. Suddenly, I know without any doubt that my tattoo is composed of obsidian somehow carved into my skin. The mark begins to burn, slightly at first, then getting hotter and hotter until the searing pain makes me scrunch up my face and suck in a breath.

Obey me, I command the magics. *Serve me.*

The scorching pain lessens a tiny bit.

I focus harder, squeezing my eyes shut so tightly it almost hurts, aiming all my willpower at the mark on my back. *Work, dammit, work.* It has to, or I'm about to be ravaged by Talos.

The burning diminishes even more, and the pins and needles prick me with less force. *Yes.* I funnel every ounce of energy I have into taking control of the magics, though I have no idea how to do that. I trust my instincts and do whatever feels right.

The pain fades away.

But a new sensation, like a thousand tiny slithering snakes, takes its place. The magics are fighting me, I know. All I have to do is keep after it, keep struggling, keep commanding those magics to heel for me.

And pray I don't die in the process.

Chapter Twenty-Eight

Max

I'M STANDING IN AN EMPTY FIELD IN THE UNSEEN, ALONE, WITH TWO moons glowing in the sky above me and the forest encircling me. I'd followed my instincts, not even trying to figure out where they led me, because trying to interpret a telepathic signal seems like a direct route to insanity. This must be where Harper is. Why else would I be led here?

Yes, that's right. She's invisible. And so is the palace of the obsidian fae.

I scrub my scalp with both hands as if I can rattle understanding into my brain. How did I cock it up? I must have done, since I see nothing in this field.

Unless…the palace actually is invisible. Or underground.

Possibly both.

"Maximus, you naughty boy."

I turn around and groan when I see exactly the person I knew I would see.

Hathor shuffles up to me, her shoulders slumped and her hair and make-up a mess. She's wearing a white tunic that hangs down to her knees, but it's smeared with dirt and, I think, blood. In this light, with only the milky glow of two moons to illuminate her, I can't tell for sure.

"What happened to you?" I ask. "No offense, Hattie, but you look like hell."

"That's what happens when the hounds of Hades destroy my home." She spits those words, though her voice is more hushed than I've ever heard it. "What did you do to bring this on me?"

"I brought it on you? That's rich. You've hunted me mercilessly, sending your ruddy vampire and that Valkyrie bitch to retrieve me." I point a finger at her. "If you hadn't done that, your temple would still be standing."

Yes, I'd watched the entire complex crumble to dust after that obsidian fae wanker took off with Harper. I desperately struggled to save the individuals trapped inside the structure, winding up bloodied and covered in dirt-infused sweat, but I couldn't save any of them. The magics that toppled the palace ensured they would die, as surely as if they'd been run through with endued swords. They hadn't even tried to run away, bound by their ensorcellment to the goddess.

"My worshipers are dead," Hathor tells me, and I swear she's crying. "So are my bounty hunters. I have nothing left. Nothing, do you hear?"

"Can't express how much I don't give a toss about that. You're alone?" I grunt with a hint of sour laughter. "About bloody time you had to fend for yourself. Now sod off, Hattie."

"You have never called me Hattie before." She lifts her perfect godly nose and sniffs. "I don't appreciate it."

"I'm in a foul mood, so do yourself a favor and get out of my sight."

She glances around like she's searching for something. "Where is your beloved? Has she abandoned you?"

And naturally, Hathor sounds pleased by the prospect. Smugly pleased.

"One of the obsidian fae took her," I say. "He's the blighter who destroyed your temple."

"The obsidian fae? Are you certain, Maximus?"

"Would you stop calling me that? My name is Max."

She waves a hand to show me how little she cares about what I want. "Oh fine, whatever. You must be confused because the obsidian fae are a myth."

"No, you are wrong." And yes, I feel smugly pleased by that fact. The nasty goddess is not omniscient after all. "I've seen an obsidian fae. They are real."

Hathor hugs herself, rubbing her arms. "The rumors say they have a sort of king who calls himself Talos."

"Fascinating. Now piss off, would you? I'm busy."

"Doing what? Admiring the sky?"

"If you must know, I'm trying to locate the palace of the obsidian fae."

And utterly failing at the task. If that Talos wanker lays one finger on Harper, I will rip his limbs off his body. Assuming I can ever find his palace. *Bugger.*

"Maybe I can help," Hathor says. "I am a goddess, after all. My powers are far more vast than yours."

This is perfect. I need the help of the woman who has made my life hell for centuries. She ensorcelled me so often I lost track of how many times—and of all the depraved acts she forced me to commit. She also forced me to enjoy them. I should use Harper's sword to slice Hathor's head off her neck.

But I do need help. And she is powerful.

First, I need an answer to one question. "Why did you track me down? You know you can't ensorcell me anymore."

"I was…um…" She hunches her shoulders, still hugging herself, and flashes me a scowl. "I missed you, all right. There's no one around to entertain me."

Laughter erupts out of me, the bitter and completely unamused sort. "You're lonely? That's perfect. About time you learned to live without a horde of minions who adore you only because you've got them under your thrall." I pat her arm and give her a sarcastic smile. "Chin up, Hattie. I'm sure you'll drum up another horde soon."

She scowls again. "Do you want my help or not?"

I sigh. "Yes, fine, assist me."

Hathor shoos me out of the way and raises her arms high above her head, hands spread. She starts chanting in the old tongue, the one used by gods, mages, and sorcerers. It's also employed during the forging process. But Hathor is using it to…help me. The idea that she volunteered to do that and demanded nothing in return must be a sign the worlds are about to implode.

The air inside the clearing thickens and shimmers like an air mass roiling in waves above hot pavement. The pressure increases too, pressing on my eardrums.

A black structure pops into view, hunkering low to the ground.

Hathor aims a self-satisfied smile at me. "There. I've saved the day, haven't I? You may kneel and kiss my feet now."

I would laugh, but I know she's not joking. She sincerely thinks I want to kiss her feet. Instead, I give her the thumbs-up sign my mortal friends love to use. "Good job, Hattie."

She flaps her arms. "That's all I get? I reveal Talos's palace to you, and that's it?"

"Tha—" I cut myself off just in time since I'd been about to thank her. *Ruddy moron.* I have definitely spent too much time around mortals. "You've done well, but I don't need your assistance anymore."

She lifts her chin, eying me over the tip of her nose. "So, you don't need any backup while you storm the palace of the incredibly powerful lord of the obsidian fae?"

I grumble a few curses in various languages. "All right, fine. Come with me."

Hathor rolls her shoulders back and smiles with haughty satisfaction.

We approach what looks like the front of the structure, which seems to be carved out of pure obsidian. I decide this is the front based on the fact it's concave, though I see no seams like a door might have. I place my palms on the surface and move them in circles, hunting for a mechanism to open the door.

"Oh for Ra's sake," Hathor snaps. She shoves me out of the way. "Let me handle this."

She chants again, and the door grinds open.

It disappears into the wall. Beyond the opening, I see a dimly lit corridor.

"You may kiss my feet," Hathor says. "I really think you ought to this time since I've literally opened the way for you."

Rolling my eyes at her, I hurry down the corridor.

The clapping of her sandaled feet assures me Hathor is following, whether I like it or not. Well, at least her powers might come in handy.

I follow the tether that connects me to Harper, having no idea where it might lead me. Doesn't matter. I need to find Harper, and I don't care what obstacles I must get past or how many obsidian fae I need to destroy in the process. I conjure the fire obsidian stone, clutching it in one hand while I summon Harper's sword.

Where is she? I can't lose her. I won't let that happen.

Something cold pulses down the tether. Fear, I realize. Harper is afraid. And alone.

I'm coming, hold on.

And that bastard Talos is about to die.

Swerving around a corner, I run faster and faster until flames burst out from my skin and form a trail that stretches behind me. The fire obsidian stone warms in my palm, setting off a tingling that spreads outward and intensifies until it consumes my entire body and merges with my natural fire. The flames transform into an array of shimmering, writhing hues like a train of brightly colored fire dragged after me. My skin gives off the same multicolored flames.

I see an open door ahead. A chamber.

And I hear chanting.

Someone howls like a banshee.

Harper.

I speed through the doorway and skid to a halt, the flames whirling around me in the wind created by my sudden stop. The fire on my skin dwindles to a low burn that clings to my skin.

Harper is on her knees, her arms stretched out, her fingers spread, and her palms aimed at the being who lies crumpled on the floor in front of her. She's breathing hard, and sweat runs down her face.

The being on the floor cups his genitals, or what I take for his genitals since his hand is over his groin. He roars, "Seize her!"

A pair of obsidian fae who had hidden in the shadows leap forward, reaching for Harper.

I rush at them and swing her little sword. One fae's head tumbles to the floor. I swing again, and another fae head rolls across the obsidian floor. Will that take them out for good? To make sure, I kick their heads as far away from their bodies as I can.

Then I tell Hathor, "Seal the doors, will you?"

She does it, pulling up a shimmering, translucent barrier that fills the doorway.

I drop to my knees beside Harper. "Are you all right?"

Perspiration still streams down her face, but she manages a weak smile. "I'm okay. Stopped that creep before he raped me."

Suddenly, I realize she's naked—and shackled.

I touch the shackles, intending to test them for a spell that might stop me from removing them. But the second my fingers contact the metal, the shackles disintegrate into powder with a puff of fire that emerges from my fingertips. A puff of multicolored fire.

After I help Harper get to her feet, I conjure her clothing and pull her into my arms.

She hugs me tightly, burying her face against my chest.

All the while, that obsidian fae bastard cups his balls, or whatever his kind have, and glares at me.

"Can't get up?" I ask. "What a pity. Must be cold lying there on the floor with your balls in your hands. Well, at least they're not in your mouth."

Harper lifts her head to gaze up at me. "You came."

"Naturally. You are my fated mate, after all." But she's become so much more than that, and I still haven't figured out what exactly that means. "Are you sure you're all right?"

"Yes, I'm positive." She hoists herself up on the tips of her toes to kiss me. "I've never been happier to see anyone in my life."

"I'm happy to see you too. But we should do something about the balls-less wanker on the floor."

"He still has his testicles. I threw a big old ball of something-or-other at him." She eyes the fae lord, and her lips twitch upward. "It must've really hurt, considering that he wailed like a baby when I did it."

"I only heard a howl, like a banshee. Was that him?"

"That was me. I screamed when I threw the ball of whatever at him. My howling probably drowned out his pathetic noises."

Although I'd rather keep holding Harper, I move away from her to loom over the lord of the obsidian fae. "You must be Talos. It's not at all a pleasure to meet you, though it will be a pleasure to remove your head."

I raise the sword.

"Wait," Harper says. She comes up alongside me. "I need to do it. He's the one who murdered my best friend thirteen years ago. I'm sure he's the one who ordered his goons to torture me too."

"You're right. You should destroy him." I hand her the sword. "He's all yours, love."

She raises the blade, preparing to strike, but hesitates as she bites down on her lip. Just when I think she might change her mind and opt for mercy, she slams the blade down on Talos's neck.

The fae lord's head rolls across the floor like a gruesome bowling ball.

Harper tosses the sword away and tucks herself under my arm. "Are you sure that will kill him?"

"Can't be sure of anything since I have no idea how that sword is able to remove an elemental's head."

Hathor sniffs. "Toss them all over a boundary. Then you can be sure."

Why didn't I think of that? I raise my hand, about to make the bodies disappear.

The walls pulsate like we're inside a giant heart that's just begun to pump multicolored blood. It sounds that way too, like the heartbeat of a giant being. Even the floor pulsates beneath my feet.

Harper jerks her head up. "What's going on?"

"No idea." I hold her tighter with one arm while I wave my other hand to vanish the bodies, but nothing happens. "We need to get out of here. Get your barrier down, Hattie."

The goddess flicks her wrist toward the doorway. Her eyes widen. "I can't release it. Someone or something else has commandeered my magics."

She doesn't sound offended by that fact. She sounds frightened.

What in the multiverse could scare a goddess? Or seize control of her magics?

I mutter an oath.

Talos's head rolls across the floor, moving faster and faster toward his body until it snaps into place on his neck. The dark-red streaks in his flesh begin to pulsate in sync with the entire chamber.

Hathor backs up to the wall, cringes, and staggers away from it. She comes up beside me and Harper and wraps her arms around herself, sidling closer to me.

A terrified goddess is a very, very bad sign.

The three of us back away from the fae lord's body.

His eyes spring open, his gaze veering to us.

Talos vaults to his feet and cracks his neck. "That hurt, but not as much as what I shall do to you."

He's glaring at Harper when he says that.

"Filthy light magics," he hisses, stalking closer, still focused on Harper. "How did you transmute dark powers into light magics? Tell me, or I will decapitate your lover the way you so blithely did to me."

The sword she'd used to do that lies on the floor between us and Talos.

I swing my hand out to whisk the sword into my palm.

But Talos grabs it first.

He points the sword's tip at me while still looking at Harper. "Choose, mortal. His head or your secrets."

"I don't know how I did it," she says. "I wanted to stop you from raping me, so I summoned all the magics you force-fed me. It worked. That's all I know."

Talos makes a ticking motion with the sword while he speaks in an almost sing-song tone. "Time is running out for you two. Tick, tock. Tick, tock. My patience wears thin."

Part of me wants to point out he's mixing metaphors, but that's irrelevant at the moment.

"Your little trick," Talos says, "cost you a sizable chunk of the energy I worked so hard to infuse into your worthless mortal body. You'll need to simmer for a while to replenish the magics before I can ingest them." He flicks his yellow gaze to me. "And you're in luck, incubus. Sex with you empowered those magics faster and more thoroughly than any of the suffering I caused her. Who knew?" He moves a touch closer, tapping the sword's tip on my chest. "Here's your assigned task. Fuck her until she's so full of ripe magics that she can't speak or move. If you fail… Well, I'm certain you can guess."

He slashes the sword in the air inches from my throat and makes a noise that's clearly meant to sound like my head getting sliced off.

Talos turns his attention to Hathor. "As for you, goddess, I have no use for an arrogant female who cares only for her own pleasure. Shall we find out if this blade can sever your head too?"

Hathor shakes her head furiously.

"Didn't think so," Talos says. With a vicious smile, he waves his hand—and the heads of his two minions reattach themselves to their bodies. As the two fae rise, their lord commands, "Take these three to the bridal chamber. Once the salamander has done his job, the handfasting ceremony will commence." He growls out a sigh. "Again."

The guards herd us toward the doorway.

Behind us, Talos calls out, "No more tricks or heads will roll, literally. Or perhaps I'll cut your hearts out instead. That might be more entertaining."

And I thought Hathor was the maddest being in the Unseen.

Chapter Twenty-Nine

Harper

THE FAE GUARDS DUMP US IN MY "BRIDAL CHAMBER" AND LEAVE. THE doorway grinds shut. Max, Hathor, and I stand there exchanging clueless looks for a minute or two. Well, at least I don't feel like the ineffectual dunce in the room. If a goddess and an incubus can't figure out what the hell to do, that puts us all on the same playing field. A nice level one.

Yeah, we're all pathetic. Fabulous.

Hathor looks at Max but waves a hand toward me in a pretentious gesture. "Go on, Maximus. Fornicate with her."

"With you watching?" he says. "Piss off, Hattie."

"Stop calling me that." She sighs melodramatically. "Honestly, how can you be such a prude? You love orgies as much as I do."

"No, you ensorcelled me so I'd do whatever you wanted and enjoy it. After the spell wore off, I hated myself for all of it."

Max hates himself for what Hathor made him do? I want to hug him, but I doubt he'll like that with Hathor standing right next to him.

"We're not feeding Talos," Max says. "That means no fornicating of any kind."

"Max and I need to have a talk," I tell Hathor. "Go over there—into the corner, facing the corner—and cover your ears."

"What?" the goddess balks. "I am a queen, revered by—"

"All the ensorcelled people you forced to revere you. Get over yourself already. Nobody here is going to bow down before you." I gesture toward the far corner of the room. "So get your ass over there and do what I told you to do."

Max lifts his head, one brow arched. His mouth gradually slides into a sexy smile.

Oh yeah, I just got bossy with a goddess.

Hathor huffs, whirls around, and stomps into the corner. She does not, however, face into the corner. She leans back against the wall, folds her arms over her chest, and watches us over the tip of her raised nose.

Whatever.

Max slings an arm around my waist and pulls me into his body. His voice turns hushed and sensual. "I love the way you ordered the goddess around like she's a child. That was the single sexiest thing you've ever done, and the most satisfying comedown I've ever witnessed. Hathor deserved it."

"Glad you approve." I slip my arms around his torso. "But how are we going to stop Talos? I'm scared, Max, which doesn't put me in the mood for sex."

"Even I can't get in the mood." He throws a scowl in Hathor's direction. "Cover your ears and shut your eyes. This is a private conversation."

I glance in the goddess's direction just in time to see her slap her hands over her ears. She shuts her eyes too, but I think she might be cheating a little bit. I think I see a sliver of an opening between her apparently shut eyelids.

"We need more power," I say. "Maybe we can get that without sex."

Hathor gasps. "No sex? You should at least give me a good show if I'm to be stuck here in this hovel with you two."

"Zip it," I snap.

The goddess puckers her lips.

"It's worth a try," Max says. "You did contact me telepathically. No sex involved."

Hathor moans with a touch of whining in it and slumps down to the floor. Sitting there on her high-and-mighty rump, she crosses her arms again. "If you're not going to do anything worth watching, I might as well take a nap."

The goddess shuts her eyes, leaning her head against the wall.

Max takes my chin between his thumb and forefinger, urging me to turn my head toward him. "I'm scared too. But together, we might have the power to stop Talos."

I gaze into his eyes, letting myself fall into the swirling, liquid colors in his irises, their coppery brown shade merging with threads of gold and silver and a touch of white. I've seen white in his eyes before, and it meant fear. A little fear can be good, but if he's as freaked out as I am, it might hinder our efforts to defeat Talos. So I keep my gaze locked on his while I slid my hands up his chest, over his shoulders, to link them at his nape. The heat of his body melts the chill in me. I spiral down, down, down into the whirling depths of his eyes.

An invisible rope snaps taut between us. I feel it, almost hear it, though the sensation exists only in the supernatural bond that joins us. Weight bears down on my chest, but it's not a physical pressure, and I suck in a shaky breath, overwhelmed by the power of this connection. His eyes pull me deeper into the bond, setting off a prickly tingling that sweeps over me from head to toe and dives under my skin to awaken parts of me I've suppressed for so long. Max has awakened me like no one else ever could. What we have is more than sex.

And we're about to prove that.

I lean into his body, tipping my head back so I can maintain eye contact.

He lowers his head, never breaking the link between us. His eyes smolder a brilliant red, the rims of his irises sparkling with pure, iridescent silver. Inside his pupils, copper sparks ignite and flicker.

The pressure in my chest intensifies, making it hard to breathe. Tears prick at my eyes, but I feel no pain, only the sweet pleasure of connecting with Max. My shallow breathing triggers ringing in my ears, but I know how to get more oxygen.

I boost up onto my tiptoes and press my lips to his.

The first contact of his lips on mine affects me like a potent drug, and I moan with the most intense satisfaction I've ever known. Parting my lips, I moan again when he slips his tongue inside, starved for the taste and feel of his mouth. He plunges his tongue deep, wrapping his arms around me, our bodies molded to each other. We don't grope or fondle each other. Though our tongues tangle, we don't turn this into a scorching-hot kiss either. We explore each other lazily like we have forever to do this, like we're not on the cusp of being destroyed by a mad fae lord.

Everything else drifts away from us.

I know he feels what I feel, this deep bond that suffuses us down to our souls and binds us in ways I may never fully understand. I know he experiences that with me because I sense it. We are connected. Bound, but not by enslavement ensorcellment. We chose this binding.

A wave of pure, heartbreakingly beautiful emotion surges out of Max and into me, enlivening my body, my mind, and the magics in my tattoo. It burns with a flurry of prickling pains, but even that can't diminish what we're sharing at this moment. The fervency of what Max has just given me spurs me to push everything we both feel back into him.

He gasps into my mouth, his body going rigid.

Maybe he hasn't penetrated by body physically, but he is inside me.

I latch on to the sensations and let go of everything else.

Those pins and needles stab into the tattoo harder and sharper and hotter than ever. Though I wince at the pain and tears trickle from my closed eyes, I cling to Max and to that extraordinary passion that has nothing to do with sex. A rush of intoxicating magic engulfs me and gushes into Max, creating a feedback loop that fuels us both like never before.

Max freezes, our mouths still fused.

I open my eyes.

And he's staring straight into mine. His irises blaze with metallic shades that swirl and flame.

For several seconds, we stay like that. Frozen. Our gazes locked. Both of us struggling to catch our breath in the wake of the fervid bond we just sealed.

Max peels his mouth away from mine and sets me down on my feet. He wipes a hand across his mouth. "That was…unexpected. I feel stronger than ever."

"So do I."

We both glance at the corner where Hathor is leaning against the wall.

The goddess clambers to her feet. "Let's all take our clothes off and get into bed. The strength of the magics you two invoked has me fired up, and I guarantee sex with a goddess will be fantastic."

"Afraid I'll have to decline your generous offer," I say. Does she seriously think I want to have a threesome with her? *Yech*. I don't even like the woman.

"Bugger off, Hattie," Max says.

"Why have you started calling her Hattie?" I ask.

"To annoy her."

Oh yeah, I should've guessed.

Max leans in close, one side of his mouth twitching upward. "That got me fired up too. After we defeat Talos, I'm going to fuck you for days."

Maybe that statement should irritate me, but instead, it makes me feel warm and tingly all over.

I stuff my hands in my pants pockets and chew the inside of my lip while I consider our situation. "Talos told me obsidian is condensed dark magics. The power lies dormant until it's activated. Wonder if I could do that to all the obsidian in this palace." I glance around at the vast quantities of the stone all around us. "I'd rather test my theory on one piece of it, but I'm guessing you and Hathor can't conjure anything right now."

"No," Hathor whines. "I am impotent."

"Look on the bright side. You get to see how mortals live."

She bursts into tears.

Oh, whatever. I don't have time for the histrionics of a whacked-out goddess.

"I can't conjure either," Max says. His eyes widen for a heartbeat like he's just remembered something. He reaches into his pocket, pulling out a black stone with rainbow colors in it. "Lindsey gave me this. It's fire obsidian. She thought I might be able to get more power from it since I'm bound to elemental fire."

"Does it work?"

"Yes, but now I'm thinking it will be of more use to you. Our connection might allow you to tap into the fire energy of the stone."

He offers me the rock.

I hold it in my palm, feeling the odd warmth and silken texture of it. The colors embedded in the black stone begin to writhe, but I sense it's not a bad thing. This stone might contain dark magics, but I can harness them. I've done it before. Once. And that single effort drained me.

But I'm not alone anymore. I have a goddess on my side, the scary-strong magics in my tattoo, and a soul-deep connection with a powerful elemental. The palace might be dampening her powers and Max's, but with the three of us banding together, maybe we have the exact right amount of magics.

We also have a weirdly pretty chunk of fire obsidian. Which I have no clue how to use.

"Anybody got an idea?" I ask. "I'm all ears because the only plan I have is iffy at best."

Max shrugs.

Hathor shrugs.

Great. I've got a powerful elemental and a frigging goddess on my side, but they have zero ideas. Guess it's my plan or nothing.

Why couldn't I have just stayed home and watched soap operas instead of flying to Michigan in search of a portal? No, I wouldn't undo anything that's happened. I found Max, and that makes all the suffering worthwhile.

I grasp Max's wrist and turn it so his palm faces up, then I drop the fire obsidian stone onto it. "You should keep this. You're the fire elemental, so you'd know how to use the stone better than I do."

He closes his fist around it. "Tap into our connection. It will strengthen us both as it did a moment ago."

Nodding toward Hathor, I ask him, "What can she do?"

The goddess jumps up, huffing. "I am all-powerful. I can do anything."

"Okay," I tell her, "get us out of here, then."

Her mouth crimps. She kicks the wall with her sandaled foot, hisses at the obvious pain the action caused, and whimpers.

"Yeah, that's what I thought."

"What is your plan?" Max asks.

"To call it a plan might be a slight overstatement. Just follow my lead while I wing it."

Max nods.

Hathor pouts for a couple of seconds, then nods.

The hidden door grinds open, and six fae guards march into the room. They shackle us, but my tattoo throbs when they do that like it wants to disintegrate these bonds.

Not yet, I tell the magics.

The throbbing subsides.

We are marched out of the bridal chamber to the throne room, and our guards leave us there—alone. Max walks up to the doorway, carefully touching his palm to what looks like an open space, but multicolored sparks crackle against his palm. The sparks web out across the doorway. When he retracts his hand, the sparks vanish.

"It's warded," Max says. "We're trapped in here."

Of course we are. Talos wouldn't have it any other way.

A shape on the floor, at the base of the throne dais, catches my attention. It almost blends into the obsidian beneath our feet. I walk over to the item and pick it up.

It's the sword the fae gave me.

My tattoo pulses, the sensation transforming into a burning prickle that spreads through my entire body until it reaches my hand.

A shiver scurries down my spine, and I turn to face the doorway.

Talos struts through the wards and straight to me.

Max and Hathor start to walk toward us.

But the fae lord throws one hand up, halting them mid-step. They struggle against the spell that's frozen them in place, but they can't get free. Talos flicks his wrist, sending Max and Hathor flying backward until their backs hit the wall. They hover a few feet off the floor, still imprisoned by magic.

I have to do this alone. Maybe that's appropriate since I'd been alone most of my life until the day I met Max. The crazy chick nobody wanted around, not even my family, is not alone anymore.

"Kneel," Talos commands.

I square my shoulders and lift my chin. "Screw you."

He glances down at the sword in my hand and chuckles with menacing sarcasm. "I created that sword. Do you think I would give you a weapon that can destroy me?"

The sword's hilt quivers in my hand, quivers with a power that wants out.

He surges closer, forcing me to bend my head back to see his face. "I gave you that sword so you could dispatch anyone who tried to prevent you from reaching me."

I should have known, shouldn't I? Maybe I'm still laboring under the enchantment he put on me, the one that pushed me to find the Unseen. I'll never be truly free until Talos is gone forever.

The words of Ken the oracle whisper through my mind.

You belong to the obsidian fae, he'd said. *The darkness without will soon consume the light within. Once that happens, you will cease to exist as a mortal with free will. They will command you like a marionette.*

I can't let that happen. I won't.

You were destined for this before you were even conceived in your mother's womb, Ken had told me. *What must happen will happen, but the outcome is yours to affect.* The oracle had warned me that I shouldn't assume I understood what he meant. Super helpful, yeah. But his final words echo in my mind now.

Seek the light, but do not fear the dark. Sometimes the truth lies within it.

Today, I'd realized the darkness and the light exist in symbiosis. They need each other to survive—like two sides of one coin, as Ken said. I've learned to harness the dark magics and convert them into light magics. I used that power to subdue Talos earlier.

"Kneel," Talos commands me again.

What must be done will be done. The meaning of Ken's statement suddenly hits me, like a bolt of lightning striking down from a clear blue sky.

Talos raises his hands, holding them parallel with the floor, and thrusts them downward.

My knees buckle. A power I can't fend off forces me to kneel before the fae lord. I grit my teeth against the overpowering force that still bears down on me. Tapping into the magics within me, I struggle to escape—struggle and fail. The effort leaves me gasping for air and sheathed in sweat. I need to grab on to my connection with Max.

The second I try, Talos flicks his wrist.

An invisible fist clamps around my throat, choking me.

"No more delaying," he growls. "Sex would have been the more enjoyable way to ingest the magics, but I've grown tired of you and your insubordination. I made you what you are, and now I will unmake you."

He drops to his knees in front of me, grasps my face roughly, and opens his mouth.

That power, the blackest I've ever felt, forces my mouth open. I fight it, but my jaw might break if I don't stop. I have no choice, so I surrender.

For now.

I reach out for the link that binds me and Max, sensing it hovers just beyond my magical reach. If I don't connect with him right now, before Talos unmakes me, I won't get another chance. So I focus all my energy, all my will, on seizing that telepathic rope.

Talos seals his open mouth over mine.

My tattoo burns with such heat and strength that tears sting my eyes and the scalding agony forces me to choke back a cry. The magics within the tattoo barrel through my veins and push up into my throat, erupting through my mouth. The foul taste of it makes me gag, and no matter how hard I try to stop it, the power flows into Talos through our joined mouths.

The entire palace begins to vibrate, the shock waves coursing through my body. Through the tears that blur my vision, I see the walls start to pulsate like before, only this time the pulsation grows and grows and grows. The floor shakes so much I'd fall down if not for Talos holding me up with his cold hands on my face and his cold mouth attached to mine.

Max, I need you.

With every iota of free will I have and every scrap of magic I still command, I latch on to our bond and feel for the power of the fire obsidian stone, the power inside Max. But my energy drains away like water through a sieve. Talos is consuming everything inside me.

Serpents of dark magic swirl out of Talos and up through the ceiling.

I know where those magics are going. I can feel what he's doing. The dark energies pouring out of him will deluge the entire Unseen—and then the mortal world. As my eyes shut without my permission, I hear the worlds screaming. Light magics can't fight back, so all that's left is for them to shriek and pray for salvation.

The sword is still in my hand. Talos claims it can't destroy him. But does he really understand the power he's ingesting? Which of us understands it better? The fae who created it, or the mortal who has lived with it for thirteen years? Talos will not have his enslaved worlds.

Every word Ken had spoken to me replays in my weakening mind, and I know what I must do.

While the magics stream out of me, I flip the sword around so its tip points toward me, and I grip the hilt in my hand.

Max, forgive me.

CHAPTER THIRTY

Max

DARK MAGICS CHURN AROUND US, THEIR CLAMMY TONGUES DART-ing out to taste the wards that keep me and Hathor pinned to the wall. The tremors and pulsations in the stone rattle my brain and body, chattering my teeth and making it hard to see what's happening between Harper and Talos. The power inside her is siphoning into him, that much I know.

What will become of her once he's drained the magics?

Max, forgive me.

Harper's voice whispers in my mind. What is she asking forgiveness for? Talos is the one who needs to beg for absolution. The magics gushing out of him have spread beyond this palace, threatening to devour every last bit of light magic. The sky will darken to match his soul if he even has one. The bastard had planned to ravage Harper's body, sexually, to get the power he forced her to ingest. Now, he's ravaging her in a different way, by tearing the magics out of her by force, heedless of the fact he's sucking out her life too. I can feel it happening to her, but I can't stop it.

The bastard has already tormented her with dark magics for thirteen years. He will not hurt her anymore.

I kick and beat and claw the ward around me until blood trickles down it from the lacerations on my hands. I'm breathing so hard my ears ring, and I would stumble and fall if not for the magics confining me.

I glare at Hathor. "Do something, you worthless cow. You're a bloody goddess."

She shakes her head slowly, her eyes large, her face pale. "My powers have been vanquished."

Why is Harper not fighting off Talos's power-sucking magics? She has the sword in her hand. Maybe it can't kill the bastard, but it could help her escape. Slice his head off, gain some time, get away. Maybe the wards around me and Hathor will crash down when that happens, maybe not. I don't care as long as Harper escapes.

Talos tears his mouth away from hers, breathing hard, his chest heaving. He glances around the chamber, then turns his gaze up to the ceiling where the darkest magics are swirling out of the obsidian walls and up through the roof.

He throws his head back and cackles. "The worlds shall be mine!"

"You don't have all the power yet," Harper tells him. "Take it all, I don't want it. Kill me, I don't care. I've had enough of being your pawn."

She can't mean it. She wants to give him all the magics inside her? That would grant him unimaginable power and turn two worlds into a playground for the fae lord. This must be part of a plan. But what does she mean to do? Why hasn't she chopped his bloody head off? It might not kill him, but it would give us more time to figure out how to get rid of him.

Harper slides one arm around Talos's midsection and presses her open mouth to his.

She still holds the sword in the other hand.

Magics flood out of her into him, through him, rocketing in all directions and out of the palace to devastate the Unseen.

I beat the ward with my fists, blood trickling down the barrier, and roar.

Harper's eyes are still open. She swivels her gaze to me.

My hand throbs, and I realize it's the fire obsidian stone causing the sensation. I'd forgotten I was holding it. The telepathic bond between us has weakened somewhat, but I clasp the stone tighter and funnel its power through me, down the invisible line that connects us, and straight into Harper.

Too late, she murmurs in my mind. *Have to do this.*

A chill crackles through me, as hard and cold as a block of solid ice. I still have no idea what she means to do, but an intuition warns me she doesn't care what she must sacrifice to stop Talos.

Harper raises the sword behind the fae lord, holding it with the blade sticking out from the bottom of her fist, aimed toward Talos's back.

And she plunges it into him, to the hilt.

Her body jerks. She freezes, still clutching the sword.

Talos tears his mouth away from hers, his eyes bulging, his mouth gaping. He gasps, wheezes, splutters, but does not move away from her. He arches his back as if he's trying to get away but something prevents it. The fae lord claws at his chest, which remains plastered to Harper's body.

Blood spreads across his chest—and hers.

It must be his blood. He won't let go of her, so she's getting his blood on her. Why doesn't she get away from him?

She tugs on our connection, wanting more power from me. I open the floodgates and send a torrent of magics to her, not giving a toss if I exhaust myself to the point of death. She needs it, and I give it. To rid the worlds of Talos, I will sacrifice anything.

Except for Harper.

Her hair lifts away from her shoulders, rising higher and higher as if a massive amount of static electricity courses through her, around her, inside her. The surrounding air begins to coruscate with black sparks, then it transmutes into a shower of multicolored particles, and finally, it transforms into pure white.

Talos screams, his back arched as far as possible while he remains glued to Harper.

I've never heard any being scream with the depth of agony and sheer fury that's coming out of Talos.

His body ripples as if it's become liquid.

And still, Harper does not move.

I shout her name, but she stays as motionless as a statue, not even blinking.

The body of Talos, lord of the obsidian fae, dissolves and splashes onto the floor in a puddle of glimmering darkness. The liquid siphons away into…wherever the remains of someone like him go. The remnants of his powers, the essence of his obsidian soul, appear as a mist that fizzles out amid a cloud of snapping sparks. He is gone, forever.

But Harper still hasn't moved.

And suddenly, I see why.

The sword she had driven straight through Talos's emaciated body is wedged in her chest.

"No!" I roar as the wards around me and Hathor come crashing down.

I race to Harper, falling to my knees beside her, my breaths sharp and short and my ears ringing again.

Blood has soaked her shirt and her hands, which are coiled around the blade. Her face has gone paler than ever, as pallid as death itself.

"No, Harper." I brace her body with my arm around her shoulders. "I'll get the sword out, and you'll be fine. Don't worry." I brush sweat-soaked hair away from her face. "We'll get you to a vortex. You're strong and healthy, so it will work."

She turns her head in slow motion and looks at me. "Too late."

I shake my head, but I can't see anything. My surroundings have become blurry. Only when a salty tang seeps between my lips do I realize tears are running down my cheeks. I keep my arm around her while I grasp the sword's blade and pull. It won't come free. Won't budge at all.

"Dammit," I snarl. "Hathor, get over here and hold her so I can—get the bloody thing—"

Hathor rushes to us, dropping to her knees behind Harper. She wriggles closer until Harper's back is flush with her front, and then she grasps Harper's shoulders.

"No," Harper says, her voice weak. "Stop, Max. It's over."

"It is not fucking over."

Moving in front of her, I grasp the sword's hilt and pull, careful not to pull too hard. The blade slides out little by little.

Harper's face contorts with pain.

I get the blade free and hurl the sword away. It whacks down on the obsidian floor and spins away from me.

Harper sags against Hathor, and a breath gusts out of her, seeming to deflate her entire body.

The walls begin to shiver, their many colors coruscating and throbbing. I hear throbbing too as if this palace is a living thing struggling to survive without its master. Its heartbeat grows erratic as the shuddering in the walls spreads into the ceiling and the floor, convulsing the edifice from the inside out.

I don't give a damn about any of that.

Hathor shakes her head at me, her eyes glistening with tears.

"Do something," I shout. "You're a sodding goddess."

"I can't." She swallows visibly, her lips trembling. "I am powerless."

The wards protecting the palace shatter with explosive force—the real kind that detonates with deafening volume.

And the entire structure evaporates.

We crouch inside a clearing in the woods.

I scuttle toward Harper on my knees and drag her away from Hathor, cradling her to me with her head on my chest. I cup her face in my hand. "I'm getting you to a vortex."

"Won't work," she croaks.

"You don't know that. Hold on, love, hold on for me."

"Sorry, I can't."

Though she spoke the word sorry, it triggers only the barest thread of a debt between us.

Harper raises her trembling hand to touch my lips. "This isn't your fault. I did what I had to do. Someday, I hope you can forgive me."

"Forgive you? I love you, Harper."

Tears roll down her cheeks. "I love you too."

"You can't leave me, not now, not after—You just can't."

Hathor lays a hand on my arm. "Max—"

I shake her hand off and glower at her. "Leave off. Why are you still here, anyway? If you have no powers, I have no sodding use for you."

She squeezes my shoulder, a single tear painting a trail down her cheek, and then she vanishes.

"Let me go," Harper says, her eyes half-closed, her lips almost blue.

"No."

"You have to, Max." Her hand falls away from my face, hanging limp, her fingers grazing the ground. "You made me feel like I belong somewhere. You cared about me when no one else did, and you did everything you could to protect me. When I needed the power of your elemental fire, you gave it all to me. We saved the worlds, but you can't save me. This was my destiny since before I was born."

"That's rot. We found each other so I could lose you? What kind of sick joke is that?"

"I don't regret any of it. I got to love you and be loved by you, and that's all I ever needed. Thank you, Max."

Her gratitude invokes a debt between us, one strong enough to pull a thread of magic taut between our souls. Is it enough to save her?

A realization slams through me. There is a way to save her. I've done it before, and I can do it again. But I swore I never would. It's wrong to forge another being without their consent. Who cares about right or wrong? Harper can hate me after I've done this, but at least she'll be alive.

"No, Max," she says, her voice cracking. "Don't do it."

"Hush, love, it will be all right. I can fix this."

I raise my hands over her body, palms down, and chant in the old language.

She shakes her head weakly. "It won't work. You gave me so much of your magics to stop Talos that you don't have enough left to forge me. I don't want that, anyway. You have to let me go, Max."

I struggle to my feet while holding her in my arms. "Stop talking like you're dying. It's not going to happen. I forbid you to give up."

Her eyes drift closed. "I never could follow orders."

"Don't fall asleep. Stay with me. You owe me a debt, so repay it by surviving."

She doesn't respond. Her breathing is so shallow I can barely detect it.

I whisk us to the portal, activate it, and rush through it into the cave behind the falls in the mortal realm.

Harper lies limp in my arms, her head lolling backward over my elbow.

"No," I snarl, and I leap through the falls, flying us to the vortex.

We're both dripping wet when I kneel to lay her down in the center of the grassy area that houses the healing vortex.

She just lies there. Still. Barely breathing.

I throw my head back and bellow, "Tris!"

Nothing.

"Triskaideka, get your sodding arse out here before I raze the entire multiverse to find you!"

A figure appears on the other side of Harper.

The young woman has red hair and a freckled face, like Tris. "My brother's unavailable. I'm Pendi, the temporary guardian of the vortex."

I stab a finger into the air toward the woman. "Then *you* do it. Power up the vortex and save her."

She bites her upper lip and crouches beside Harper, studying her. When Pendi turns her gaze up to me, the pity on her face slices into me like a thousand tiny blades. "I wish I could, but it's too late. She's gone."

"But the vortex heals dead people. I know it does. Lindsey told me—"

"That was different." Pendi rises, her expression pained. "Tris healed a guy who's head got severed, but his soul was intact. There's nothing left inside this girl that I can heal. Whatever wicked nasty magics did this to her, they drained everything from her body. As far as I can tell, her soul is gone."

"Get it back."

Pendi bunches her shoulders, spreading her hands. "I don't have that kind of power."

I kneel beside Harper, gazing at her beautiful face, so peaceful in...death.

And I plow my fist into the ground. Earth and grass spray up and rain down around us.

"Wish I could do something," Pendi says. "If she has family, you might want to take her to them."

"She has no one except me."

Pendi reaches across Harper's body to touch my arm. "You must know what she would want. Give her the final rites she deserves."

Final rites? No, I can't do it.

"You have my heartfelt condolences," Pendi says, and she disappears.

I stare at Harper.

The sun sets, bringing the chill of night, but still, I can't look away from her face.

Why is she gone? Why did we go through all that suffering, risk our lives to find the obsidian fae, if this was how it would end?

You are so young, salamander, and so innocent in the ways of destiny.

Ken the useless oracle had told me that. I want to hunt the tosser down and rip his head from his body.

Harper wouldn't want me to do that.

But I can do something. I must do something.

I pick her up and rush to the falls, piercing the cascade and pausing for only a second to open the portal. Then I rush through that as well, too fast, bursting out with so much force that I lose my hold on Harper and tumble across the ground over and over and over, finally smacking into a tree. It hits hard enough that the tree leans over, its roots pulled out partway.

Cursing, I run to Harper and gently pick her up.

And I'm off again, aiming for the Temple of the Four Winds. I've been there once before, with Lindsey, but I've never tried to target it on my own. I pop out inside a clearing with a stream running through it.

"Sod it!" I roar, taking off again.

This time I come out on top of a high cliff overlooking a forest I don't recognize. A harpy flies past me in bird form, shrieking her displeasure that I've invaded her domain.

I hurtle us away.

And wind up inside a cave in which a gnome squats by a fire, eating meat off a bone that looks humanoid.

Hurtling again. Hitting more places that aren't anywhere I want to be. Why can't I do this? The only time I've had trouble with teleporting was when the hunger had gotten too strong. But I'm not starved now. I need to concentrate, but my thoughts are like raindrops in a tempest, whipped around so wildly that I can't catch them.

The last time this happened, Harper had calmed me.

She can't do that now.

I emerge under an enormous tree, the branches of which sag almost to the ground, forming a cocoon around me. Around *us*. Harper is not gone yet. I don't care what that leprechaun said. Cradling her to me, I rock slowly and kiss her hair. Her body still feels warm and soft, not cold and stiff like mortals do when they've passed the point of no return. I'd felt that icy stiffness when Aurelia died.

Failed another woman, haven't you? Worthless sack of pheromones, that's what you are.

I hug Harper closer, my face buried in her hair.

My pounding heart slows its frenetic pace. My breathing evens out, letting me take several careful, deep breaths. I feel…calmer.

She can't be dead. I wouldn't feel better holding her if she were.

"You're here with me," I murmur into her hair. "I can feel it."

I raise my head, shut my eyes, and focus.

The trip takes a few nanoseconds longer than it would if I were traveling anywhere else, but I've arrived. At last. I succeeded in reaching the Temple of the Four Winds. In fact, I've set us down on the portico right in front of the massive wooden double doors.

Fog shrouds the entire temple, masking the steep steps that lead up to the portico and the mountaintop itself. The temple's white stone structure seems paler this time as if the Four Winds have sensed what's happened and mourn the loss.

But I haven't lost her. Not yet.

The Four Winds have let me through their wards, so they must want to help me.

With a grinding noise that vibrates my eardrums and every bone in my body, the great doors creep inward. It's all the invitation I'll receive.

As I carry Harper through the doorway, a tepid breeze explores me with its invisible fingertips as if examining me for foul magics or judging if I'm worthy. The breeze dissipates, and I walk inside, so I assume I've passed the test. Last time I visited this place, I'd been on fire from head to toe, overwhelmed by dark magics I'd ingested to protect Lindsey.

I lay Harper down on the cold white floor.

A single being appears, floating slightly above the floor. Her flowing robes drag on the stone beneath her. A breeze I don't feel tousles her white hair, and she aims her glossy black eyes at me.

"I know why you have come, salamander," she says in her ethereal voice. "But I'm afraid there is nothing we can do."

"But you saved me once before. You even helped Lindsey spare the soul of her former lover, despite the fact he tried to kill her. Harper doesn't deserve to die. She saved both worlds from Talos and his minions."

"Indeed she did. But alas, we can do nothing for her."

"Please." I don't care if speaking that word indebts me to this being if it convinces her to save Harper. I drop to my knees. "Please do something."

"You are fortunate that no debt can be incurred in this temple." She floats closer and gazes down at Harper. "It is beyond our powers."

"What? I thought you lot were the most powerful beings in the Unseen."

"Not quite. There are other powers greater than the Four Winds." She floats backward, retreating toward the shadowy recesses of the temple. As she recedes from view, she says, "Trust in yourself, salamander."

For a long time, I crouch there, numb and frozen. Maybe hours pass, maybe days, maybe even centuries. No, it can't be that long. Harper lies there looking as peaceful and lovely as ever.

But she's dead.

I draw her into my arms and head for the mortal world, barely noticing the trip through the portal. The second I exit the falls, I transport us to the only place I have left to go.

Lindsey jumps and yelps when I materialize right in front of her in the living room of the home she shares with Nevan. He's reclining across the length of the sofa, his shirt unbuttoned. Lindsey is straddling his lap, her fingers still holding the button she's just unhooked on his trousers.

"Don't you ever knock?" Nevan asks.

Then they both notice Harper, the way she's limp and pale, her head hanging backward, her eyes closed.

"Oh God," Lindsey says, scrambling to get off her husband.

Nevan helps her stand up.

Lindsey rushes to me, her expression so full of empathy and sorrow that my throat constricts and lays a hand on my arm. "Max, I—What happened? Is she..."

"Dead." My voice sounds dead too. Everything inside me has gone still and cold. "The vortex didn't work. The Four Winds won't help. It's over, and I've lost her."

"I'm so sorry."

And I know she means that. It's not simply a platitude. More than anyone else, she understands loss. But I can't let her commiserate with me now. Can't think about what's happened yet.

I push my arms out, thrusting Harper at Lindsey. "Take her. She needs to have a proper…whatever mortals do with the…you know what I mean."

"Yes, I do."

"I'll take her," Nevan says.

Lindsey steps aside, and her husband gently transfers Harper into his arms.

"Don't leave, Max," Lindsey says. She grasps my arm. "You shouldn't be alone, and you'll want to be here when we lay her to rest. Does she have family?"

"None that ever wanted her. I'm all she had."

"She has all of us now, and we'll take good care of her." Lindsey throws her arms around me. "Promise me you'll stay."

My gaze veers to Harper, cradled in Nevan's arms. "I've done enough damage to the women I loved."

Before either of them can speak, I whisk away.

CHAPTER THIRTY-ONE

Harper

WHERE AM I? NOT IN MY BODY, THAT'S FOR SURE. I REMEMBER DRIVing that sword through Talos and straight into my own chest. Yet the memory of that excruciating agony seems like something that happened in a movie instead of in reality. Anything to stop Talos, that had been my mantra. Now I'm floating around like a ghost, observing life from a disconnected vantage.

Am I dead?

If so, this is not the afterlife I'd hoped for. I've been dragged here, there, and everywhere in the Unseen and now in the mortal world. Max and I formed a deep connection, even a telepathic one, but this is not heaven in any sense of the word. I've watched, helpless, while the man I love carried my body in his arms and tried to bring me back to life. He even tried to forge me. I must be dead, right? Why else would Max do that? I see his grief, but I feel disconnected from it. He has sunk deep into the loss and piled on more of that self-loathing he believes he deserves.

Max asked Lindsey and Nevan to take care of my body. Now, he's leaving them.

Where is he going this time?

Since I can't stop him from dragging me around in his wake, I'll find out soon enough. Not that I want to drift anywhere else. Max had cried while I lay dying in the obsidian palace. He begged me to stay with him. I wished I could do that, but I'd known I couldn't. Even now that his outward grief has lessened, I sense the pain inside him.

He blames himself. Of course he does.

Max and I hurry back to the portal and cross over to the Unseen, then he goes back to his lair. He sits in one of those big chairs and gazes straight ahead at nothing, his shoulders slumped and his face ashen beneath the surface bronzing. His eyes glisten with new tears, but he sucks in a breath through his nostrils and rubs the moisture away with the heels of his hands.

"Bollocks," he says, and his voice hitches on that word.

I want to fold my arms around him and kiss away the pain. Instead, I'm forced to float above him. Damn, I wish I could figure out how to float just above the floor rather than six feet overhead.

Soon I'll be six feet under.

Am I really dead? I don't feel like I am, but nothing else explains the fact that I'm floating overhead and following my lover who can't see or hear me.

When Max was bouncing around the Unseen, struggling to target his teleportation to that big white building in the clouds, I had tried to make him hear me. I screamed as loud and as long as I could. He never noticed. And since my throat didn't hurt after all that screaming, I decided that must mean I'm dead.

Yet I still don't feel dead.

How would that feel, anyway? It's one of those things you have to experience to understand, I imagine. Will I move on eventually and go into the afterlife? Heaven or whatever it is. I don't want to move on. I want to stay with Max forever.

We just found each other. I haven't known him long, but already I love him. Why didn't I realize that until I lay dying in Max's arms? At least I'd told him. To die knowing Max never realized how I feel about him would be eternal torture.

Max jerks forward, his elbows on his knees, and lets his face fall into his raised palms. "Why did you have to do that, Harper? Living as a slave to Talos would've been fine with me as long as I had you."

No, he wouldn't have wanted that. He'd been a slave to a Roman emperor, a slave to an evil sorcerer, and a slave to the goddess Hathor. He needed freedom. If my death spared him from a new enslavement, I'm glad I died.

I manage to float down a little bit, just enough to stretch my hand out and pretend I can touch the top of his head. "I'm here, Max. Things will get better, trust me. It'll take time is all."

He bows his head even further, stabbing his fingers into his hair. "I can't do this alone."

Can't do what? I need to ask him, but I have no voice.

Rising, Max zips away again, towing me along behind him.

We emerge inside a small clearing full of beautiful flowers unlike anything in the mortal world. The purple blossoms are huge, and they glitter with flecks of copper. Above us, the sun burns in the sapphire sky.

Max squats on a boulder. He opens his palm and conjures...

A gun.

Has he found an endued weapon? Please no. I can't explain why, but I'm positive that pistol is endued and that he plans to use it on himself.

"No, Max, don't do it. For me, please, don't."

He raises the gun to his temple and squeezes his eyes shut.

"Stop, Max, please," I shout, though he can't hear me.

Maybe I can contact him telepathically. Why didn't I think of that earlier? Distracted by dying, I guess.

He drops the gun. It thumps onto the ground.

And he cries. His shoulders shake. He stumbles away from the boulder and collapses on the ground amid the beautiful flowers.

I gaze down at him and try to float closer, but I can't do it. So I position my floaty self directly over him. Time to try telepathy. I look at him, though he has his eyes closed, and do my damnedest to beam my thoughts straight into his stubborn mind.

Hear me, Max, please.

Focusing every ounce of energy I have on the task, I urge him to see and feel my presence.

Nothing happens.

I love you, Max. I'm here, I'm okay, it's not your fault I'm gone.

His eyes flutter open. He gazes up at me, though I'm not sure he sees me.

If I can't make him hear or see me, maybe I can at least help him feel better and make sure he never tries to hurt himself. Do elementals have an afterlife? Will I go to the same place where he goes?

Max gazes up at me like he sees…something. Or maybe senses something. "I want to believe you're all right, but I can't do anything except miss you."

"I miss you too."

"Please come back to me, Harper." He exhales a long sigh, his entire body sagging. "You can't, though, can you?"

"Don't give up on me."

Can he hear me? No idea. But I feel something coming down that telepathic link between us. It's faint at first but grows stronger and stronger until a wave of warmth floods through me. I know what this feeling is.

It's love. Deep, undying love.

"Why did you have to leave me?" Max asks.

"Oh Max, I'll always be with you."

He pushes himself up into a sitting position, bowing his head. "You wouldn't want me to destroy myself, so for you, I'll try to find a way to stay alive. Actually living might be impossible, but I won't do what I just considered doing."

Thank God. Relief rushes through me, and I desperately want to hug him and kiss him and go back to his lair so we can have sex for hours and hours. I'll never get to do that again, will I? No more kissing Max. No more lying in his arms.

I still don't feel dead, but then, I have no idea what that feels like. I'm probably in denial. Soon, I'll accept my fate. Won't I?

Something tugs at me.

Max gets up and rubs his neck, his head still down.

Tug, tug, tug. I know some force is determined to drag me away from Max, but I don't want to go. Not yet. If that force intends to haul me off to heaven, it will have to wait. I need to keep an eye on Max for a while, until I'm one hundred percent positive he won't do anything rash.

He sighs and disappears.

Two forces yank me—one trying to drag me after Max, the other trying to haul me somewhere else. I fight the pull that wants to take me away from Max, fight it so hard my head hurts. How can my head hurt when I have no body? Screw the answer. I keep battling that pull even while everything inside me throbs with gut-wrenching pain.

I lose the battle.

That force yanks me away from the world and slams me into a dark place.

A thumping noise, soft at first, grows louder. A breeze whispers around me in a regular rhythm while that thumping becomes regular too. I see a faint glow, nothing more than a pinpoint, but it gradually widens until the glow fills my vision.

"She's breathing," a voice says.

Who is that? Not Max. Where am I? God, I hope I haven't been abducted by evil creatures from the Unseen again. Will it be granite fae this time? Evil creatures from the Unseen. That sounds like a great title for a nineteen fifties horror movie.

"Harper," that voice says, "take slow, deep breaths. Easy, don't rush it."

The being who speaks to me is female, I think.

"Good," she says in a soothing voice. "That's right, breathe slowly. Open your eyes whenever you're ready. No rush, but we are excited to meet you."

Her words of encouragement give me the boost I need to do exactly that. I peel my lids apart little by little, and it seems to take hours before my eyes are fully open. Light surrounds me, the glow of it so bright I squint for a while before I can see anything.

I'm lying on a bed. Inside a room I don't recognize.

A pregnant woman and a muscular man stand beside the bed, watching me with expectant looks.

"Harper, how do you feel?" the woman asks.

"Okay, I think." I push up on my elbows. "Where am I? And who are you?"

The woman sits down on the edge of the bed near my feet. "I'm Lindsey O'Rourke, and this is my husband, Nevan."

Her husband moves to stand beside her. He settles a hand on her shoulder.

Lindsey. Nevan. I remember Max mentioned them.

I clear my throat, which suddenly feels dry and scratchy. "Could I get some water, please?"

As soon as I speak the word please, I realize I might have made a big mistake. Is this the mortal world or the Unseen? I don't even know if these two are the same Nevan and Lindsey that Max mentioned.

"I'll get that water," Nevan says in an Irish accent. "Lindsey will help you get acclimated."

Nevan leaves the room, and Lindsey scoots a little closer to me. "How are you feeling? You can stay lying down if you need to."

"No, I'd rather sit up." And I do that, shimmying backward until I'm leaning against the headboard. "Um, what happened?"

She bites her lip for a moment before answering. "We thought you were dead, sweetie. No pulse, no breathing, nothing. But you didn't feel cold and stiff, which made us wonder. So we took you to one of our elemental friends, Ennea."

"I met her. She's a fae witch."

"That's right. She believes with all her heart that you and Max are fated for each other. Ennea determined that you were not dead, so we brought you back to our home where we've been watching over you and waiting for you to wake up." Lindsey clasps her hands on her lap, eying me like she's worried about how I'll react to the rest of what she needs to tell me. "How long does it seem like you were asleep?"

Nevan returns with a glass of water, handing it to me.

I sip the water and say, "Must've been out for a day or so. I had an out-of-body experience, I guess. Something tied me to Max, and he was dragging me all over creation."

"Uh-huh." Lindsey exchanges a glance with her husband, then gives me that funny hesitant look again. "Sweetie, you were out for five weeks."

I stare at her without blinking for so long that my eyes start to burn. Then I blink furiously, struggling to comprehend the meaning of her words. Five weeks? No, I just left Max—and he'd just left me with two people who looked a lot like Nevan and Lindsey. My astral vision or whatever it was had been a little hazy the first time I saw them.

A phone rings elsewhere in the house, and Nevan trots off to answer it.

"No, it can't be that long," I say to Lindsey. "I destroyed Talos yesterday."

Lindsey shakes her head. "Five weeks have gone by. You were like Sleeping Beauty, seeming dead but not really gone. Pendi, Ennea's sister who's in charge of the healing vortex, thought your soul was gone, but Ennea knows more about that stuff. And she said your soul had left your body but was still tethered to it. Do you have any idea what woke you up? It wasn't a kiss from Prince Charming, I'm sure."

"I don't know." My thoughts rewind to when I floated above Max in that beautiful little clearing. "I kept trying to make Max hear me, and I thought maybe he did, subconsciously. Then something forced me to come back here."

Lindsey gives me a knowing smile. "Maybe it was a kiss from your Prince Charming after all. The supernatural kind."

I had felt a rush of warm, sweet love right after Max begged me to come back to him and I swore I'd try. Could that have been the telepathic kiss that woke me from my death-like slumber? But that couldn't have happened five weeks ago.

"Where is Max?" I ask.

Lindsey's smile fades. "We don't know. Everyone's been looking for him, but even the oracles are having no luck."

"Does that mean he's...gone?" I can't make myself speak the word destroyed. If he conjured another endued weapon...

She lays her hand over mine on my thigh. "No, sweetie, he's not dead. We can tell that much. Travis swears he can sense Max is out there somewhere, and the oracles agree." She rubs her forehead and sighs. "But somehow, he's camouflaging himself from everyone. Even Hathor tried, but she couldn't find him either."

"Hathor? She probably wants to ensorcell him again."

"I don't think so," Lindsey says. "She seemed genuinely concerned."

Worrying about Hathor can wait. Right now, I need to track Max down. "Maybe I can find him. We have a telepathic connection."

"Do you? Wish I had that with Nevan so I could stop him from buying the wrong kind of toilet paper. He always picks the absolute cheapest one that's like sandpaper. Who knew a former sylph king would be such a cheapskate?"

Yeah, that's slightly more info than I needed about these people.

"Nevan won't let me go to the store with him," Lindsey says. "He thinks being pregnant means I can't walk anymore."

"Uh-huh."

She pats my hand. "Sorry, I'm babbling. What can I do to help you find Max?"

"I think I need to do this on my own."

"Sure, but maybe you should eat something first."

"Good idea. I am really hungry all of a sudden."

"Do you feel like you can walk?"

"I think so."

Lindsey stands and offers me her hands while I slide off the bed and get to my feet. I take her hands because my legs feel a little shaky. After standing there for a minute, I feel the shakiness fading away. I take a few steps, still holding on to Lindsey's hands, but I have no problems with it now.

"I can walk on my own," I say.

"Let's go to the kitchen, then."

She leads me there, though not while holding my hand, and tells me to sit down at the table. I watch her prepare scrambled eggs, bacon, and toast for me. I offer to help since I feel weird letting a very pregnant woman cook for me, but she dismisses the idea. We chat while she whips up my food, and we laugh a lot. She recounts all the humorous moments she's had with Max, including how they met, but things get more serious when she relates the story of the two times they saved the worlds together.

Max and I saved the worlds too.

I need to find him, but Lindsey has a point about my need to eat. When she sets a plate and a big glass of orange juice in front of me, I gobble it up in record time. No food has ever tasted this good. I'm still hungry, so she gets a dozen blueberry muffins out of the freezer and thaws them in the microwave for me.

And I gobble those up too, all twelve of them, along with a big glass of milk.

"Wow, you weren't kidding," Lindsey says, watching me from across the table while I wolf down the last muffin. "You really are starving."

Full at last, I lean back in my chair. "Guess almost dying really took it out of me."

She gives me that oddly wary look again. "Um, you were actually dead, Harper. Your soul hadn't moved on, and something weird was going on inside you, but you were definitely not among the living anymore."

"That's impossible. I was in a coma or something."

"Afraid not."

I open my mouth, but it takes a few seconds before I can summon any words. "What do you mean something weird was going on inside me?"

"Nobody could explain it or decide what it was. Some kind of wonky energy was hiding inside you, keeping you from crossing over. You were deceased but not dead-dead."

"Sure, that makes sense."

Wonky energy? Yeah, total sense.

Nevan marches into the kitchen, straight to Lindsey, and picks her up.

"What are you doing?" she asks. "We can have sex later, honey. I'm busy helping Harper."

"You're about to go into labor," he informs her. "Bob called to tell us so. I've put your bag in the car."

"Oh." She glances at me. "I guess we need to split. Nevan insists I have this baby in a hospital with doctors and nurses there to fuss over me."

"It's okay," I tell her. "Don't worry about me and Max. I'll find him."

"You'll need an elemental to take you through the portal. Max obviously doesn't want to be found."

"Go pop out your rug rat. Let me worry about the stubborn salamander."

Nevan rushes his wife out of the house.

He rushes back in a minute later, rips a drawer open, and seizes a pair of keys. Tossing them to me, he says, "Take our truck. Lindsey insists. We're taking the car. All you need to do is turn left out of the driveway until you reach the first intersection, then turn right. That'll take you straight to the rock shop."

"Thanks."

Nevan dashes out again.

A moment later, I hear a car engine rev up, followed by the sound of tires rolling down a gravel driveway.

Time to find Max.

I drive their big, brand-new pickup to the shop and park badly, since I don't give a hoot about the parking laws right now. Somebody beeped at me when I swerved into the entrance to the parking lot, but I ignored it. I fling the door open without bothering to shut it again and sprint up the hill, through the rock garden, and down the trail to the falls.

Though I'm breathing hard, I don't pause to catch my breath. I climb over the wooden railing around the falls and the pool below it, then I clamber onto the rock ledge to sidle over to the cave entrance. Without a second's hesitation, I leap through the cascade into the cave.

How do I open a portal? Maybe I should shout for an elemental, but an instinct inside me takes over, and I heed it.

Moving closer to the rear wall of the cave, I raise my palm.

The portal telescopes open.

How did I do that? No idea. All I know at this moment is that I need to hunt down Max.

I dive into the portal.

Chapter Thirty-Two

Max

I'M LYING ON MY BACK IN THE GRASS, SURROUNDED BY FLOWERS THE color of Harper's hair, staring up at the sapphire sky that's almost the same color as Harper's eyes. A few clouds roll by. Birds make noise in the trees. I've never enjoyed the sound of birds, not here or in the mortal world. Their noises are incredibly annoying. Today, I find it even more irritating, though I can't explain why. Oh yes I can. Everything annoys me because my life sucks, as Lindsey would say, and it will go on sucking until the universe implodes.

When you have nothing to live for, immortality bites the big one.

But I'm still not sure what "big one" that phrase references. I learned it from Lindsey, and all she told me was that "it means something is really, really awful." Well, that's my existence now. Awful. Monumentally awful.

For weeks, I've hidden anywhere and everywhere I could hide to keep my friends from finding me. They want to "help," which means driving me insane with one of two activities—commiserating with me while talking about Harper or trying to cheer me up while talking about Harper. Neither option holds any appeal for me.

I destroyed her. Maybe I hadn't forged her, because I couldn't, but I had killed her as surely as I had destroyed Aurelia. Maybe I'm cursed. Or maybe I just suck the big one.

No, it's *bite* the big one. Christ, I can't even curse myself properly.

Shutting my eyes, I let the sun scorch me. If I stay like this, maybe the sun will burn me to a crisp and the wind will scatter the charred bits of me into outer space.

"Max, wake up. It's me."

Oh, merda. I'm hearing things again. Hearing *her* voice. Will these bloody hallucinations never end?

"Go away," I mutter.

"I kind of thought you'd be happy to see me." The hallucination of Harper makes an irritated noise. "Open your damn eyes, Max. I rose from the dead or whatever so I could track you down. We're supposed to have a big reunion with lots of kissing and, preferably, lots and lots of sex. And you tell me to go away? Sheesh, I should've stayed comatose."

"Not talking to you. After a few minutes, you'll disappear."

"Dammit, you dragged me around like a ghost chained to your sorry ass for five weeks. The least you could do is look at me before you tell me to leave."

This is by far the most vivid and bloody aggravating hallucination I've ever had.

I crack one eye open.

Harper stands there with her hands on her hips, fingers drumming, lips puckered. "Well? Got anything to say besides, 'go away'?"

"You're a mirage. I no longer speak to people who don't exist."

"I am not a mirage, you pigheaded salamander."

"Don't think 'pigheaded' is an appropriate slur to use against a salamander. Maybe I'm salamander-headed."

"Ugh." She throws her hands up. "You are the most frustrating, arrogant, salamander-headed ass on the planet. Any planet."

The vehemence in her words spurs me to open both eyes.

My hallucination of Harper stalks up to me, bending from the waist to stare into my eyes. "What do I have to do to convince you I'm not a mirage?"

"Not sure it's possible to prove that."

She kicks my leg. "Get up. Now. That's an order."

By the gods, this is a bizarre hallucination, even for me.

I push up into a sitting position, yawn, and get to my feet. Stretching my entire body, I yawn again. "I hate it when mirages interrupt my naps."

The illusory Harper grasps my face, hoists herself up on her tiptoes, and crushes her mouth to mine. This feels…amazingly realistic. Her lips are warm and yielding but demanding at the same time. She licks at the seam of my mouth, and my cock jerks as if the real Harper is pasted to my body. And she smells like Harper too. Feels like Harper. I push my tongue between her lips, and she tastes like Harper too.

She pulls away but stays on her tiptoes, sliding her hands down to my shoulders. "Believe me now?"

"I—" Gazing into those lapis-blue eyes, I want to believe it. I need her to be here, to be real, but my mind can't quite accept it might be true. "But you can't be here. You died in my arms. The vortex didn't work. I couldn't forge you. Harper Goode is dead."

"Maybe I'm not exactly like I was before, but I am real. I am me." She touches her lips to mine again, though only for a heartbeat. "It's me, Max. I came back for you."

"Why?" I sound as baffled as I feel because I don't get second chances like this. I destroy everything I love, and I love Harper Goode.

She laughs delicately. "Why did I come back to be with you? Duh. I love you, Max. That's the only reason I need."

"I love you too, but—" I swallow but the tightness in my throat gets tighter. "This doesn't make sense."

"You still think you don't deserve love or a second chance." She grasps my face again, forcing me to look at her, though I try to turn away. "You damn well better accept it. Whether it's a miracle or fate, we've been given another chance. I'm not going to waste it, and I won't let you waste it either. Your sexy red ass belongs to me."

"My arse is only red when I'm in salamander form. I doubt that's sexy."

"Okay, maybe not. But you are adorable in lizard form, and I love every side of you." Her lips kink up on one side. "Even when you bite me while you're hiding in my bra."

I stare at her for a moment, an excruciatingly long one, while I try to reconcile my past with the future it seems we've both been gifted with for reasons I cannot fathom. She deserves everything, but I…don't. Am I really going to walk away from her because of that? Maybe the fact she's here, now, proves I've earned this second chance.

Maybe I am a stubborn arse, but I'm not that salamander-headed.

She's here. She loves me. Why am I complaining about that?

I wrap my arms around her and hoist her off the ground, spinning us around and around so fast that the world becomes a blur. She laughs and throws her head back, grinning, while I do the same. We levitate above the ground, drifting higher and higher, as high as I feel at this moment. Is it euphoria? I've never experienced that before, not without ensorcellment.

But this is real, not a sham. Harper is real and alive and in my arms.

Once we return to the ground and stop spinning, I hug her close. "How this is possible, I don't know. But I won't turn my back on it. On us. On you."

"About damn time. Thought I'd have to literally kick your ass to knock some sense into you."

"That won't be necessary." I nuzzle her cheek. "Now it's time for that kissing and shagging you mentioned earlier."

She grins.

And I kiss her.

"Better hold off on that for a minute," a male voice says.

We stop kissing but don't end our embrace. In unison, we turn our heads to the side to look at the being who has spoken.

Ken the oracle stands there, an arm's length away.

Bob the oracle stands beside him.

"What are you lot doing here?" I ask. "We're busy."

"You'll want to hear this," Ken says. "Unless you no longer want to know how Harper survived death."

I turn toward Ken, though I keep one arm around Harper. "Well, go on. Tell us."

"She was right when she said she's not exactly like she was before." Ken glances at Bob, the oracle who had once issued the Janusite prophecy. "Why don't you tell them, Bobby? You know the salamander better than I do."

"My name is Max," I say. "Not 'the salamander.' Max."

Ken rolls his eyes.

"Ignore him," Bob says. "He's just miffed that I foresaw the Janusite and he didn't."

Harper huffs. "Is anyone going to explain? Or do I need to kick your foreseeing asses?"

I do love it when she threatens violence. It makes me want to drag her back to my lair and shag her for the rest of eternity. Not that her mortal body could stand that. Unless...

"Someone had better tell us what's happened to Harper," I say. "Before I flame out and scorch both of you."

"Yes, yes," Bob says. "Here's the deal. Harper is no longer mortal."

"Well then, what in the multiverse is she?"

Ken frowns at me. "Watch your language. You're in the presence of oracles."

"Bugger off, Ken. You're a bloody annoying arse, do you know that?"

"Quiet," Bob says, his voice booming through the clearing with unnatural power.

We all shut our mouths.

"Harper is not mortal," Bob says. "She has become immortal—like you, Max. The magics inside her prevented you from forging her, so she hasn't become an elemental. But she does have elemental power. Still, she's not an elemental. She is...an immortal human with powerful magics."

"Wonderful," I say with great sarcasm. "The clears it all up, doesn't it?"

"She's immortal, Max. That means only endued weapons or magically enhanced poisons can kill her. Harper will live as long as you will, provided you two stop getting into so much trouble."

Ken shifts his gaze heavenward, shaking his head. "I don't foresee that happening anytime soon. They're just like those mortals you love to visit. They can't stop themselves from intervening when the worlds are in peril."

"Sitting idly by is not in their nature," Bob says. "Not for Max and Harper, and not for Lindsey and Nevan either. Destiny can't change who they are."

I scratch my cheek, wincing because I can't believe I'm about to discuss this with two oracles. "So, ah, if Harper is immortal, does that mean her body is, ah..."

Bob chuckles. "You two can have all the sex marathons you want. Her body can handle it now. She's a lot more durable than your average human."

I glance at Harper and grin. "Brilliant."

She bounces on her toes. "When can we get started on those marathons?"

Ken clears his throat. "You might want to tell him about Lindsey first."

The oracles vanish.

"What about Lindsey?" I ask. "Is she all right?"

"Sorry, I forgot. Lindsey is in labor."

"Why is she doing bloody housework? She's pregnant."

Harper clamps her teeth down on both her lips, snorting while she tries not to laugh. "No, Max, being in labor means she's about to have that baby any minute. Nevan took her to the hospital."

"You've met Lindsey and Nevan?"

"Sure. You gave my body to them, remember?"

Bugger. I'd almost forgotten about that. Harper's miraculous return distracted me from everything else in the multiverse.

"I, uh, didn't mean to abandon you," I say. "But I thought you were…no longer living."

"Yeah, you thought I kicked the bucket. I know." She moves in front of me and clasps both my hands. "Let's zip on over to the mortal world so you can meet Lindsey and Nevan's kid."

"All right." I tug her hands to make her move closer. "But as soon as we do that, we're whisking ourselves straight to my lair."

"Can't wait for that."

I study her for a moment, wondering how much her resurrection has changed her. "Can you teleport now?"

"Yeah," she says like I've asked a stupid question. "How else did you think I got here? Took me three hours to figure out how the zipping thing works, but I've got it now. I can open a portal on my own too."

"Not sure that's a good thing. I might wind up chasing you all over both worlds to keep you out of trouble." A sobering thought occurs to me, and I ask, "Can you cross the boundaries in the mortal world? The hospital is outside of them."

Ken flashes into view beside us. "Yes, she can. Forgot to mention that before. She's immune to the boundary magics, just like you. Adios."

He flashes out again.

I don't understand how or why Harper is immune to boundaries, but I don't give a toss. We can go anywhere we like, together. That's all I need to know.

Throwing my arms around Harper, I take us to the portal. We step through it, and I transport us directly into the hallway of the hospital where Lindsey and Nevan had told me they would go when the time came. It's come. Today.

Maybe I'm not a blood relation, but I still feel like I'm about to become an uncle or…something. I've glamoured into a more mortal-friendly appearance. And yes, I conjured clothing for myself. I even conjured those awful shoes.

When we get to the hospital, Nevan meets us in the cramped room where a nurse told us to wait. He says we can't see Lindsey until after the baby is born. That might take hours or days. He orders us to stay here in this dreary little waiting room. I become fixated on the clock on the wall, with its tiny arms that tick off the seconds and minutes—and hours. I stop counting after the twelfth complete revolution of the minute hand. Why do mortals refer to those little arms on the clock as hands? They look nothing like that. Hands have fingers.

I tell Harper that, and she grabs my arm to drag me down onto the chair beside her. "You have a bad habit of being too literal, Max."

"But those appendages on the clock resemble arms, not hands."

"Stop trying to make logic where there isn't supposed to be any."

Grumbling, I do exactly that. I stop trying to understand mortals. It's pointless, isn't it? They're all insane.

Finally, Nevan comes out to inform us the baby has arrived.

We follow him to Lindsey's room, where she's reclining on a bed in a semi-upright position. Nevan perches on the bed's edge beside her. She holds a newborn child in her arms.

They both look happier than I've ever seen them.

Babies are much smaller than I remember, but then, I haven't seen a human infant in over two thousand years.

Lindsey waves for us to move closer. "Come on in. You guys missed the main event, but the after-party is still going."

I hold Harper's hand as we cross the threshold and go around to the opposite side of the bed from where Nevan sits.

Lindsey smiles at me. "This is our son, Max."

"Have you named him yet?"

"Yes," she says with a laugh. "His name is Max."

My mouth drops open, but I can't speak. She named her child after me? Why?

Lindsey offers me the baby, who's swaddled in a blanket. "Here. Hold him."

"No, I…can't. What if I break him?"

"You won't."

I accept the child, cradling him the way I'd seen Lindsey doing a moment ago. The tiny boy looks up at me, his blue eyes pale and luminous. He has Lindsey's eyes but Nevan's dark hair. The nose looks like a combination of the two.

"This will get bloody confusing," I say, "if your child has my name. How will little Max know you're shouting at him and not me?"

"His middle name is Max," Nevan says. "The first name is Liam."

Even giving their child my name as the middle one makes me feel oddly anxious.

"We want you to be Liam's godfather," Lindsey says.

"Me? Why?" Did I say that out loud? Bollocks, I did. "What is a godfather? The only reference I'm familiar with is that ridiculous film about men who shout a lot and cut off the heads of large animals. Tris made me watch it once."

Lindsey laughs. "I'm talking about a different kind of godfather. We want you to be Liam's guardian, sort of like an honorary uncle."

"Oh." I gaze down at the child in my arms, feeling a strange heaviness in my chest. I'm meant to care for this child as if he is my family. As if his parents are my family. "I'll do my best not to disappoint you."

"You could never disappoint me, Max."

I hand the child back to his mother.

Lindsey and Nevan are, I suppose, the closest approximation to a family that I've had since the day I died and became an incubus. But they're not all I have anymore. Now I have Harper too—and that irritating little leprechaun, Tris, as well as his less irritating sister, Ennea. Should I count Janus as part of my surrogate family? I can't quite bring myself to do that. The bloke still annoys me endlessly.

As if he heard my thoughts, Janus appears near the foot of the bed. He looks at the baby Lindsey holds, and then he does something that stuns me so badly my mouth falls open—so far that I feel a draft coming in.

Janus grins and laughs.

"Congratulations," he says. "Your child is as beautiful as you, Lindsey, and I am certain he will prove to be as strong, compassionate, and steadfast as his parents."

My mouth gapes open even further when Lindsey suggests Janus hold the child and his eyes tear up when he takes little Liam in his arms.

A god crying? Blimey.

Well, Janus is Lindsey's ancestor. He never saw his own child be born and grow up. He'd been imprisoned in the Temple of the Four Winds before the mortal he loved realized she would be having his child. At least now he gets to see his tiny descendant become a man.

Harper and I leave a little while later but promise to visit often. We return to the Unseen, to our lair, and get started on those sex marathons Bob had mentioned.

Whatever Harper has become, physically and magically, I don't care. We're together, and that's all I need.

Chapter Thirty-Three

Harper
Six weeks later

THE SUN BEAMS DOWN ON ME FROM ITS HIGHEST POINT IN THE SKY, HER-alding today as the summer equinox, the longest day of the year. Well, here in the mortal world it's the equinox. I still have no idea if the Unseen realm has a similar thing or if the world there moves in a perfect circle around the sun. Or if it moves at all. Maybe the sun revolves around the planet. Or maybe it's all magic that no one can understand.

I'm relaxing in a lawn chair that can sit upright or tilt backward, with my bare feet on the footrest. The chair leans back just enough that I can lounge here while the sunshine bakes my skin. No longer do I need to worry about sunburn because my immortal, unkillable body is not suscep-tible to ultraviolet rays anymore. I found that out a few days ago when I fell asleep in this chair while Max went off on a secret mission and Nevan and Lindsey had gone to the store to buy groceries, taking their new son with them.

Yep. I'm virtually invincible now.

This afternoon, Max is reclining in a chair identical to mine that sits a couple of feet away from me.

I can't resist rolling my head to the side so I can admire his supernatu-rally hot body. He's naked, the way we both prefer him to be. We're on Lindsey and Nevan's property, surrounded by woods, so we can both go naked if we want. Our friends don't mind. And yeah, I've gotten to know Lindsey and Nevan as well as Travis, Ennea, Bob, Ken, and even Pendi, the sister of Ennea and Tris. I still haven't met the infamous Triskaideka, the snarky leprechaun who became Max's good friend thanks to their mutual acquaintance with Lindsey.

Naturally, Max denies he and Tris are friends. He denies Travis is his buddy too.

But everyone else knows the truth.

Ennea and Pendi keep telling us Tris is "unavailable," and when Max pesters them for more info, they tell him it's not their place to reveal Tris's reasons for not being around right now. They swear he'll be back, eventually.

Max gets up and stretches his entire body.

I love watching him do that, but I love it even more when he sprawls on the grass and closes his eyes, soaking up the sun like only a salamander can. His copper-sheened skin glistens, highlighting all those beautiful muscles and making me want to drag my tongue over every last one of them. His manly equipment looks just as mouthwateringly good when he's relaxed as it does when he's aroused and ready for a marathon feeding session. I never would've imagined I'd want to nourish a ravenous beast with my body, but damn, I can't wait for our next round of Feed the Beast.

The new me can handle at least nine straight days of sex, interrupted only by the occasional need for me to consume actual food. Yeah, I still have to do that. But I also know I can wait at least four days before I get hungry enough that I need food.

Max has never looked hotter or been so well-fed—or so happy.

I've never been happier either.

But I'm dying to know what secret mission he went on the other day. Despite my best attempts to seduce him into telling me, he has stayed mum. All I get from him is a smirk and an offer to "shag" me until I forget about everything except his body and the many ways he can make me scream.

So yeah, I forget about it for hours and hours.

Today, I am determined to get an answer.

I pick up my plastic water cup, remove the lid, and dump the ice-cold contents onto Max's sizzling bod.

He jerks upright, his legs still stretched out on the grass, and splutters. "What did you do that for?"

"Tell me about your secret mission."

Max rises to his knees and crawls toward me, leaning over my chair and my legs to get his face close to my cleavage.

I'm wearing a string bikini, so I have plenty of cleavage for him to ogle.

He glances at my breasts, slides his tongue over his lips, and finally meets my gaze. "No, *dulcissime*, I will not tell you. But you'll find out as soon as Lindsey and Nevan get home."

"Well, I guess I can wait that long." I hook my leg around his hips. "You've been calling me *dulcissime* since the day we met, but I still don't know what it means."

"It's Latin for sweet." He slips an arm around my waist and pulls me into his body, unfurling it to his full height with me glued to him. "Even when you were trying to kill me, I knew you'd be the sweetest meal any salamander could enjoy."

"Nobody but you gets to feast on me. All those other salamanders better find their own fated mates." I rake my tongue over his chest, giving his nipple a light pinch with my teeth, which makes him growl softly. "You're mine, Maximus."

"Yes, I am. And I love it when you call me Maximus." He slides his hands down to my bottom. "No one but you gets to call me that."

A big pickup truck rolls up the driveway, emerging from the woods that surround the long gravel path to the road. Lindsey, Nevan, and baby Liam are home.

Luckily, Max hasn't gotten hard yet. His rod is getting bigger, but he's not fully aroused yet. Nevan does not like it when Max has an erection in his presence.

We walk over to the truck to greet Lindsey and Nevan, and to help them carry the groceries into the house. All three of us insist Lindsey and Liam go into the house and get comfy on the sofa instead of the new mom lugging grocery sacks. Lindsey told me yesterday she loves Max like a brother, and she's thrilled he found me, so I'm not surprised when she grins at me and Max like she's tickled pink.

By the time we've unloaded everything and put all of it away in the kitchen, more guests arrive. Bob, Ken, Janus, and Ennea waltz out of the woods first. Every single one of them has the ability to cross the boundaries in the mortal world, most of them having been granted that dispensation by Lindsey before she gave up her Janusite powers. The god Janus gave Ken the same privilege.

The gang gathers around the barbecue grill while Nevan cooks up hamburgers and sausages.

Yeah, it seems strange to watch a former sylph king grilling for his family and friends. I didn't know Nevan back when he was king, but I bet he looked super-hot giving orders to his army. I said that to Lindsey once, and she told me with a secretive smile, "No comment."

I took that to mean yeah, he had been super-hot giving orders—and yeah, Lindsey had jumped his bones after every time she heard him commanding his army.

Everyone is telling jokes and laughing, but some instinct makes me glance toward the trees.

Two beings saunter out of the shady woods, heading toward the group.

I recognize Travis, but the other guy isn't familiar. He stands almost as tall as Travis, and though he has plenty of muscles, he's not quite as outrageously buff as either Travis or Max. His skin is a normal, suntanned shade instead of bronzed or copper-sheened. As they come closer, the sunshine lights up the new guy's bright-blue eyes. Under the suntan, I notice faint freckles on his face. He has fiery red hair that kisses the shells of his ear.

Max is busy instructing Nevan in how to grill a sausage properly, like an incubus has any idea about such things.

I nudge Max with my elbow.

He looks at me. "What? Can't you see I'm doing something very important? Nevan is about to scorch your meal."

"No, he's not. I'm having a burger." I point toward the two newcomers, who have almost reached the group. "Who's the new guy with Travis?"

"The what?" Max glances toward his fellow incubus, and his brows scrunch up. "I have no idea. There's something familiar about him, but…" He searches the crowd until he spots Ennea, then waves for her to come over here. When she does, he asks, "Do you recognize the bloke who's with Travis?"

She laughs like he's made a joke but seems to realize quickly that Max is not kidding. Her expression turns confused. "Of course I know him. So do you. That's my brother, Tris."

Max swings his gaze back to the hot redhead and gapes at him. "That can't be Tris. Your brother is a skinny, mangy shrimp of a leprechaun."

"Not anymore," Ennea says, smacking Max's arm with the back of her hand. "He just finished the transmutation."

"The what?"

"It's like puberty, except way more painful and a lot more dramatic."

"But Tris is centuries old. Why didn't he experience puberty until now?"

Ennea shrugs one shoulder. "He reached the transmutation time a little later than average, but not abnormally late."

I butt into the conversation, my curiosity overriding my manners. "How long has he been gone?"

"Since a week before I met you," Max says.

"Puberty only took three months? Sheesh. For mortals, it's a years-long angst-fest."

"Yeah, I've heard," Ennea says. "But trust me, the transmutation is way more painful."

Looking at Tris, I can believe that. Max said Tris used to be scrawny, and I figure he must've been shorter too since Max called him a shrimp. He must've learned that term for a short person from Lindsey. It doesn't sound like a word Max would've come up with on his own.

Travis and Tris approach us, smiling and laughing like they've just shared a good joke. Travis slaps Tris's shoulder.

Max's brows hike up while he takes in the sight of his formerly skinny friend who's now a muscle-bound hottie. "Hello, Tris. You, ah, look well."

"I'm a giganto freak like you," Tris says. "Go on, say it. We're all freaks with too many muscles and not enough brains. I felt my IQ going down every time a new muscle formed."

"Max is very smart," I say, leaning into my sexy salamander and hooking my arm around his.

"I'm no knucklehead either," Travis says, and I realize his Texas twang has faded so much that it's barely noticeable.

Tris flaps his arms. "Hey, it was a joke, ya mooks."

Ennea corrals her brother and hauls him over to where Lindsey sits on the chair I'd occupied earlier with Liam on her lap. She hands the baby to Tris, who cradles the little cutie while smiling.

Lindsey seems flummoxed by Tris's new appearance. She glances at Max, and they both shake their heads and lift their shoulders.

Okay, Tris must have *really* looked different before.

I nudge Max with my elbow. "When are you going to share your secret mission with me?"

"Right now." He steps away from the group, shoves his fingers in his mouth, and whistles to get everyone's attention. Once he's achieved his goal, he rolls his shoulders back and says, "Keep quiet and be our witnesses to this special event."

Travis raises his hand like a kid in school.

Max rubs his jaw and sighs. "Yes, Travis, what is it?"

"What kind of special event is this?"

"If you would shut up, I'd tell you."

Travis folds his arms over his chest and shuts up.

Max clears his throat. "We'll get to the event in a moment. First…" He waves for me to come closer. "Come here, Harper."

I trot over to stand beside him.

He grasps my shoulders and moves me in front of him.

Then he drops to one knee. "I needed a bit of advice on how to do this the mortal way, so forgive me if I don't get it quite right."

He can't be about to…

Max clasps my left hand, gazing up at me with the sweetest expression of hopefulness and adoration.

And I start crying.

CHAPTER THIRTY-FOUR

Max

NEVER IN ALL MY EXISTENCE HAVE I DONE ANYTHING LIKE THIS. I'D wanted to marry Aurelia, but I never got round to asking her. A sort of nausea I haven't experienced since my forging has me in its grip, and my throat has gone as dry as a desert. I clear my throat several times but still feel like I can't speak. Lindsey advised me on how to propose marriage the mortal way. I'd asked for her insight because Harper deserves the right kind of proposal, which Lindsey assured me involves "super romantic gestures" and "plenty of soppy but completely honest words" about how much I adore Harper.

I have a speech memorized, but I need to get my voice working first.

So I conjure a bottle of water and gulp down the entire contents in one breath.

Harper touches my face. "Relax, I'm going to say yes."

I make a noise, something like a growling huff. "Now you've gone and cocked it up. The surprise is ruined."

"Hate to break it to you, but everyone here guessed what you had up your sleeve before you got down on one knee."

"I have no sleeves. I'm naked."

"Yeah, I know. It's one of those mortal sayings, the kind that drives you bonkers."

I glance around at my friends, clear my throat again, and speak in a loud and authoritative voice. "You will all keep your mouths shut and let me get on with this."

Everyone nods. Most of them smirk.

Reclaiming Harper's left hand—didn't Lindsey say it's the left one?—I look into the eyes of the woman I adore. "I love you, Harper Goode, and I want to spend eternity with you and only you. Fate might have pushed us in the right direction, but we made our own happy ending." Apparently, that's a thing mortals talk about. Happy endings, or happily ever after. Sounds like rot to me, but then, I'm not human. Harper is, sort of. But I'm getting distracted from my plan, so I pull in a deep breath, exhale it, and get on with the most important bit. "Harper, will you marry me?"

"Do elementals have weddings?" she asks.

A breath explodes out of me. "Are you trying to ruin my proposal? It will be a handfasting ceremony since I am not human and we therefore cannot have a wedding with a priest or whatever they call those blokes who marry mortals. But you will have a handfasting ceremony with most of the same trappings. A dress and all that other silly rubbish. That's what Lindsey told me a wedding has. If she was having me on—"

"I wasn't," Lindsey says. "Hurry up and jam that ring on her finger."

"*Merda*. The ring." I conjure it, holding the ring in my other palm while I still clasp Harper's left hand. "Let's try this again. Harper, will you—"

"Yes," she says. "I will marry you. Or handfast with you. Whatever you call it, I absolutely sign up for eternity with you, Quintus Salonius Maximus."

"But you didn't even let me finish asking."

"I did too. A minute ago, the first time you asked. You got the whole question out then." She wiggles the third finger on her left hand. "I'm ready for that ring now."

"This is not the proper order of things." I slip the ring onto her finger. "But I suppose it doesn't matter. Just promise me you won't cock up our handfasting ceremony by interrupting it."

She smiles and draws a cross over her heart with one finger. "Promise."

I get up and haul my betrothed into me so I can kiss her.

Our friends clap, and some whistle or cheer.

Without letting go of her body, I give up Harper's lips just long enough to announce, "Thank you for witnessing this special event, but Harper and I need to go home and shag."

I whisk us straight to the waterfall behind the rock shop and leap over the railing onto the stone ledge. We're through the falls and into the portal within two seconds flat, and once we emerge on the other side, I take us directly to our lair. It used to be only my lair, but now it's become a real home for me and Harper.

She wriggles away from me and lies down on the bed, her delectable body spread out on the fur blanket. "How should we celebrate?"

"By fucking, obviously."

Her smile sends all the blood rushing to my loins, but her sweet laughter makes my chest tighten. I've gotten used to that feeling. It means I love her.

She skims her hands over the fur blanket and bends one knee, exposing the slick, pink flesh between her thighs. "But there are so many ways we can do that."

"We have the rest of forever to explore all those ways."

Since I'm already hardening, I have the requisite equipment to satisfy all her desires. And as an incubus, I can do that for weeks, months, maybe even years without needing a break. I will need to give her the occasional rest period, though. This new immortal body of hers might be far more durable than it used to be, but she's not quite an elemental.

I straddle her on my hands and knees. "How do you want it?"

"Every way imaginable."

I flip us over with Harper beneath me. "It's a good thing we have eternity together because I will never run out of ideas for how to make love to you."

"Living forever used to sound like hell, but now it feels like heaven."

For the next three days, we take each other to heaven and back more times than I can count. Who needs a clock or a calendar? Time is irrelevant to us now.

At the end of our sex marathon, I conjure food items and cook Harper a meal. While we eat, I broach a subject I've been hesitant to discuss with her. But since we're getting married, or handfasted, I know it's time. "There's something I've wanted to tell you, but I've been, ah…anxious about speaking the words."

"Nothing you tell me will chase me away. So go on, say it."

"I've told you about Aurelia. I left out a few pertinent facts because, well, I worried how you might react."

"Spit it out, Max."

Pushing food around my plate, I avoid looking at her. "That day when you threw a knife into my back, I saw your reflection in the water and thought you were Aurelia. She had the same color hair and eyes."

"But I'm not her identical twin."

"No." I scratch my head, grimacing. "I've wondered if that meant any-thing, your resemblance to her. So I asked Ken."

"He let you into his office? Guess he's not anti-salamander anymore."

"I think he's resigned himself to my presence, though I'm the only salaman-der he'll allow inside his office lair." I drop my fork and focus on Harper. "Ken told me your resemblance to Aurelia doesn't mean anything. It's a coincidence, and fate does allow for those, according to the oracle. Which means I don't love you because you look somewhat like her. I love you because you're Harper Goode, the most annoying female in the multiverse."

She pokes me in the side with her elbow. "Very funny. I love you despite the fact you're the most arrogant, salamander-headed male in the multiverse."

"I won't argue with that description of me."

"Does this mean fate made it all happen? We had no choice in the matter?"

"No, that's not what I'm saying or what Ken said." I draw her into my arms, her lush breasts crushed to my chest. "Everything that happened with Aurelia, including her forging and her destruction, had to happen. If I'd stayed a mortal and married her, you and I wouldn't be here now. You are my true love, Harper. You're the one woman in all the worlds, in all of history, who makes me whole."

"Glad to hear it. Because you're my true love too."

I kiss her so well and for so long that if we had a clock, it would probably show days have elapsed. When I finally give up her lips, I smile and pat her arse. "Now, let's start planning that wedding."

She throws herself at me, wrapping her legs around my waist and her arms around my neck. "I can't wait to pick out a dress."

"Yes, that sounds like exactly the sort of excursion I'll enjoy."

I'm being sarcastic, but not entirely. I do want to see Harper in a wedding dress. I want to see her naked after that, but I will enjoy removing that frock. Slowly. No vanishing clothes. I'll take my time.

Travis appears behind Harper.

I groan out a sigh. "Go away. Can't you see I'm about to shag Harper?"

She wriggles in my arms to turn sideways to me. "Hi, Travis. What's up?"

He fidgets, scratching his arms, and avoids looking either of us in the eye.

"What's wrong with you?" I ask. "You're acting like you've got fleas."

"No," he says slowly, "that's not the problem."

His voice, it sounds different.

The woman in my arms bursts out laughing. "Oh, this is perfect. You're both British now."

I flick my gaze to Travis and back to Harper. "What are you on about? He doesn't sound anything like me."

"Sure he does. He has a British accent."

"Well—That's—" I push away from her to scowl at Travis. "Why are you imitating me?"

Travis hunches his shoulders. "Don't know. It just kind of happened. I woke up this morning and sounded like this. It's awful."

"Speaking with my accent is not awful. Women love it."

Harper laughs again, even harder, her eyes watering. "Maybe his accent changed because of the way he feels about you."

"What way might that be? If he wants to shag me, the answer is absolutely not."

Travis's eyes flare wide. "Oh hell no, I don't want to do that."

Harper sets a hand on my arm. "Relax. I think his accent mirrors yours because he admires you and wants to be like you."

"But—" I flap my arms in the air. "I don't want him to imitate me. This is by far the worst thing I've ever experienced."

"Worse than dying? Worse than being forged? Or ensorcelled? Or—"

"Yes, I grasp your meaning." I bar my arms over my chest, refusing to look at Travis. "But I never would have consented to this."

She sidles up to me, squeezing herself under my arm so I have no choice but to lower it. "Take it as a compliment, Max. You're his hero."

Travis blanches. "No, that's not—"

"Shush," she says. "Both of you. Travis might share your accent, but he doesn't have your panty-melting voice. Well, his voice is hot too, but not as hot as yours. No offense, Travis. The point is, no one will mistake either of you for the other. You sound different."

"Hmm." I sneak my hand down to her arse, for no good reason. I love holding her soft cheek in my palm. "If he's going to sound like me, he needs to choose a better name."

Travis's mouth gapes. "What's wrong with the one I've got?"

"It's not sexy. You're an incubus now, not a mortal sheriff."

"Okay, maybe you've got a point." He rubs his chin, his eyes narrowing while he considers the issue. "How about Bartholomew?"

"That's a bloody awful name."

"Sounds good to me."

"Do you think women want to scream 'Bartholomew' while you're shagging them?" I roll my eyes. "You're hopeless."

"How about—"

"Get out of here." I squeeze Harper's arse. "I have more important matters to deal with."

Travis whisks himself away.

Harper wriggles around until she's pasted to my front side. "Why do you have a British accent?"

"After three months, you finally ask me that?"

"I was preoccupied with other stuff. Answer the question. If you don't mind."

"What if I do mind?"

She tickles my chest, which she knows makes me randy. "Come on. Tell me, and then we can get it on again."

"That's a dirty trick, using sex to make me confess." I scratch behind my ear, head bowed, and grimace. "I have no bloody idea why I sound the way I do. The change happened so slowly that I didn't notice until a nymph I got a leg over with a few centuries ago asked about my accent. She suggested perhaps my speech had changed because that's how my descendants talk. I never had any children, but my two brothers might have done, though that doesn't really explain—"

"Shut up, Max. Have you ever been to England?"

"No. It's a place in the mortal world, but that's all I know about it."

"Then how do you know all the British terms? Get a leg over, bloody hell, sodding, et cetera."

"No idea." I grasp her arse. "Can we shag now?"

"You have the most persistently one-track mind I've ever come across." She walks her fingertips up my chest like they're tiny creatures exploring me. "You told Travis you had something to deal with. What is it?"

"You, love. It's time for our next marathon. Let's start with that thing you wanted to do to me back in Hathor's temple."

She bites her bottom lip, releasing it little by little. "Do you mean it? You're going to let me?"

"Yes. It's about time you experienced everything life with an incubus has to offer." I transport us straight to the bed, with Harper on top. "Do you still want to try it?"

"Oh yes, I've been dying to do this to you." She slithers down my body until her face is above my groin. Her pink tongue glides over her lips with a leisure that makes my cock stiffen in an instant. It waves in front of her face, and she grins. "Mm-mm-mm, I'm ready to feast on you."

"So go on, *dulcissime*. Devour me."

Her smile lights up her face and my soul. I swear it must shine through the mountain above us too, igniting the entire multiverse with her lustful joy. I no longer need to worry about losing her. She's immortal, yes, but she's also mine for good—I'm hers too. We can spend as long as we want inside this lair, enjoying each other over and over and over.

After all, we have eternity.

ANNA DURAND IS A BESTSELLING, MULTI-AWARD-WINNING AUTHOR OF contemporary and paranormal romance. Her books have earned bestseller status on every major retailer and wonderful reviews from readers around the world. But that's the boring spiel. Here are the really cool things you want to know about Anna!

Born on Lackland Air Force Base in Texas, Anna grew up moving here, there, and everywhere thanks to her dad's job as an instructor pilot. She's lived in Texas (twice), Mississippi, California (twice), Michigan (twice), and Alaska—and now Ohio.

As for her writing, Anna has always made up stories in her head, but she didn't write them down until her teen years. Those first awful books went into the trash can a few years later, though she learned a lot from those stories. Eventually, she would pen her first romance novel, the paranormal romance *Willpower*, and she's never looked back since.

Want even more details about Anna? Get access to her extended bio when you subscribe to her newsletter and download the free bonus ebook, *Hot Scots Confidential*. You'll also get hot deleted scenes, character interviews, fun facts, and more! Plus you'll receive the short story *Tempted by a Kiss* and mutliple bonus chapters in both ebook and audiobook formats.

VISIT ANNADURAND.COM TO SIGN UP.

9 781949 406276